The Adventures of
CANNON
BELLE

Aaron Rosenberg

CRAZY 8 PRESS

BELLA HAD BARELY STEPPED THROUGH THE doors of Barrage Hall when she was accosted—but not by a tall figure in navy blue. Rather, it was a shorter, softer form swathed in peach and topped with dark curls who rushed her so close her first instinct was to reach for her cutlass. Good thing she had come to the ball unarmed, or she might have run her dearest friend through before realizing it!

"Isabella, there you are!" Abigail engulfed her in a quick hug, her head only reaching Bella's shoulder, then stepped back to study her at arm's length. "Let me look at you! I do declare, it is utterly unacceptable—you grow more lovely every time you go away!"

Bella laughed. "That is only your own fondness coloring your perceptions," she replied. "But I thank you for it."

There were others trying to enter behind her so she moved off to one side, Abigail gliding along beside her. Together they sought out a pair of seats with a good view of the floor, not so close to refreshments as to risk being spilled upon but not so far away as to make resupplying a chore, and with an easy avenue of escape if someone unpleasant approached.

Listen to me, Bella thought, biting back a laugh. *I'm approaching a ball as if it were a naval engagement!* Still, the two certainly had their commonalities.

Not the least of which was the officer now descending upon them, his path as unwavering as his ship had been mere days before.

For Jenifer, who captured my heart,
and our children, who stole both of ours

With enormous thanks to my excellent beta readers,
Lorraine J. Anderson, Amy Lewanski,
Christopher D. Abbott, and Peter March
and to my amazing editor,
Robert Greenberger

Chapter One

April, 1814

"SHIP AHOY!" THE YOUNG LAD IN the crow's nest of *Nature's Grace* shouted, his voice cracking with excitement—and fear. "Ship ahoy!"

"What?" The ship's captain, a fair-minded man named Giles Kendall, came charging out of his cabin, buckling on his sword belt as he went. The sun had not yet risen above the horizon, fog still skimming the water's surface, and he had been sound asleep, as had most of the crew. "Where away?"

"Hard to starboard," the lookout replied from up above, "and heading right for us!"

Racing to the starboard rail, Kendall stared out over the Mediterranean—and his face paled at the sight of the tall, angular ship speeding toward them ahead of the just burgeoning dawn. Its full brown sails caught the wind, bellying out as the ship rushed forward, seeming to almost skim across the waves, but it was the smaller, darker shape fluttering by the prow that held his attention.

It was a black flag with a skull and crossbones displayed in white. Only this one, he saw as it drew ever closer, bore a pair of cannons instead of the usual bones. And that could only mean one thing.

"To arms!" Kendall shouted, even though he knew it was most likely futile. "All men, to arms!"

Nature's Grace was a flurry of motion as groggy sailors emerged from the hammocks belowdecks and raced to the railings and the riggings, cutlasses and belaying pins at their belts, knives in their boots. Kendall himself checked that his sword was loose in its scabbard, then began to load his pistol. But the shot fell from his hand, the cast-iron ball rolling away across the deck, as a loud boom echoed over the water. Second later, something smashed through the railing not two paces to his right, careened across, and then shattered the portside railing as it made its exit.

There was no mistaking what had just happened.

"Ahoy, the ship!" a voice shouted from the approaching vessel, which had lowered its sails, letting its dying momentum carry it the rest of the way until its prow nudged up against their rail—right where there was now a gaping hole. "Toss down your weapons and surrender, or the next one won't just crease your deck, it'll split her in two!" The voice was a woman's, speaking proper King's English, and might have been sweet if not for the sharp tone and the harsh words.

Kendall growled, hand reflexively going for his sword, but his common sense soon got the better of him, and instead of drawing steel, he unbuckled and let the still-scabbarded weapon fall at his feet. His pistol, still unloaded, clattered to the ground beside it. "Do as she says, men," he called out. "There's nothing else for it now."

Every one of them knew that it was certain death to go up against the pirate captain known as "Cannon Belle."

"Another fine haul, Cap'n," Quince declared, holding up a heavy crystal decanter, its neck delicately chased in silver. "And look, I secured the best o' the lot for you!" He was a sour man with golden hair, hence the name, but he was an able first mate and loyal as the day was long.

"Thank you, Mister Quince," "Cannon" Belle Pearcy told him, accepting the decanter and a matching goblet and pouring a measure of ruby-red wine from one to the other, then raising it in his direction. "To your health." Her own thick mane of hair was black as sable and hung in a heavy plait nearly to the small of her back, swaying as she shifted with the ship, adjusting to keep her balance as naturally as breathing. The black tri-corner captain's hat atop her head was wide enough to keep her face shaded even though the sun was now casting its golden rays across the *Deadshot*'s deck, but her bright blue eyes still glittered as if generating a light of their own.

"And to yours," he answered, hoisting a similar goblet and taking a long swig. Belle took a sip of hers as well, the rich, velvety liquid sliding down her throat, then forced herself to take another, longer swallow. With honor satisfied, she placed the crystal set on a nearby barrel and moved to the railing so she could supervise the transfer of *Nature's Grace*'s goods to their own hold. The ship's crew was all behaving, which was wise—her men had by now all been trained up to be a surprisingly well-mannered lot as long as things went their way and everyone did as they were told, but all it took was one hot-head taking a swing at someone, and the whole scene would spin out of control.

Singling out the ship's captain from the crowd of sailors who had been brought over to the *Deadshot* for safekeeping, Belle approached him. He was a short, sturdy man with plain but strong features, and she was impressed by how carefully he was holding himself and his crew together.

"Thank you for being so reasonable about all this," she told him, stopping a few feet away. "Once we finish securing your goods, we'll be on our way and then you can be on yours." She favored him with a sharp smile. "We will be spiking your cannon, of course. Wouldn't want you to get any ideas about shooting us from behind and reclaiming your cargo."

He acknowledged her with a short nod. "Thank you for not overstaying your welcome," he replied. "And for keeping your men in check. Wanton looting we could not have stood for. This, this is far more . . ."

"Civilized?" she supplied, and Kendall couldn't prevent a small smile.

"Indeed."

Belle smiled back. "I see no reason why piracy must equate to barbarism," she explained, exactly as she'd told her crew many a time. "Nor why pride should overpower sense."

He studied her, though he had the decency to do so without staring and to linger more on her face than on the figure so clearly displayed in her black velvet pants, fitted white silk shirt, and red leather vest. "You are not what I had expected," he stated finally. "I've heard the tales out of the Aegean and thought . . ."

"That I'd be bloodthirsty and cruel?" She laughed, then sobered. "I am—when I'm crossed. If you and your men had resisted, I'd have slaughtered every last one of you." She sniffed. "But why throw lives away, whether yours or mine? That would be a waste, and I abhor wastefulness."

Back on *Nature's Grace*, her steward, Luke O'Dell, waved. That was the all-clear—the ship had been stripped of its valuables, and its cannons temporarily rendered inoperable. "It seems our business is concluded," she told Kendall, "which means it is time for you and your men to be on your way." She doffed her hat and swept into a low bow, as if to royalty. "Captain."

He bowed back, and though shallower, it was still that of a man to his equal. "Captain." Then, turning on his heel, he gestured for his men to follow him and led them back aboard their ship. Soon, lines were cast off and the two ships parted ways, men on both sides using long poles to separate the two vessels.

"Where to now, Cap'n?" Quince asked, joining her near where Gregor manned the wheel.

"Home," Belle replied, her gaze already fixed across the waters, where an almost forgotten country waited. "Back at last." She flashed a quick grin at her first mate. "Time to find that cove I told you about, set foot in our homeland, and spend some of these ill-gotten gains on good English soil."

He grinned back. "Aye, aye!" he agreed with relish.

They both laughed, but Belle was barely paying attention. In truth, her mind had already wandered toward home, and the scene that awaited her there.

It almost made her decide to stay at sea a while longer. But she knew she could not. There were obligations to attend, and attend them she would. Despite any desires to the contrary.

Chapter Two

"ISABELLA? ISABELLA!" A PALE SHAPE SUDDENLY flickered in front of her face, mere inches from her eyes and nose, and Bella flinched back, instinctively raising a hand to catch the offending item. The sound of her name trailed off in a gasp, and she realized that Abigail was standing there staring at her even though her mind registered the delicate silk and wood and ivory clasped between her fingers. Carefully, Bella opened her hand, releasing the carved and painted fan she had captured and offering it back to her friend.

"Goodness!" Abigail stated, snatching back the accessory and clutching it to her chest. "I thought sure you'd mangled it beyond repair! What has gotten into you during your travels?"

"I'm so sorry," Bella managed. "I— my thoughts were elsewhere, and you startled me."

"I should say so! And does your startlement now often result in violence?" her friend pressed, huffing a bit. Most of that indignation was feigned, Bella knew. Abigail Montrose did enjoy a good scene.

"It . . ." Bella trailed off, fighting to hide the smile that threatened to grace her face and to swallow the laughter that struggled to burst forth. Did her startlement often result in violence? Yes, indeed, and typically of the pistol and cutlass variety! She pictured herself slicing Abigail's fan to bits and could no longer conceal her amusement.

"Oh, you will be the death of me, Isabella Parsons," Abigail exclaimed, but her own lips quirked up. "Or at least the death of my fan!" Then she laughed. Bella was relieved. She had not truly meant to upset her friend. But her mind had wandered, and for an instant, she had forgotten which world she was in just now.

And that was a mistake she dared not make.

Obligingly, she focused upon her surroundings once more. They were in Hillington, of course, at Barrage Hall, the meeting place and entertainment venue of Lower Yorkshire County. All around them were their peers, the aristocrats and landed gentry, dressed in their finest and dancing, singing, playing, eating, and conversing with one another amid the music and the frequent to and fro of servants bearing lovely food and drink. It was a party, after all, the first ball of the season, and Bella had promised Abigail before she'd left that she would be back in time for them to attend it together.

Only, that had been months ago. So much had changed since! And now that she was here, Bella could not help but wish that she were elsewhere. Specifically, back on the *Deadshot*, her legs clad in close-fitted velvet pants rather than layers of ruffles, her sword and pistol at her side.

That was a different life, however, and one that she had to put behind her for good. Thus Bella forced herself to remember where she was—*who* she was—right now. Which is why she put on a smile, patted the seat beside her, and said, "Come now, Abbie. Sit beside me and tell me what's transpired since I left. I can only imagine what has occurred in my absence."

Fortunately, her friend needed no additional coaxing. "Well," she declared, dropping onto the bench in a flurry of silk and lace and ribbon, "you will never guess! Mary Winstead, you remember how she was pining for that merchant's son she'd met back in London? So she . . ."

Bella did her best to listen attentively, but only a very small portion of her truly cared that Mary had eloped with her merchant boy, or that Brian Fried had returned from his time overseas with a laughable mustache but an impressive limp, or that Constance and Beatrice were not speaking to each other—again—because they had both taken an interest in the same man—again. How had she ever found such things to be of any interest, she wondered. Because surely she had. She did not recall being so persistently, terribly bored in the past.

But she certainly was now.

Nor was the company likely to hold her attention, present company excluded. Oh, a few of the other young women had greeted Bella with feigned warmth when she'd entered, but while there were good manners and even perhaps some modicum of friendly regard, that was as far as it went. Only Abigail was a true friend.

The gentlemen were no better. Certainly several of them had approached already, hoping to engage Bella for this dance or that one. Sadly, they were all the same men she remembered from before she'd left, and none of them had improved any with time. The younger men were still too shallow, too foolish, too full of themselves. The older ones were too arrogant, too domineering, too convinced of their own superiority. She had declined every request thus far tonight, and doubted that would change as the evening progressed.

No, far better to sit here with Abigail instead. She was still being seen, still a presence, but with minimal effort on her part, and no commitment beyond being a receptive audience.

Her eyes darted about the room even as she listened, taking in the tall, leaded-glass windows and the heavy, oak-paneled doors, and the candles in their sconces lined up evenly on both sides to illuminate where the glow from the massive overhead chandeliers failed to reach. Her peers were busy mingling, laughing and carrying on, but Bella realized that she much preferred the bawdy sea chanties of her crew, and the roar of the waves, the whistle of the wind as it filled her sails.

That was a party! A shame that it was all behind her now.

Movement at the window captured her attention, and Bella focused on it just in time to see a broad navy-clad back disappear along the boulevard outside. And who had that been? Cutting into her friend's rambling discourse, she asked, "Abbie, is there someone new about town? Someone tall, dark, well-formed, and nautical?"

That set Abigail tittering, any imagined outrage at being interrupted cast aside in favor of conspiratorial giggling. "Ah, you've heard, have you? I might have known! Barely back a day and already setting her sights on the finest man I've ever seen!"

"Abigail." Bella tapped a finger on her friend's knee, stopping her mid-torrent. "Who. Is. He?"

"Oh, well, that would be Commander Reid," Abigail answered with only a brief, feigned pout. "Newly arrived from London, no less! A fine figure of a man but, alas, a consummate officer—meaning that he seems far too preoccupied to attend a dance and pay proper attention to any of the young ladies there." The way she stated that last bit made it clear that this was truly a crime beyond any other and should be punished accordingly. Abigail, like Bella herself, was a young lady possessed of at least moderate fortune. Unlike Bella, however, her friend had little else to occupy her time beyond occasionally visiting other ladies of her acquaintance, doing needlework, planning social engagements, and shopping for a suitable husband. There were few enough here to choose from, which was why any newcomer—particularly a handsome one—would, of course, pique her interest.

Bella, on the other hand, had more than enough to do and think about without such frivolous pursuits.

"Geoffrey!" she called out the next morning while seated at the breakfast table. The tall, stooped figure of the family butler appeared in the doorway almost instantly.

"Yes, milady?" he inquired. "More tea?" He scooped up the teapot as he approached, the delicate china almost disappearing between his enormous hands.

"Oh, well, perhaps a touch," Bella agreed, extending her cup. "But that is not why I called." She indicated the heavy ledger that lay open beside her place, and an entry marked by the latest letter from cousin Nancy in London. "What is this here? A hundred pounds for oranges? Fifty for venison? Eighty for ice cream?"

"Ah, yes." Geoffrey looked apologetic, wringing his hands together now that he had restored the teapot to its customary place. "Many of our own deer had to be put down due to illness, I'm afraid, so we were forced to purchase from neighbors. The ice cream, as you know, is one of the only things that can bring your father out of his doldrums, so that was also required. As for the oranges, your father was desirous of them, and as you know they are deuced hard to come by, especially at this time of year. It was necessary to procure them from a merchant down in Derbyshire, and I am afraid the shipping fees were rather steep."

"A hundred pounds? I should say so!" She sighed, then sipped at her tea to cover it. She could not be too angry at Geoffrey. He did his best when she was away, but of course he was still only staff despite his many years of loyal service. If her father insisted upon a purchase, Geoffrey could hardly gainsay it. Only she could do that—when she was in residence. Which had not been the case, of late.

Well, that ended now. "I will deal with any such extravagances in future," she insisted, and Geoffrey bowed. She could not mistake the relief on his face. Now he would not have to struggle with balancing his master's cravings and demands against the practicalities of maintaining their household. That was Bella's job.

Fortunately, it was one she was more than capable of handling— and had been, even before her recently acquired career. Although it seemed that had grown more challenging in her absence, due to her father's whims and excesses.

As if summoned by her thoughts, a second figure emerged through the door, this one as hunched as Geoffrey but far shorter and far thinner, a small, frail figure whose wisps of white hair and puzzled expression suggested he had just awakened from a bad dream.

Bella only wished that were the case.

"Good morning, Papa," she said dutifully, rising from her seat to cross the room and embrace him. But gently—William Parsons,

Baron Roderick had never been a robust man, but in recent years, he had grown nearly skeletal, a shadow of his former self. "Would you care for some breakfast?" She escorted him to his seat across from her and then poured him tea.

"Ah, yes, thank you, my dear." He beamed up at her. "How kind." Reaching for the sugar, he dumped several teaspoons of it into his tea in rapid succession, stirring rapidly, then took a sip. Isabella could not imagine how his mouth did not pucker at such cloying sweetness, but he merely nodded and sipped again. At least he seemed content. She returned to her own seat and went back to perusing the household accounts while nibbling at toast, having her tea, and keeping an eye upon her father.

"Are there any oranges, by chance?" Lord Roderick asked. He looked up at Geoffrey with childish glee. "I do love oranges!" Bella had to stop herself from barking at him for throwing away money on such foolishness.

Commanding a pirate ship had almost been a relief compared to this!

After breakfast Bella changed to a walking-about dress of soft blue-gray that nicely offset her trim blond curls and drew attention to her eyes. As she set a hat atop her head, she recalled how her best friend had shrieked upon seeing her last night. "Your hair!" Abigail had cried, gloved hands nearly going to Bella's head but then retreating to her own chest instead. "What happened to all your long, lovely curls? Is this the work of that new maid? If so, she should be sacked at once!"

"No, no, she had nothing to do with it. I simply grew tired of them," Bella had replied airily. "I feel worlds lighter now." She twirled for effect. In truth, she had hated to cut her hair after growing it long for all those years. But fitting those dangling tresses beneath her sable wig had proven next to impossible, and she had been more concerned about protecting her identity—and therefore her life—than soothing her vanity. Besides, she *did* like the way they looked now. Sophie was proving to be a treasure, particularly at dealing with this new, shorter hair. And it saved so much time in preparation!

"Well, it is rather fetching," Abigail had agreed, then laughed. "Leave it to you, Isabella—you go away on holiday and come back practically a different person!"

More than you know, Bella had thought, a little sad at the fact that she had to keep such a secret from her oldest and dearest friend. But there was nothing for it—Abigail was a notorious gossip, utterly unable to keep a secret. Even one that could put lives at risk.

Pushing all that from her mind, Bella gathered up her purse. "Daniel!" she called, and the family coachman appeared. "Please collect the trunk in the hall for me," she instructed. "I am conveying it to Mr. Keats." He bowed and departed at once to see to it. A few minutes later he returned to escort her to and into the waiting carriage.

The family solicitor, Solomon Keats, had a handsomely appointed office on the second floor of one of the buildings in town, just above a tailor. Daniel pulled the carriage up by the door and helped Bella out, then she waited as he unstrapped the trunk, hefted it down, and carried it inside and up the stairs. Once at the top, she knocked twice.

"Come in!"

Bella pushed the door open and gestured for Daniel to set the trunk inside. "Thank you, Daniel," she told him. "You may return to the carriage. I shan't be too long, I think."

"Ah, Miss Parsons!" Mr. Keats had risen from behind his desk and crossed the thick rug to greet her. "Welcome home! How lovely to see you, as always. I trust your business went well?" He took her hand in both of his and clasped it warmly. Bella smiled in return. She had known him her whole life and considered him almost an uncle—which was why she did her best to ignore the way his gaze

had changed as she had grown older, or how he held her hand perhaps a second too long.

"Always a pleasure, Mr. Keats," she said instead, kissing his
cheek before gently extracting her hand and gliding to the nearer
of the two chairs before his desk. Taking the hint, he returned
to his own seat, though he continued to regard her fondly—and
slightly hungrily—once they were both seated. "And yes, thank
you. Though there were some difficulties at first, they have all been
dealt with satisfactorily now. We should begin to see proper returns
again soon. In the meantime, I have brought some additional funds
to add to the family account." She indicated the chest, which sat
behind them where Daniel had left it.

"Oh, yes? Very good." The solicitor leaned forward. "I do not
mind telling you, Miss Parsons, in all confidence, that some of
your father's recent expenditures have been . . . peculiar, to say the
least. And ill-advised, but that is the limits of what I may accom-
plish, to advise against it."

"Of course. Rest assured, now that I am returned, you will see
an immediate cessation to such purchases," she promised. "In the
meantime, that should be more than sufficient to clear any recent
debts and cover expenses for some time." It had better be—the
trunk contained the bulk of her captain's share from the *Deadshot*'s
many successful raids and was full of coin and jewelry and items
like candlesticks and goblets and dueling pistols. Nothing that
could be readily identified, however. She had made sure of that.

"I am sure. You are an excellent steward of your father's interests." It was clear that Mr. Keats was bursting to ask where such
newfound wealth had come from if not the embattled holdings
she had gone to visit, but as a gentleman, he could not. And as
the family's confidante, even if he had asked—and even if she had
answered truthfully—he would have been honor-bound to keep
her secret.

Bella was not about to trust her life to that honor, however.

Instead, she rose to her feet. "Thank you, as always, Mr. Keats,"
she stated as she moved back toward the door. "I am grateful that

my father and I can continue to rely upon you."

She was gone before he could catch hold of her hand for another lingering good-bye.

At least that is settled, Bella thought as she relaxed back into the carriage and listened to the crack of Daniel's whip ordering the horses into motion again. Her family's estates had always before now been enough to provide a comfortable living, especially for such a small household as they had at Crestmont—provided such interests were properly managed and they did not indulge in extravagances like hundred-pound shipments of oranges! She had expected this additional money to take care of that and allow them to continue with a greater sense of security than before. Besides which, she would be keeping a tighter grip on the purse strings from now on, so that her father could not make any more wild purchases. As a result, she had fully expected their home and estates to be once again secure.

Which should have meant that the need behind her recent foray into piracy was now at an end. For some reason, that thought had made Bella almost want to weep even as they had returned to the land of her birth.

Now, however, she was no longer so sure what would happen next. Could she trust in the monies from their foreign investments arriving in time to protect them against any further surprise expenses? What if the house took damage in a storm, or a horse went lame, or the carriage axle snapped? What if one of the staff chose to marry, with the family of course expected to shower them with gifts and even a private home? What if her father took ill and required expensive medicines from London or abroad? Her recently acquired loot would maintain them at their current levels for a time, but would that be enough?

And was she merely looking for excuses? She had sworn that her piracy had been a means to an end, that being to return safely home and rescue her family from disgrace and ruin. She had accomplished that. Even if they had to sell some of their livestock or some of their lands, they could almost certainly manage without her resuming that villainous occupation.

Which was not to say taking to the sea once more would not allow them more protection against any ills. More to the point, it would also ease the strange yearning she had felt since she'd set foot back on land and exchanged her hat and trousers for a wrap and a dress.

The question was not one she needed to address at the moment, at least. Bella concentrated on staring out the carriage window instead, studying the town and how it quickly gave way to countryside as they headed for home.

"Why, Isabella!" The high, shrill voice made Bella wince, but she managed to smooth that expression away even as she turned. "How lovely to see you again!"

"And you, Constance," Bella replied, leaning in to brush cheeks with the other young woman and then with her sister and companion. "And dear Beatrice. How are you both?"

"Oh, we are fine, just fine," Constance answered quickly, holding both of Bella's hands and leaning back. "Now let me take you in! My, you did get some color, didn't you? Such a sight! And your hair! Where did you holiday again, that they thought shorn scalps were in fashion?" Beatrice tittered, the sisters' dark eyes glittering with malice, and Bella gritted her teeth as beside her Abigail grumbled just loud enough for her to hear.

"It was an island in the Mediterranean," Bella replied after extricating herself. "A lovely place, warm and sunny." She shuddered slightly, and only partially for effect. "Coming back to the damp and cold and fog was quite a shock, I can tell you! And, of course, such weather as this does horrors to one's complexion, not to mention digestion—but I'm sure you don't need me to tell you that!"

The tittering turned to gasps, both girls' eyes flying wide as the rapid succession of insults sank in. "Well, I never!" Constance declared, gathering her skirts and flouncing off, Beatrice right behind her.

"That may well be the problem!" Bella called after them. "A little fresh fruit would work wonders!" The sisters did not give any indication that they had heard.

Abigail, however, burst into laughter. "Oh, you are wicked!" she exclaimed, face still red from humor. "But they deserved that!"

"They always did," Bella agreed, trying and failing to tamp down her own grin. It was true—the Tremont sisters were vain, nasty, grasping creatures, always ready to find fault with others in order to make themselves look better.

As some of the only other presented young women in their circle, Bella and Abigail had been forced to tolerate the pair, at least in public. Now Bella found she simply couldn't be bothered to pretend any longer.

"I heard," Abigail confided, leaning in close so that only Bella would hear, "that they fired yet another lady's maid. Can you imagine? That is at least the third in as many years. Such ghastly behavior, because you know they will not give a good reference, either. How are the poor girls to find new employment after that?"

"How indeed?" Bella agreed. But her mind had turned, not to maids, but to men instead. Specifically, men she knew: Quince and Gregor, Luke O'Dell and Isaac, John Wynn and Tom and all the rest. Men who had thrown in with her on the *Deadshot*, who had sailed under her command, and who had trusted her to keep them safe and bring them fortune on the open seas.

Men who had followed her back here to England, where any one of them might be tried, convicted, and hanged for their crimes.

What would happen to them now? They could sail the ship themselves, but none of them had the necessary flair for command, the drive required to lead a crew to prosperity. Or, sad to say, the wit to keep the Royal Navy off their backs.

If she left them now, they would all perish. And it would be her fault. They were her men, and thus her responsibility.

Accordingly, she turned to her friend. "Abbie, I'm afraid I must dash," she said. "Some of my father's affairs—well, it appears I may need to settle them in person. In London."

"Oh, no!" Abigail clutched her hands. "You cannot leave again! You've only just returned!"

"I know, and I shall again, and soon," Bella promised. "But for now, it's urgent I go."

A gleam came to her friend's eye. "And what about Commander Reid?" she asked slyly. "What if he were to finally attend a ball, only you were not here to draw his attention?"

Bella smiled. "Perhaps some other time." She pressed her cheek to Abigail's, hugged her briefly, then turned away. "Keep a weather eye out for me," she suggested and then strode from the ballroom as swiftly as her gown would allow, leaving her friend to puzzle over that last phrase in her wake.

"Whither away, Cap'n?" Quince asked. She was in her customary place just to the side and a pace or two behind Gregor, where she could watch the ship sail without disturbing his view of the waters ahead.

"I'm not certain yet, Mister Quince," she admitted, then laughed. "But there is a whole new sea here for us to explore and plenty of ships upon it for us to capture. I think it's high time we found a few of those."

"Sounds good to me," her first mate admitted. "Besides, the men were starting to get fat and lazy sitting around spending all their wealth. Time to whip 'em back into shape again." He turned serious for a moment. "Didja hear about the new naval officer, though? Sent up from London, straight from His Majesty, with orders to hunt down any pirates along the coast. A Commander Reid, I think."

"Indeed." Belle considered that then smiled, hands going to her hips just to the sides of her sword and pistol. "Sounds like we'd best be ready for him, then."

This time it was Quince who laughed. "Oh, I'll make sure the lads are ready," he promised and marched off, already bellowing orders.

Belle observed as her crew leapt about, dancing to the first mate's tune, and the *Deadshot* sped across the waves like the deadly predator it was. For now, they seemed alone on the high seas, but she knew that would not last—nor did she want it to. After all, where was the thrill in a chase with no one to chase—or be chased by?

"Very well, Commander Reid," she said softly, glancing back toward the retreating shores of home before turning to face forward again. "I believe I'm ready for that dance now."

Chapter Three

BELLE WAS STANDING BY THE RAIL, overseeing the transfer of goods when a shout shattered the calm sea air. "Cap'n!" It was young Isaac, up in the crow's nest on lookout. "Sails!"

"Where away?" she replied, already hoisting herself up onto the rigging and beginning to climb.

"Port and aft!" the lad replied, his voice cracking.

Scowling, Belle hooked one arm through the ropes halfway up, snatched up her spyglass, and yanked it open even as she raised it to one eye, squinting to focus where he was gesturing. Sure enough, a speck of white against the green and blue suddenly leapt into larger view, resolving into an array of sailcloth, all full near to bursting from the wind off the English shore. It was a good-sized ship, too, its three full masts and squared sails marking it as a frigate, which could only mean one thing. "Royal Navy!" she hollered, slamming the spyglass into her other hand to collapse it and then stuff it back into its leather holster at her belt as she half-shimmied, half-dropped back down to the deck. "Quince! Finish up and let's be gone!"

"Aye, aye, Cap'n!" her first mate responded, then turned to the rest of the crew still over on the merchant ship with him. "You heard, lads!" he bellowed. "Step lively, lest you're wanting to explain to the Navy why we're out here nicking these bales and crates!"

That jolt of fear added a kick to everyone's steps, and a short time later Quince and the others were leaping back across to the *Deadshot* and hauling the gangplank after them. The whole while,

Belle had kept one eye on the proceedings and the other toward the shore, where that frigate had loomed larger with each passing second. It had just come hull up as they cast off lines and shoved away from the now-emptied merchant vessel, and she was able to make out its flag, with its tell-tale red cross quartering white and the Union Jack a splash of color in the upper left quadrant. The fact that she could make out the ensign with the naked eye meant her own Jolly Roger must now be visible to the approaching ship as well. Bother. "Lay on the sailcloth!" she shouted. "Put our back to the wind and let's crack on!"

The crew cheered and set to work with a will, no more eager to face a sea court than her. It was a rare thing for "Cannon" Belle Pearcy to run from a fight, but this was one she knew she couldn't win—a standard frigate might have as many as forty cannon, though they could hold up to fifty, whereas the *Deadshot*, though more heavily armed than most schooners, still managed only a dozen. Nor were hers as heavy as the frigate's. But even with two sails to three, and riding low in the water from their fresh cargo, Belle's ship was the faster of the two, provided she had the wind on her side. She was counting on that to get them all away safely.

The frigate was clearly making for them now, its prow aimed right at their stern, but as the minutes marched on, Belle was relieved to see that it was no longer gaining. And then, little by little, it fell back, dwindling in size so slowly she worried that might only be wishful thinking. She was finally convinced when she could no longer make out the ensign's design, and then not even its colors. It was only once the frigate was again a mere spot on the ocean, though, that she turned to her crew and smiled.

"Well done, lads," she told them all. "I'm sure they thought they had us, but it'd take a sharper crew than that to catch us, eh?" They cheered. "Now let's make for home. We'll take the long way round, just to be sure, and then it's shore and celebration and drinks for all!" That brought even more cheering, and the deck was a lively place as they tacked sail and brought the ship around in a long arc that would point them well away from where they'd found that merchant, and where the frigate might still be waiting.

One crew member was not whistling and singing and laughing, however, and he sidled up to her as she stood near Gregor at the wheel, his customary scowl upon his face. "First time we've seen a naval vessel this close in," Quince commented, his long blond hair ruffling in the breeze.

"It is that," she agreed, not at all put off by his manner, for she knew Quince to be trustworthy as well as competent. Every captain should have a first mate willing to ask them the hard questions, if only to make sure they did not forget to ask those themselves. "Must be that one you mentioned, sent by London to track us down."

"Must be." He frowned, rubbing at his chin, which he kept scrupulously bare perhaps in defiance of the typical image of a bearded pirate. "What was his name again? I've clean forgot it."

I have not, Belle thought but did not say, for she saw no reason to tempt the fates by uttering it aloud. The name rang in her head, though, clear as a bell—or a warning trumpet.

Bella stepped down out of the carriage and bit back a curse as her dress hem snagged on the runner, tangling about her legs and nearly spilling her out upon the muddy ground. Blazes, but she forgot how hard it was to move in all this fabric! Give her back her velvet trousers any day! If only she had not needed to come into town today, giving her a little time to get her land legs once more, but yet again her father had overspent and she was forced to meet with their solicitor to discuss the situation. She managed to keep from falling, but in doing so dropped her reticule. Damn and blast! She lunged forward, trying to catch it before it struck the dirt—or worse—and growled as the heavy velvet bag slipped through her fingers—

—only to watch a larger, more weathered hand catch it an inch above the ground.

"Oh!" She straightened to find a man rising to stand before

her, the bag in his hands. And this was quite the man! Tall, broad-shouldered but trim-waisted, those attributes well-displayed by the fitted navy-blue jacket hanging open over a white waistcoat and breeches, his dark hair tugged back beneath his bicorn to show off a strong, handsome face with noble features and dark eyes alight with interest. The hint of a smile tugged at his lips, and his bare cheeks were slightly weathered from sun and sea.

"I believe this to be yours, madam," he stated, presenting the bag with a slight bow. The unadorned gold epaulets on his shoulders proclaimed his identity as clearly as a card, yet Bella pretended not to know it, for they had not yet been introduced. Still, she smiled and curtsied as she accepted the reticule back, her gloved hands almost but not quite brushing his bare ones.

"Thank you so much, kind sir," she told him, careful not to let herself simper, for she hated such behavior. She did reward him with a warm smile, however. "I do appreciate it."

He answered with a deeper bow, sweeping the hat off his head and revealing that his dark hair had a tendency to curl about the ears, which she struggled not to find charming. "Nicholas Reid, at your service, if I may be so bold."

"Isabella Parsons, a pleasure," she answered. Daniel had stepped out from behind the coach door to present himself at her side, a silent but visible chaperone, and Bella quickly introduced him as well. She was pleased to see that her new acquaintance did not behave as so many gentlemen would have, acknowledging the coachman with a nod but without a glance as he was not of their social class. Instead Reid turned and met Daniel's gaze and even offered his hand, which was accepted with some surprise.

"Are you new to the area, Captain?" Bella asked, and was quietly amused to see Reid frown and nearly sigh. "Only, I do not recall seeing you before."

"I am only lately arrived, yes," he returned gamely enough. "This past month or two, my crew and I have been quartered at the docks in Riverside." That was a smaller town only a short ride from Hillington but right where the river met the sea. As a result, it was not only an active port but the location of the region's Royal Naval barracks, though those had been in disuse for as long as Bella could remember. "And it is only Commander, I am afraid," he could not resist adding, though he at least managed to do so without visible rancor.

"Oh, I apologize!" she said, pressing a hand to her mouth and not missing the way his eyes followed that gesture, lingering a moment there before flashing up to her eyes and then away. Well, now! "But surely you must come to the ball tomorrow night!" she urged. "It is here in town at Barrage Hall, of course, as all our simple country entertainments are. There you will have a chance to meet all your new neighbors—and I daresay you will garner much attention, both for your novelty and for the smartness of your uniform."

He laughed. "It is good to know what qualities I have to offer," he said, his eyes lively and that hint of a smile tugging at those lips again. This man was dangerous! Especially since he followed that with a tilt of his head and added, "I hope that, if you are also in attendance, as you seem to be suggesting might be the case, you will reserve for me at least one dance?"

How could she respond to that but to nod and say, "It would be my pleasure, Commander."

"Excellent!" His smile broadened and he offered a final bow before clapping his hat back onto his head. "Until tomorrow eve, then." He turned on his heel and was gone, long, strong strides carrying him down the street without haste but still at a good, steady clip.

Bella watched him go, admiring the way his figure filled out the back of those breeches. Dangerous, indeed!

Chapter Four

BELLA HAD BARELY STEPPED THROUGH THE doors of Barrage Hall when she was accosted—but not by a tall figure in navy blue. Rather, it was a shorter, softer form swathed in peach and topped with dark curls who rushed her so close her first instinct was to reach for her cutlass. Good thing she had come to the ball unarmed, or she might have run her dearest friend through before realizing it!

"Isabella, there you are!" Abigail engulfed her in a quick hug, her head only reaching Bella's shoulder, then stepped back to study her at arm's length. "Let me look at you! I do declare, it is utterly unacceptable—you grow more lovely every time you go away!"

Bella laughed. "That is only your own fondness coloring your perceptions," she replied. "But I thank you for it."

There were others trying to enter behind her so she moved off to one side, Abigail gliding along beside her. Together they sought out a pair of seats with a good view of the floor, not so close to refreshments as to risk being spilled upon but not so far away as to make resupplying a chore, and with an easy avenue of escape if someone unpleasant approached.

Listen to me, Bella thought, biting back a laugh. *I'm approaching a ball as if it were a naval engagement!* Still, the two certainly had their commonalities.

Not the least of which was the officer now descending upon them, his path as unwavering as his ship had been mere days before.

"Miss Parsons," he proclaimed, sweeping into a deep, formal bow. "I am happy to see you are a woman of your word. And I do not believe I have had the pleasure of meeting your charming companion?" Though he was alone, here in the presence of so many onlookers it was allowed to introduce oneself to a young lady without being thought reprehensible or, worse, ill-mannered.

"Commander Reid, may I introduce Miss Abigail Montrose," Bella replied. "Abigail, this is Commander Nicholas Reid of His Majesty's Royal Navy."

"Delighted, Miss Montrose," Reid told her, bowing over her hand, but his eyes immediately returned to Bella's. "Miss Parsons, I believe I was promised a dance tonight. Might I be so bold as to lay claim to it now, before you are no doubt assailed by others demanding your attention?"

She laughed and rose to her feet, setting her reticule on the seat to hold her place. "How could I refuse such a noble and considerate offer, Commander?" She turned to Abigail. "I hope you will excuse me for a moment, Abigail."

Her best friend feigned a pout, though her eyes sparkled. "I will be forlorn, of course," Abigail sniffed, "but somehow I shall endure." She winked. "Especially if you return with punch."

"Consider it done." Bella let Commander Reid lead the way out to the floor, her hand resting lightly upon his, and then turned to face him as they settled in among the many other pairs assembling for the first dance of the evening. "Are you always so daring, sir?" she asked as the music began and they stepped toward and around each other, twirling in time, their hands still held gently between them, connecting them yet also maintaining the proper distance required by decorum.

"When I have an objective in sight, certainly," he replied with a small grin. "I hope you will forgive me my forwardness. I am a military man, and accustomed to the need for swift and decisive action."

"There are many who would say such behavior was antithetical to social niceties," she pointed out, able to focus her attention on him as her body went through the familiar steps of the dance all on its own. It did not surprise her at all that the commander was light and sure on his feet, his steps graceful and smooth. She suspected he would be deadly with a blade, especially with the way his eyes remained focused on her face the whole time, sharp and intent.

"And are you one of those?" he asked now. "For if so, I will endeavor to moderate my behavior."

That drew a laugh from her, and his own smile broadened, his eyes crinkling in pleasure. "Am I? Not at all! No, I applaud anyone who knows what they want, what they must do, and sets their sights on achieving it." As she had done when she had made the rather strange decision to turn to piracy. Not that she'd had a choice at the time! It had literally been "do or die" then, or at least "do or be ravished or ransomed or some other horrendous fate," and she had determined to accept none of those. Instead she had laid her own course, unconventional as it might be, and had turned what could have been a torment into a triumph.

Commander Reid was studying her, and Bella realized with a start that her chin had risen and her lips had firmed into a thin line. She forced herself back to the present, back to Barrage Hall and the ball, and back to her previous smile. "How are you finding Hillington and its environs?" she asked as sweetly—and demurely—as she could manage.

A rapid blink of the eye was the only indication that he had noticed her sudden shift. "Most agreeable," he answered easily, bowing as the dance ended and they returned to their starting positions. "Especially the company."

"You flatter me, good sir," she told him, curtsying. "Thank you most kindly for the dance. Now I believe I promised my friend refreshments as recompense for abandoning her."

"Well, we cannot have you go back on your promise," he stated, and offered her his arm. "Would you permit me to accompany you?"

"Of course." Together they quit the floor, allowing other couples to take their place, and headed back toward the edge of the room, veering away from where Abigail waited and angling toward the nearest refreshment table instead. There Bella's companion insisted upon pouring two crystal cups full of punch and then carrying them as they returned to their seats, where he presented one to an appreciative Abigail.

"But you did not get one for yourself!" she pointed out. "You must rectify that, and then join us!"

"It would be my honor," the commander stated, bowing. "I shall return momentarily."

No sooner had he stepped out of earshot than Abigail turned to Bella, eyes sharp as a hawk's but smile bright as the sun. "Spill, my dear," her friend whispered. "Do we like the handsome Commander? Because you certainly seemed all smiles just now, and he could barely tear his eyes away from you! Trust me, the room is already abuzz about it!"

Yes, Bella had felt some of those eyes upon her as they had danced, and not all of them as friendly as Abigail's. Hillington was not a large community, and thus there was a dearth of eligible young men to be had. For her to have already claimed some attention from the newest—and most appealing—would seem a coup to many, and an injustice to others. For now she merely allowed herself a small, smug smile. "He is acceptable thus far."

"Acceptable!" Abigail swatted her friend's shoulder with her closed fan. "If that is all, step aside and allow me to take a turn! I'm sure he'll be far more than acceptable to *me*!" She was laughing as she said it, but Bella knew there was some truth behind the jest as well. Which was why, when the commander returned, she favored him with an expression of feigned concern.

"Abigail was just lamenting the lack of suitable dance partners," she informed him after giving him barely enough time to take a sip from his cup. "And I believe I hear the musicians gearing up for the next dance."

Her hint was not subtle, nor was he slow to apprehend—or to rise to the occasion. "Then perhaps, Miss Montrose, you would allow me the pleasure of this dance?" he told a beaming Abigail, handing his mostly untouched cup to a passing manservant and bowing to her as he offered his hand. The dip of his head to Bella, however, made it clear that this was being done more as a favor to her than out of real interest on his part, and she acknowledged that with a nod and a smile a touch warmer than she had originally intended.

The two departed for the dance and Bella watched them go, though her mind quickly wandered. She exchanged polite greetings with other neighbors and acquaintances as they strolled by, pleased at least to not have to deal with the Tremont sisters, who were away visiting an elderly relative for a fortnight. There was no question that Barrage Hall was pleasant, with its high ceilings lit by glittering chandeliers and its tall windows framed by lacy curtains and its vast rooms filled with happy, laughing people. Yet, Bella found her heart yearned for the salt tang of the sea and the wide-open space of the glittering blue water, and the gentle roll of the *Deadshot*'s deck beneath her feet.

At least she had re-acclimated to dry land! It would have been terribly embarrassing to have tripped over her own feet during the dance because she was still adjusting her footing to the imagined sway of a deck at high tide!

When Abigail returned after the dance, she was alone—and fuming. "That Penelope Sinclair!" she declared, flopping down in her seat. "Can you believe the nerve! The dance had only just ended—the music still hung in the air!—when she declared, loudly, 'Oh, if only I had someone to dance with! But all the good men are spoken for, or else not willing to attend me!' So of course your dashing Commander—"

"He is hardly my *anything*," Bella interrupted, only to be tutted at as if by a spinster aunt.

"Oh, I think he is, Isabella," her friend confided, her dimple showing as she smiled. "He might have been dancing with me, but I am not blind—I saw how it was done for your approval and nothing more." She pouted, though only for an instant, for Abigail never could hold anger for long. It was one of the things Bella treasured about her. "I would be severely put out if I did not love you so." This was accompanied by a fond pat to her hand. "So, anyway, your dashing Commander of course immediately offered his services—though he made sure to glance my way for permission first. And"—she lowered her voice even more, as if they were discussing deep secrets rather than ball gossip—"he bade me request that you reserve the last dance for him."

Bella smiled at that, despite herself. First *and* last dance! Partiality indeed! "Then he shall have it," she declared, and raised her cup to toast and seal the matter. Abigail giggled and did likewise, and the two of them settled back in to people-watch and gossip and poke gentle fun at their peers, which was often far more fun than the dancing itself.

"You have been rather popular this evening," Bella said as she faced "her" commander once more. It was the final dance of the evening, and he had indeed made good on his request, appearing beside her to offer his hand.

"I apologize," he told her, with a quick grimace that vanished almost as soon as it had appeared. "Such was not my intent." He glanced about them before leaning in and adding, in a softer tone, "I had not realized there would be so many ladies in desperate need of a dance partner."

"Oh, yes, you have landed in a veritable garden of unwed young women," she answered with a smile. "We are all of us available, and thus all desperate to find a good man."

That earned her a calculating gaze whose frankness made her flush slightly. "You do not strike me as desperate at all," he told her as the music began and they fell into step. "Quite the contrary. You seem very self-possessed, as if you could take or leave such things. Which," he added, smiling, "I find extraordinarily appealing."

"Do you now?" Bella laughed. "That is good to know, for it is true that I have been said to be headstrong and proud. 'Accustomed to having my own way,' is I believe the popular term." She swept around him, her skirts swishing to the motion, and he matched her step by step.

"I have yet to see any pride beyond what must be considered justified," he responded. "Nor have you seemed headstrong, only confident." He grinned, and the expression made his eyes crinkle again. "But we have only just met."

"Indeed." Bella grinned in return. "And yet I feel a bout of such willfulness coming on."

She deliberately increased her pace, still keeping her general motions in time to the music but upping her own tempo, adding an extra step, an extra twirl. Reid raised an eyebrow but echoed her, staying in time with her movements. They were still in their place in line, yet Bella saw some of the other dancers looking their way, and a few faltered as they muddled their own steps, unsure if they should be pacing her or the music or both.

That only urged her on. She sped up yet again, now stepping twice to the other pairs' once, twirling in between, and yet still Reid kept up. Good. She liked a challenge.

Dancing was normally warming, under all the layers and lights. Now she was positively aglow, her skin damp from perspiration, only the recent shortening of her curls preventing them from becoming a sticky mass atop her head. Yet Bella felt more alive than she had all night, and she laughed aloud as they spun together, her and Reid, out of synch and yet still in step with those around them. That felt like her whole life described right there, outwardly still in line but inwardly moving to her own beat, refusing to be constrained by the rest yet somehow still fitting in, and she was flushed but grinning when the music finally ended and they came to a stop, her heart beating wildly as she curtsied to her partner.

Commander Reid was breathing heavily as well, and his face was shiny with sweat, but his eyes were alive and still dancing as he bowed. "A fine, spirited way to end the ball," he told her, offering his arm to escort her back to where Abigail waited. "Thank you, Miss Parsons, for a most pleasant evening, and a welcome relief from the norm."

"Thank you, Commander Reid," she replied as they reached her friend and disengaged. "Sometimes, you simply have to let the lady lead." She could already see from Abigail's expression—half shock and half glee—that the gossiping had also accelerated to reflect her own feverish pace. "I fear I must now bid you good night."

"Of course." He bowed to them both, then turned and disappeared back into the crowd, which was already beginning to disperse. He did not do so with the haste of a man trying to distance himself from a dangerous reputation, at least not to Bella's eye, but who could be sure? Only time would tell.

For now, she patted Abigail on the arm. "Come, we will find our coaches," she suggested, leading the way toward the door and enjoying how the crowd parted for her, much like the sea before her ship's prow. "Best to depart now, so they can talk about me in peace."

Abigail was still laughing about it the next morning. "La, the whole room practically erupted!" she crowed, accepting the cup of tea Sophie had poured her and stealing one of the small sandwiches Margaret had prepared exactly how she liked them. Bella had invited her friend over to Crestmont for morning tea and they were comfortably ensconced in the sitting room, just the pair of them and her lady's maid. "Lady Sarah was near to apoplexy! 'Does she imagine this to be a race?' I heard her say. 'Men are not interested in women who can outpace them!'" She tittered as she imitated the county's most venerable—and most crotchety—widow, her brown curls dancing about her head.

Bella laughed as well, eschewing the sandwiches in favor of a small apricot tart. "Yes, well, who says women are interested in slow men?" she retorted, making her friend quake with laughter. But she shook her head. "Ah, Abigail, I fear I am becoming a bad influence on you," she warned. "You should take care lest my bad reputation rub off on you." She said that only half in jest, for in truth she worried about her effect on her friend, and not just from her behavior at the ball. What if her other identity, the occupation she had thought to shed yet had been loathe to give up, were to be somehow revealed? Would Abigail be censured as well, for their close association? Bella hoped not. Though of course she hoped never to get discovered for her own sake as well.

"Pah, as if I care what those old fusspots have to say!" Abigail protested. She grinned. "Besides, while they might have been scandalized I heard a few closer to our age say they admired your spirit—and more than one gentleman mutter that he'd be happy to have a go at keeping up with you!"

"Hmph. They can but try." There was only one gentleman whose opinion Bella was concerned about at the moment. She suspected it would be some days before she knew whether he had in truth been as unaffected by her behavior as he'd claimed, and cursed herself for caring so much.

Still, her heart skipped a beat when, after a discreet knock, Geoffrey entered. The family butler was carrying a silver tray, the worked metal circle all but disappearing atop his enormous hand, and on the tray was a single letter, addressed to her.

"Ooh, mysterious!" Abigail declared, rising from her seat to plop down beside Bella instead as she accepted the small, tidily addressed missive. "Who is it from, and what do they say?"

Bella unfolded it and read aloud, for she had only one secret she kept from her closest friend. "My dear Miss Parsons," she began. "I hope you do not consider me overbold in stating again how much I enjoyed your company last night. Never have I had a dance so invigorating, and only partially from the pace. If it pleases you, I would very much like to call upon you and your father at some point in the near future. Yours cordially and with great spirit, Nicholas Reid, Commander."

"Oh, very nice!" her friend stated after the recitation was done. "Not at all afraid to tell you he likes you, that's certain! And 'you and your father'—he's been asking after you! Considerate, too—if your father is present, there's no question of impropriety." She tapped

Bella on the arm with her fan. "He's up for a little racing, hey?"

Bella laughed. "Now I know I am rubbing off on you," she said, "for surely you were never so coarse before." But she found she was beaming, too. Yes, there was no question of his interest, and she had to admit that she returned it in full. But how much more complicated that made everything!

Still, where was the fun in life without a few complications?

Chapter Five

THE LETTER—AND ITS REPLY, WHICH SHE had sent that afternoon, returning the compliment about their time together and extending an invitation to dine with them at Crestmont a week hence—was still on Belle's mind two days later, only gone now were cushions and tea sandwiches and Empire dresses, replaced by oiled wooden railings and hard tack and trousers. Though she missed Abigail's sunny company, Belle had to admit she preferred the scenery here on the *Deadshot*'s deck—especially now, with a fat French merchant ship floundering in their sights.

"Ahoy, the ship!" she heard Quince shout as they pulled up alongside the *Mère de Nacre*, their warning shot having snuffed out any fight the poor traders and sailors might have possessed. "Stand down and prepare to be boarded, or suffer the consequences!"

A tall, skinny man with a high forehead and a long face, presumably the captain, stomped over to the railing, hands raised to show them empty. "We surrender," he called back, his English heavily accented but easily understood. "We offer no resistance, and ask only for mercy."

"And mercy ye shall have," Belle announced, wrapping one hand around a line and swinging up onto the railing to face her fellow captain across the narrow gap. "Behave, do as you're told, and you'll all be free to go soon enough, and unharmed."

The captain nodded and gestured his men back as the grappling lines were tossed across and made fast. The gangplank followed, and soon her crew was over and beginning to haul goods up from the hold.

They had only brought a handful of items across, however, when Belle heard the cry she'd been half-expecting. "Sails!" shouted Isaac from the crow's nest. "Three-master, to starboard!" That was out at sea, and she cursed as she yanked free her spyglass and scanned the horizon. There! It was a frigate, sure enough, and she did not think it her imagination that its ensign was white quartered by red. Damn! How had he found her again, and so quickly!?

Quince was already hurrying up to join her near the rail. "It's that commander again, has to be," he agreed to her unspoken question. "And this time he's got the wind at his back, driving him on. No chance to outrun him, or dart past toward the open water. We'll have to go shoreward, but he'll be here afore we can get safely away, even if we cut ties now."

Her first mate had already turned and taken a deep breath, preparing to give that order, when Belle stopped him. "No," she said, her mind racing. "You're right, we can't outrun him, not this time. So we'll outthink him instead." Quickly she outlined what she had in mind, and Quince's sour face split into a rare smile.

"Aye, that might do the trick," he said. "And if not, well, at least we'll have given it a rum go!" Then he was leaping over to the *Mère de Nacre*, calling the rest of their men over there to him as he went. Belle grinned and turned her attention to the merchant captain, who had since identified himself as one André Laurent and who was watching the commotion with a bemused look upon his long face. "I must beg your patience a while longer, good sir," she told him, making sure her voice carried across the water. "But I assure you, we still intend to leave you and yours in peace—only a little later than originally planned."

That seemed to satisfy Laurent, at least, for he did not interfere as Quince took command of the other ship's wheel and the men scaled the riggings and began playing out the sails. A handful of others continued the work of unloading, only now they were doing so across two moving vessels instead of two anchored ones. The two ships ground against each other, scraping both hulls, but thanks to echoed commands they were able to keep both sails trimmed to match, and though the lines strained, they held.

The *Mère de Nacre* was not a particularly fast ship—which was how the *Deadshot* had caught her in the first place—and so even at her swiftest pace they had not advanced far before the frigate pulled up within hail on the merchant's far side. "Ahoy!" came the shout from that vessel, in a voice Belle had already begun to know well. "This is Commander Reid of His Majesty's *Diligent*. Yield the ship and surrender yourself for judgment!"

"No thank you!" Belle shouted back, perching high up on the *Deadshot*'s rail so that she could make out Reid on his own deck beyond the *Mère de Nacre*'s. She took care to keep her voice as deep and rough as possible, and was glad the wind was strong enough to send her black braid whipping about her head. They were so near that she saw his eyes narrow in recognition, but trusted that it was merely the famed pirate Cannon Belle he saw, and not his recent dance partner.

He seemed surprised by her open defiance. "Surrender," he insisted again. "Or—"

"Or what?" she retorted. "You'll open fire through innocents? Even if they are French, I think not."

When he visibly fumed she threw her head back and laughed. It had worked! She had thought that a naval man, and especially one as honorable as Reid, would not be willing to fire upon a civilian ship, even if England and France were still battling in the War of the Sixth Coalition. Which was why, rather than doing the expected and cutting their target loose so they could run, she had instead ordered the *Mère de Nacre* hauled in close. The two ships were sailing as one now—and as long as they continued this way, with the *Diligent* on their far side, the merchant acted as a shield, keeping the *Deadshot* safe.

"I ask you to reconsider putting these good people in harm's way," Reid tried again, clearly exasperated by this strange turn of events. "It is highly dishonorable."

"More or less so than piracy?" Belle countered. "And I am not putting them in harm's way, for I am not the one threatening them. You are."

That caused "her commander" to jam his bicorn down more firmly on his head and turn away from her to spit orders to his crew. A moment later, the *Diligent* let her sails fill again and the frigate leaped forward, racing ahead of the paired ships.

Her crew cheered at this, but Belle silenced them with a gesture. "We've not won free yet, lads," she warned. "That was just the first step. There's more to come."

Sure enough, the *Diligent* heeled about, jibing to swing wide and circle around in front of them so that it could approach the *Deadshot* from its unprotected side. The frigate's square rigging was not ideal for such maneuvers, however, and it was going from windward to leeward, making such a turn a slow and cumbersome process.

At the same time, Belle signaled Quince, who nodded and swung the rudder over a notch, Gregor matching him so the *Deadshot* and the *Mère de Nacre* both jibed as well, wearing ship to angle farther toward the shore. This forced the *Diligent* to widen its arc, lest the paired bowsprits pierce it broadsides before it could complete the turn.

But while the *Diligent* was describing a wide arc, the *Deadshot* and the *Mère de Nacre* were executing a much tighter circle, using the *Deadshot*'s hastily dropped anchor to help hold them in place as they wheeled about together. It did not hurt that even the *Mère de Nacre* was smaller than the frigate now trying to loop around them.

Still, Belle held her breath, gauging her own ship's position and speed against that of the frigate. She had the weather gauge but it would be a near thing indeed.

At last the *Diligent* completed her semi-circle. Now she was facing them and on their shoreward side. But the frigate soon discovered that it had another problem, or at least the same problem as before—thanks to her own maneuvering, Belle had kept the

Mère de Nacre between herself and Reid's vessel. All three ships were now more or less in a row and facing into the wind, with the *Deadshot* on the seaward side and the *Diligent* caught between the merchant ship and land.

That was what Belle had been hoping for. Of course, if she ran the frigate would give chase—except she had a plan for that as well. "Now!" she shouted. Quince and the boys leaped back across, tossing the grappling lines over first and tugging the gangplank after. Then Gregor spun the wheel and the *Deadshot* turned, falling behind its two escorts as its sails no longer caught the wind—and then tacking hard across the wind, toward the shore.

Which ran the pirate ship straight behind the backside of the frigate that had been pursuing it.

Quince glanced her way, a question evident on his sour face, but Belle shook her head. Even with their smaller guns a solid broadside from them now, straight up the *Diligent*'s unprotected stern, would devastate the naval vessel. She could not bring herself to do it, however, and told herself it had nothing to do with Reid being aboard the ship. No, she just didn't believe in butchery, or unnecessary violence. Yes, that was the only reason.

As they passed behind the frigate she saw the helmsman haul on the wheel, trying to bring the *Diligent* about, and tensed. If they managed the turn they'd be in a position to fire a full broadside at the *Deadshot*, and at this range there was no way they would survive such an onslaught.

But the *Diligent* had been too focused on her prey. She had not paid attention to other details—like how close they'd drifted to shore, or the depth of water. Belle winced instinctively when she heard the crunch of a hull grinding against sand and rock, but then had to repress the urge to cheer. This was why she'd angled them so close to land. She'd known there were shallows lying in wait here.

A pity Reid had not.

With its shallower keel, the *Deadshot* skipped easily across those same shallows, gliding past the *Diligent* close enough they could almost touch. The crew rushed to the stern and opened fire with their muskets, and their commanding officer followed behind, claiming a space along the taffrail. Despite the hail of bullets Belle hopped up on the *Deadshot*'s rail and grinned as she passed Reid, who had the decency to call to his men, "Belay firing!" Then, as the firing ceased, he tipped his hat. "Well played, madam," he called out. "Your reputation for boldness is well deserved."

"You are too kind, commander," she shouted back, and swept off her hat in a bow—though carefully, so that her long black wig remained in place. "Thank you for the dance!" Then they were clear and the *Deadshot* continued on, leaving the lightened *Mère de Nacre* to slowly correct its course and the *Diligent* to carefully kedge off the shoal, using small anchors on boats to pull itself out of the shallows and back to deeper waters.

The crew all let out a cheer then. "Here's to Cannon Belle," Quince shouted. "Cleverest captain in the German Ocean!"

Belle bowed and spun about. "Thanks, boys!" she told them all. "Now let's be off before the good commander comes looking for another round!"

There'll be time enough for that, she told herself. After all, Reid had made it clear he was up for a race. And as long as he let her lead, she was optimistic about her odds of coming in first.

Chapter Six

"AND HOW ARE YOU FINDING HILLINGTON, Commander?"

Bella did her best not to laugh at the question, the same she'd asked him over a week before, but did meet Abigail's amused glance and roll her eyes just a little. It was a perfectly reasonable line of conversation, of course. Very proper, and very safe. Also, more than a little bit boring.

In fact, much like Stephen Montrose, who'd voiced it.

They were gathered in the parlor at Crestmont, awaiting the call to dinner. Reid had arrived exactly on time, as befitted a military man, and handsome as ever in his sharp uniform. Bella's father had been on hand to receive the young officer, and she'd been pleased that Lord Roderick was having one of his better days, fully aware of his surroundings and other people, if mildly distracted by the stray thought or a wisp of air from the open windows showing off the room's view of the sea beyond.

"Commander Reid, may I present my father, William Parsons, Baron Roderick," she explained, and Reid had bowed perfectly, crisply.

"Lord Roderick, it is a pleasure to finally meet you," he'd said. "Though I've only been in Yorkshire a short while, I've already become well acquainted with your good name."

"That's most of kind of you, Commander. Most kind," her father had replied, beaming. "Glad to meet you as well, and pleased you could join us for dinner. You're from somewhere a bit south of us, I take it? Devon, unless I miss my guess."

Reid had not bothered to hide his surprise. "Well spotted, sir! Indeed, I grew up in Plymouth."

Bella's father had clearly been delighted to have so astounded their guest. "Yes, well, used to travel all over the country in my youth," he'd explained. "Have an ear for dialect, can tell a Plymouth man from a Dover lad from a Norwich fellow, I'll tell you that much! It's all in . . ." His discourse on pronunciation had been thankfully interrupted by Geoffrey entering to announce the rest of their dinner party's arrival, and Bella thought she'd detected a hint of gratitude on Reid's face as he'd turned to welcome the other guests. Though had there been some disappointment as well? Foolish man, to think he'd rate a private dinner with just her and her father so soon!

No, she'd keep him on the hook a little longer, lest he find matters too easy to hold his interest!

Abigail he'd already met, of course, but Bella quickly introduced him to her best friend's two companions. "This is Stephen Montrose, Abigail's elder brother, and his wife Deborah. Stephen, Deborah, may I present Commander Nicholas Reid."

"How'd you do?" Stephen had quickly followed his greeting with, "So sorry, Bella, but our parents send their regrets. Not quite up to it tonight." He'd known her her whole life, and so could get away with the familiarity of that nickname, especially here in such intimate company.

"I'm sorry to hear that, please send my regards." Though, in truth, she had not been surprised. The elder Montroses were rarely willing to leave their own home. Bella glanced around. "And no Edmund?"

That had earned a laugh from Abigail. "No, the little scamp is under house arrest," she'd answered. "For breaking another vase by bowling indoors!" Edmund was the youngest Montrose, all of twelve and full of energy. Bella quite liked him and his boundless enthusiasm, though she was always glad to send him back home after an evening. Simply being around that much energy was exhausting!

One person remained to be welcomed, however, having entered just behind the Montroses, and now Bella held out her hand, beckoning him to join her. "And this," she told Reid, "is a fellow officer. Commander Nicholas Reid, may I present Commodore Nathaniel Ayers."

"Commodore." Reid saluted the grizzled older man sharply. "It's an honor, sir. I've heard of your exploits off Gibraltar. First class, sir."

"Ha, thank you, lad," Ayers replied, returning the salute with a cheery nod and a rap of his cane on the floor. "You'll have to tell me all about your ship. Been too long since these old legs were on deck."

The two naval men were still comparing notes when Geoffrey ran the bell for dinner, and Bella was glad she'd invited the Commodore. He was an old friend of her father's, of course, and an absolute dear, even if half the town thought him standoffish. They just hadn't taken the time to get past that crusty exterior, was all. But she had grown up listening to his tales of the sea and his many naval campaigns—when he'd returned home after being released from active service, Ayers had found Bella half-wild, her mother recently deceased and her father too beside himself to cope, and had taken it upon himself to become her godfather and give her discipline the only way he knew how, by treating her like one of his sailors. She'd learned most of the regulation rope knots before she'd learned to write her name, along with several other valuable skills, and the retired officer was still like a second father to her.

"I'd say he's won the Commodore's approval," Abigail whispered to her as they entered the dining room and took their seats. Bella was at one end of the table, of course, and her father at the other, with men and women alternated between them in proper fashion. And Ruth had clearly been as sharp as ever, because the table had already been shortened to account for the elder Montroses' absence.

Dinner conversation came in waves between courses, and it was during one of those that Stephen asked Reid his thoughts on their community. So like Stephen, struggling manfully to project confidence and worldliness and almost but not quite succeeding.

Reid, of course, handled the question with aplomb. "I find myself liking it more and more the longer I am here," he answered, with a quick glance and a wink at Bella, and she smiled but maintained her own poise. She was the hostess here, after all—it would not do to giggle and simper just because some handsome man was showing her such favor! Still, she felt her cheeks flush, and only a little from the claret they were sipping with their *duck a l'orange.*

"If only it weren't for those blasted pirates, eh?" Ayers said, draining his glass and setting it down with a thump. "Though I suppose they keep you busy, what?"

"They do at that," Reid agreed with a grimace. "I've come close to catching one a time or two, but the blackguard has slipped through my fingers each time."

Bella leaned forward. "Oh? Which pirate was it?" she asked, feigning ignorance. "Anyone we'd have heard of?"

He frowned but was evidently too well-bred not to answer: "The one they call Cannon Belle."

"The woman? I daresay!" That was Stephen again. "But I heard of her being down near Tunisia?"

"She was," Reid agreed. "Terror of the Mediterranean, for all that she's a relative newcomer—as feared as old Raven Mane or that other villain, Hemlock, and both of those at least have died or gone to ground, while she's still very much a going concern. For some reason, she's relocated up here, though. Hit several ships in the German Ocean recently." He scowled. "As I said, I've had a run-in with her once already. Close enough to leap across, if not for the risk of being shot mid-jump."

"That sounds awfully dangerous," Abigail opined. "I hope no one was hurt?"

Reid's scowl lessened, becoming more thoughtful. "Oddly enough, no," he answered. "It was all surprisingly civil. But I'd heard private reports of such about her previously. Ruthless as needed but never more. Daring, though, no question of that. Bold as brass and twice as lively." His gaze rose to rest upon Bella, and she did her best not to notice, lest he make the obvious comparison.

Instead she laughed, ducking her head, and twirled her wine glass. "A female pirate captain!" She smirked. "What will they think of next, hm? And how can one possibly sail in petticoats?"

The commander's brow arched, and she could guess he was trying to reconcile that seemingly vacuous comment with the headstrong woman he'd danced with a week before. Good. Bella wanted to keep him guessing. That way he was off balance, which made it easier to maintain control. And less likely he'd tumble to her secret.

Though it was a shame she had to resort to such devices.

Fortunately, Stephen launched into a longwinded explanation of some business he'd conducted for his father in Tunisia a few years back. That led to Bella's father and the Commodore reminiscing about some early trips they'd made overseas, in their shared youth. And then Abigail expressed interest in the fashions of that time and place, even dragging the usually closemouthed Deborah into the conversation. Bella herself was only too happy to discuss frills and sashes and shawls for a time, if only to lead the talk away from tales of her own alter ego.

After dinner, Stephen and Deborah lingered only a short while before making their excuses—their infant daughter, Clara, was home with the nanny, and they wished to tuck her in for the night themselves, which one could hardly argue against—and retiring for the evening, forcing a visibly disappointed Abigail to depart with them. That did leave exactly four, however, which was the perfect number for cards, and so Bella soon found herself seated around the table with her father, the Commodore, and Commander Reid.

She'd played many times with the first two, of course, and knew their individual styles well—her father played with flair but little attention to detail, launching elaborate attacks but often forgetting his turn or the other cards that had been laid out, while the Commodore played like an old seadog, close to the chest, begrudging every lost point. Bella's own approach was daring, taking risks that paid off well half the time and doomed her the other half.

Reid, she quickly learned, was an adept player but a cautious one—not as cagey as the Commodore, and quick to respond, but slow to make the first move and too careful by half. They were paired together for one round, and did well only because Bella took charge and he adapted to the cards she'd set forth, but the next round he led off and his approach was so hesitant, so diffident, that it was all she could do not to sweep the cards from the table. Her own play grew more erratic as a result, compensating for his lack of daring by pushing hers to the limit, and they lost that round badly.

"Ah, the enthusiasm of youth," the Commodore commented with a familiar chuckle after, gathering the deck to reshuffle. "When you don't bother playing to win because you know you'll get plenty more chances later."

Reid nodded, but that only made Bella bristle more. "I always play to win," she remarked sharply, though she couldn't help calming some when the older officer patted her hand.

"I know you do, and I've always admired that about you," he told her gently. "Sometimes, though, the best way to win is just to stay in the game."

That was sound advice, Bella knew. Just not any she cared to follow. Because who wanted to stay in the game if all you were doing was muddling along, keeping barely afloat? All or nothing, that was her style—a blaze of glory, either way. Being a pirate certainly hadn't changed that. If anything, it had only increased such behavior in her. She'd expected more circumspect play from the two older men, but was disappointed that Reid's had also followed that model. He'd seemed so confident at the ball, and on the water!

She hoped this didn't bode ill for their continued association, but time would tell.

Chapter Seven

Two weeks later, Bella was far less sanguine about her prospects with the handsome naval commander.

"Gah!" she declared, stabbing her embroidery as if it stood between her and precious cargo. "He is just so infuriating!"

Abigail produced something between a snort and a giggle. "I thought the two of you seemed to be getting on quite well at dinner." The two of them were in the Crestmont sitting room again, ostensibly attending their sewing. Bella had asked her friend once why they almost always wound up at her home, to which Abigail had replied, "no siblings to contend with, less interference from parents, more comfortable couches, the fresh sea air, and better sandwiches." None of which Bella could refute.

She did scowl at her friend now, however. "Yes, yes, he was very good that night. But that was ages ago!"

"And you've not heard from him since?"

"No, of course I have," Bella was forced to allow. "He sent a very nice card the next day, thanking us for having him and expressing a desire to visit again when convenient. Convenient!" Her cloth was beginning to resemble a lace doily, given the number and size of holes she was creating in it. "What would convenience have to do with anything?"

"He is being considerate," her friend pointed out. "Which is very thoughtful of him." She tapped a finger against her lower lip. "And you have seen him since, have you not?"

It was rare for Abigail to be the voice of reason, and Bella found she did not like it, though it did not make her love her friend any less. "Twice, yes. Once on the promenade and once on our way from church. Both times only briefly." She tossed her ravaged cloth aside and flopped back in her seat. "Perhaps I've somehow lost his interest?"

That did earn a full-on snort. "Fat chance of that!" Abigail set her own needlework aside and shifted over to nudge Bella's shoulder with her own. "He *is* a busy man, you know. All that sailing about, chasing after pirates. One in particular."

"Not that he's got even the slightest chance of catching her," Bella muttered. "But yes, I know he has his responsibilities. I suppose I just expected more . . . passion? Enthusiasm? Daring?"

Her friend laughed, though not entirely unkindly. "You've been reading too many of those romances," she teased. "Expecting him to sweep you off your feet within minutes of your first encounter! Has he done anything inappropriate?"

"No, curse him!"

"Anything that would suggest he is no longer interested, beyond being too circumspect for your tastes?"

"Well, no . . ."

"Then the only problem is that he is behaving exactly as a gentleman should?"

"When you put it that way . . ."

"Good. Then it's settled. Your commander is still yours, and you are simply being impatient for him to declare his devotion." Abigail patted her hand. "He will. Just give him time."

Bella laughed. "You make it sound so simple." Yet, as she stood to retrieve her embroidery and see whether it could be salvaged, she had to wonder. Was her friend right? Was it just a question of impatience? Certainly, the dashing commander had done nothing wrong. If anything, most would agree with Abigail that he was being honorable and considerate.

Yet Bella couldn't help feeling something was lacking. Surely he could be a little more passionate, a little more daring, without putting either of their reputations at risk?

Perhaps, she decided, she would simply have to be daring for the both of them. That, at least, was something she could do.

"Ship ahead, hard to starboard!" Isaac called down. "Merchant, by the look of her!"

Belle grabbed up the spyglass and aimed it off that side, studying the waters of the German Ocean. After a second, she spotted the dark shape of ship and sails. "I see her!" she announced. "Excellent work, Isaac! Gregor, point us toward our fresh prey! The rest of you, get ready!"

The crew cheered as the *Deadshot* swung about, angling across the waves, and Belle felt her own blood thrill at the prospect of taking this new ship. This was what her romance with Reid had been missing, this excitement, this sense of being alive! She'd felt it at the ball, when they'd danced, and even a milder version thrumming through her as they'd talked. There had been a hint of it at dinner that night, though significantly more muted. But nothing since. Was she losing interest in him instead of the other way round? Yet he was as handsome as ever, as engaging, as witty, as attentive. What more was she looking for?

Something like this, she decided, leaning on the rail as her ship leaped forward, its sails filling as the wind shot it across the water like an arrow, straight for its target. She wanted a relationship that felt like this, all the time.

The ship ahead had grown just large enough to see with the naked eye when her lookout shouted down again, only with a different message: "There's a second ship!"

A second ship? Belle's heart raced and her breath grew short. They'd never taken two at once before! Could today be the day to correct that?

"What sort?" she shouted back. "Another merchant?" Sometimes a cargo was too vast for a single ship, and so it was divided among two or more, all headed to the same port and the same owner. That was what she was hoping.

The other possibility was far less pleasant. The Royal Navy did sometimes issue an escort for important ships, or whole convoys. She had no interest in fighting over her prize, and especially not with the far bigger and stronger HMS *Diligent*. An apt name for the ship and its captain, she thought with a grimace. Not the HMS *Daring* or the HMS *Bold*. Merely diligent.

When Isaac did reply a moment later, the lad's voice contained something other than excitement, however. This was more like confusion—or fear.

"It's making for the first one," he answered. "I think—I think it may be like us."

Another pirate. Belle cursed, but knew she had only one option here. "Heave to," she told Gregor, who quickly spun the wheel, killing their momentum even as Quince ordered the sail lines slackened. "Let's see exactly what we're dealing with." It did no one any good for them to charge in headlong, not when they could wait and see instead. It was entirely possible this other ship wouldn't manage to take the merchant, in which case the *Deadshot* could swoop in and finish the job for them. Or they would, but would be weakened by the merchant's resistance—Belle and her crew had no problem taking from another pirate, in a situation like that.

Still, she hated waiting. Her fists beat against the rail as she stood there, eager to pounce.

She could see both ships clearly through her spyglass now. The second one was definitely a pirate, and a big one, larger even than a frigate, and with red-brown sails that looked eerily like dried blood. Its Jolly Roger was still too faint for her to make out more than white blobs on black, but it was bearing down on the hapless merchant like a shark after a school of fish. The merchant ship was trying to run, but it didn't stand a chance—out there in the open water, its smaller size put it at a severe disadvantage.

Then she heard a distant boom, like thunder. Only she knew it was not, even before she saw the flash from the other pirate's flank.

"They've fired upon the merchant!" Quince stated. Belle hadn't even noticed him at her side, his spyglass aligned with her own.

"And not a warning shot, neither—that holed the hull, and right above the waterline." It was a risky shot, since a little lower and the merchant would begin sinking, possibly before it could be boarded and stripped bare. But it certainly let them know their pursuers meant business.

Sure enough, the merchant ship let its sails go slack, slowing in the water so the pirates could more easily overtake them. Belle imagined she could hear the bump as the two ships brushed against each other, and she watched the dark swarm of pirates clambering across onto the captured vessel.

From here, it seemed forever before that same mass of bodies reversed course, flowing back onto their own ship. Belle knew from experience, though, that to the pirates—and their victims—it would seem barely a dozen heartbeats, everything happening in a mad flurry of motion.

At last the exodus ceased—and, beside her, Belle heard her first mate whistle under his breath. "What?"

"Nobody moving on deck," he answered, and she trained her own glass on the merchant ship to confirm what he'd said. He was right, of course. There was no one there. But she hadn't seen any captives being dragged across, either. So where was the merchant captain and his crew, and any passengers? She felt a chill despite the bright sun overhead.

A moment later, they watched as the pirate ship began to pull away. It was still too close to see much daylight between them, however, when a series of flashes erupted along its side—and produced an answering shower of debris from the merchant vessel.

"They're sinking the ship!" Belle declared, unable to prevent the horror from emerging in her words. "Those utter bastards!" There was no reason to destroy the merchant ship, the pirates were clearly going to get away clean. But it also confirmed her awful suspicion regarding that empty deck.

No one had been standing there before there was no one left alive. The pirates had already slaughtered everyone onboard.

"Aye," Quince agreed, his own tone flat—though more inured

to it, he'd never been one for wanton violence either, at least not as long as Belle had known him. If he had, she never would have kept him on, let alone as her second. "And I'm not surprised, now I can see their flag clearly." Belle looked for herself, and saw what he meant—the *Deadshot* had drifted just a little closer, allowing her to make out the Jolly Roger's details. Its skull had a shark's jaws, gaping wide and ready to devour. "That's the *Hunger*, it is," her first mate continued. "Captain Ravenous, they call its master. He takes no prisoners, and leaves naught behind but wreckage."

"The *Hunger*?" Belle had heard of it, before they'd left. "But I thought they were busy cutting a bloody swathe along the Ionian and the Adriatic?"

"Aye, and we were in the Aegean and Mediterranean, afore we came here," Quince pointed out. "Guess we ain't the only ones took to cooler waters."

"No, I suppose not." She glanced over her shoulder to where Gregor awaited orders. "Back to shore, Mister Gregor. No point picking over the remains, and I don't think any of us fancy a swim." The merchant ship would be almost completely underwater by the time they could reach it, even if there was anything left of value. Plus, Belle had no interest in picking her way among corpses. At least the *Hunger* hadn't seen them, and was moving away, so she didn't have to worry about fighting off that ship, too.

The whole incident was troubling, though. Belle had known they'd face competition here, of course. She'd fully expected it once she'd made up her mind to take to the water again. She hadn't anticipated someone like the *Hunger*, though. They'd have to be a good more cautious now when they spotted potential targets, to make sure they didn't wind up as victims to the bigger pirate ship themselves.

And, unfortunately, cautious wasn't something Belle did very well. As her naval commander was no doubt beginning to learn.

Chapter Eight

THE FOLLOWING SUNDAY FOUND BELLA IN church. She had always enjoyed attending in her youth, but a few years prior their beloved pastor had retired. Bella was less fond of his replacement, but still made an effort to be present when she could, particularly on those Sundays when her father was feeling up to attending as well.

This was one such day, and the two of them occupied their pew at the front. Abigail and her family were in the row immediately behind, allowing the two friends to exchange pleasantries before services began. As was often the case at such times, Bella found herself envying her closest friend. The Montrose pew might seem crowded to some, with Mr. and Mrs. Montrose, all three of their children, plus Deborah and even little Clara all squeezed in together, but Bella thought that far cozier than her own nearly empty row, used by just her and her father. As an only child, she was, of course, used to such things, but rarely felt the lack as keenly as there in church, especially since she had no doubt some of the town's newer residents would be eyeing those empty spaces with covetous distaste. Still, there was nothing for it.

A loud clearing of someone's throat announced the entrance of Mr. Barnes, the rector, followed closely by his wife. Mrs. Barnes claimed pride of place in the front corner of the pew across from Bella's own, nodding to her as if they were equals. In the church itself, Bella could do nothing but nod back politely, for here the rector's wife did indeed take precedence. Fortunately, with the service about to begin there was no time to engage in conversation with the woman, but Bella resigned herself to enduring such afterward.

Mr. Barnes was a large man, though not a tall one, with a heavy face that turned red from the power of his sermons. He was much given to shouting for effect, and his deep voice did thunder impressively through the nave. Bella thought his sermons more than a touch histrionic, and often wondered how well the rector followed his own advice to give generously and act selflessly, but she could hardly fault the advice itself. Indeed, as a pirate she often exhorted her victims to behave in much that same fashion!

After services concluded, she waited for the crowd to thin before rising and taking her father's arm to guide him down the aisle and back out into the late morning sunlight. They could have exited immediately behind the rector and his wife, of course, but she preferred to surrender that prerogative in favor of giving her father more time to gather his senses, and not having to push their way through the impatient throng.

Abigail and her family were already outside, Clara having started to fuss before the sermon had even ended and Edmund fidgeting as well. Indeed, all but the elderly and those with difficulties walking had already exited before them, which Bella did not mind in the least.

There was still, by necessity, the formal gauntlet to be run. Mr. Barnes made a point of speaking to each and every parishioner as they left, and he certainly was not about to let his most illustrious attendees escape unnoticed or unannounced. "Lord Roderick, it has been too long since you have graced us with your presence!" the rector's loud voice boomed out, making sure everyone nearby heard. "And Miss Parsons, how lovely to see you as well! You were away again recently, I believe?"

"Mr. Barnes, Mrs. Barnes, always a pleasure," Bella replied, offering her hand to them both. "Yes, I was. Attending to family matters." She had no wish to say more, especially in such a public venue. "It was a wonderful sermon, as always," she stated instead, changing the topic to one she knew the rector could not refuse.

As expected, his face pinked with delight. "Ah, that is most kind of you, madam," he told her, bowing deeply. "Most kind." The last few parishioners had now gathered at the doorway, and so Bella was able to smile and lead her father down the front steps, making room.

"As pompous as always, I'd say," was the first thing Abigail whispered once Bella and her father had joined the Montroses upon the lawn. "To hear him speak, one would think the good rector the very paragon of human kindness."

Bella smothered a laugh behind her fan. "Careful, Abigail," she warned. "To besmirch a pastor while still on church grounds seems almost blasphemous. I would hate to worry over the safety of your soul."

Her friend giggled along with her, though discreetly. "Can't have that, can we?" She swatted at Edmund, who had just tried to steal her fan. "Stop that, Eddie!" But her little brother only laughed, darting away.

The Commodore sauntered over just then, with that peculiar gait that was a combination of both a life at sea and the injury that required his cane. "Morning, all," he announced in his gruff voice. "Fine day for it, hm?"

The others all greeted him, for Mr. and Mrs. Montrose had known the old seaman nearly as long as Bella's father had, and they were all on good terms. But after the initial welcomes, Bella found her gaze wandering, along with her thoughts. She swept the crowd, taking in all the attendees—and perhaps searching for one in particular.

The flash of blue on white soon drew her eye, and she smiled upon seeing a particular hat atop a dark-haired head. She'd thought the naval detachment might be present for services this morning, and if so, how could their commanding officer not do the same?

"Come, Abigail, let us walk a bit," she suggested, and her friend was quick to take the meaning of her statement.

"Can I come too?" Edmund asked quickly, and of course, they could hardly refuse. Thus the three of them excused themselves, Bella knowing her father was in good hands with both the

Montroses and the Commodore at his side.

They paused briefly on their route to extend condolences to the Grants. Colin and Abigail were longtime residents of Hillington, and she owned and operated the local bakery while he managed the local flour mill. Flour was notoriously combustible, however, and there had been a fire at the mill recently, though at least no one had been seriously injured. The mill was closed for repairs at the moment, but Mr. Grant assured them that it would be up and running again soon.

Bella and her two companions continued on their way. As they approached the naval contingent, however, Bella saw that her intended target was now standing a few feet away from his men and conversing with a gentleman she did not recognize. Reid turned at their approach, and if his smile was only a notch above polite she fancied his eyes shone a bit more brightly than that.

"Miss Parsons, Miss Montrose," "her" commander stated, stepping forward to greet them. "Lovely to see you both this morning. And I do not believe I've met your gentleman friend." This was directed at Edmund, who giggled, the sound a perfect echo of his sister's.

Abigail did the honors. "Commander Reid, allow me to introduce my younger brother Edmund. Eddie, this is Commander Nicholas Reid of the HMS *Diligent*." The two shook hands, Edmund standing as straight as possible in an attempt to look taller, his efforts at seeming serious offset by the grin that split his features and woke a responding twitch in Reid's own lips.

"A pleasure, sir," Reid said, his voice revealing none of that amusement. Then he pivoted slightly, making space for the gentleman beside him to join their group. "And may I, in turn, introduce Mister Charles Basil-White, recently out of London by way of Leeds. Sir, this is Miss Isabella Parsons and Miss Abigail Montrose. And Mister Edmund Montrose, of course."

Hands were shaken and bows and curtsies made all around, and Bella took stock of the newcomer. Basil-White was nearly as tall as Reid, if not as broad-shouldered, with fine features and auburn hair handsomely curled. His fine clothes spoke to both wealth and taste, being of the highest quality and most fashionable cut without being ostentatious. His smile was warm, and his hazel-eyed gaze sharp and clear.

"Ladies, sir, it is a pleasure," he stated, his voice higher than Reid's and faintly accented but no less pleasant. "And your arrival spares us from a less than cheerful discussion, making you all the more welcome."

"Oh?" Bella glanced between him and Reid. "I hope you did not find the sermon lacking? Or our town itself, for however long you have been here?"

His answering chuckle was rich and warm. "For the former, I will beg your indulgence, as I am not the most attentive of church-goers," he replied. "But as for the latter, no, I can assure you that everything I have seen here thus far has been very much to my liking." His eyes never left hers as he said this, making his inference clear, and Bella smiled both at the obvious flirtation and at the furrow it caused in Reid's brow. Nothing like a little competition to stir a man's interest!

"We were discussing the recent rise in piracy in the area," Reid commented gruffly. "A ship was attacked a few days past, and there were no survivors."

Bella knew all about that, of course, but still did not have to feign the shiver such a mention caused. "Oh, how awful!" She focused upon Reid. "I am sure you will do everything you can to capture the culprit, however."

He inclined his head to acknowledge the compliment. "I shall indeed. My men are already on high alert, but with two such predators now circling our waters, it may not be enough."

"Two?" that was from Abigail. "Then this is not the one you were already pursuing, the woman? You had said before that she seemed uncommonly civil for her given career." She fanned herself. "I confess myself relieved, for I would not think one of our sex so vicious."

Basil-White chuckled again. "I would argue that women are,

if anything, more capable of cruelty," he stated, "but then, as an unattached gentleman, it may be my views are somewhat biased. For the want of a good woman and all that."

"Oh, we are quite capable of cutting a man down; that much is true," Bella readily agreed, even as Abigail pouted. "But we prefer to let our victims live so that we may torment them again in future."

"Indeed." Their new acquaintance's eyes were alight. "Then I am even more pleased to have such a hearty constitution if it allows me to look forward to such frequent assaults upon my nature."

"These attacks are no laughing matter," Reid interjected, his face and voice stern with quiet rebuke. "Many lives were lost."

"And that is dreadful," Bella agreed. "I pray you will bring those murderers to justice and swiftly."

That seemed to assuage him, and after a few moments of quieter talk she and Abigail turned to go, having to all but drag Edmund with them. "It was a pleasure meeting you, Mister Basil-White," she said as they made their good-byes. "And I trust we will see more of you soon. And you, Commander. Please do not let your duties make you a stranger."

Reid's bow was crisp and correct. "I assure you, I will do my utmost to prevent that," he stated, but his tone felt cooler than in his previous addresses to her. Perhaps that was merely due to having a larger audience, but Basil-White's "You will, have no fear!" felt far more enthusiastic.

"Well!" Abigail commented once they were safely out of earshot and headed back to their respective parents. "That hardly seems fair, Isabella! You might let me have one of them, at least!" She tapped Bella on the arm. "Whichever one you toss aside will be fine, I assure you."

Bella laughed and hugged her friend. "I promise, as soon as I have done so, he is all yours." She couldn't refute her friend's intimation, either. It was already abundantly clear that Basil-White had some interest in her. Nor was she inclined to rebuff the tall, handsome, genial gentleman so soon, especially when he was showing himself willing to press his suit more actively than the commander beside him.

Competition indeed, and if Reid did not step up, he might find that he had been well and truly lapped, and not just when it came to naval engagements!

Chapter Nine

SEVERAL DAYS LATER, ABIGAIL WAS AWAKENED by her lady's maid, Nellie, with a brief message. And a short time after that, she emerged from her bedchambers to find an irritable Bella pacing about the Montrose's best sitting room.

"Goodness, someone is impatient!" Abigail declared, crossing to the table where Nellie had already set out a breakfast service. "And hungry," she added, seeing that several of the tarts had already been consumed, or at least poked at.

"I have been here upwards of an hour already!" Bella replied sharply. "Did my note not say to be ready at once?"

Her friend laughed and did a little twirl to show off her riding habit. "And so I am, as you see! 'Dress quickly for a ride,' you said, and I have. But where are we riding to, and why?"

Bella wanted to stay angry, but she never could manage that in the face of Abigail's habitual cheer and so laughed and hugged her friend instead. "I thought, it being a fine day, that we might take the gig to Riverside," she suggested. "And discover what ships may be docked there."

"Ah, I see." Her friend tapped her on the nose. "Ships such as one HMS *Dilligent*, perhaps?"

"That would be one, yes." Bella stuck out her tongue. "If he will not take time to see me, then I must go see him instead! And surely two young ladies riding to the docks will not pose a problem or present an indiscretion. Even Lady Sarah has been known to ride along the beach on occasion."

"Yes, yes, all very respectable," Abigail agreed easily, accepting the cup of tea Nellie had poured her and a scone slathered with gooseberry jam. "And very bold, but not too much so. I approve, and you know I'll never turn down the chance to admire a whole shipful of handsome young sailors. But not before breakfast. I'm sure your commander and his crew will still be there when we arrive."

There was clearly no budging her, so Bella surrendered, taking a seat herself and claiming one of the aforementioned tarts she had already mangled. After all, there was no sense letting good food go to waste!

Riverside was less than an hour from Hillington, and it truly was a fine day, bright and sunny and just warm enough to not require a wrap. Bella handled the gig's reins with aplomb, spurring her horse on to a steady trot—no reason to look too eager! The ride generated a pleasant breeze, and she and Abigail talked and laughed along the way.

The town sat just within the point where land gave way to sea, at the very mouth of the river. Most of the coastline above it was too steep and too rocky for an adequate landing, which was why Hillington itself had been built where it was, not along the water's edge but back a ways, where the ground was more level and more suitable for gardening. But the riverbank sloped down nicely, allowing Riverside ready access to the waterway, and its edge was lined with docks. As Bella and Abigail passed along the streets and buildings and approached the water beyond, they could see a few ships moored there, including two bearing the Union Jack.

Two?

Bella looked again, but there was no mistake. Two Royal Navy frigates were docked there, and from this distance, she could not distinguish between them.

Abigail had noticed as well. "I say, is there a second Commander

Reid?" she whispered. "Perhaps he has a twin brother? Then we can both have one!"

"Shush," Bella warned, biting back a smile. "It could just as easily be his old, ugly, hunchbacked, and hook-handed uncle, and then where would you be?"

Only a few dockhands were about, unloading crates and barrels from a lone merchant ship, and Bella ignored them, making for the nearer of the two naval vessels. She reined in where dock planks met dirt and hopped down, offering Abigail a hand after. Together, the two of them stepped onto the dock and proceeded toward the ship. Several figures in Navy blue were visible upon its deck, and as they drew closer, she thought the one nearest the gangplank must be Reid. Then she had chosen aright, and this was the *Diligent*!

They continued their approach, but after a moment, Abigail tapped her on the arm. "Look," her friend said, waving her fan at the ship's stern. There, painted across the scrollwork above the rear windows, was the ship's name: HMS *Dutiful*.

Dutiful? But she could clearly see now that she'd been right and that it was Reid there upon the deck. What was going on here?

A cry from the ship indicated that they had been spotted now as well, and Reid glanced up. So did the person with him, who wore a matching coat. Ah, conferring with the other ship's captain, then! Yes, that made sense.

The pair approached and then descended the gangplank, striding forward to meet them, and Bella saw that she'd been right, for the newcomer did indeed have the navy coat and white waistcoat of a commander.

Those had been expertly tailored, however, to fit a figure such as no man had ever displayed, and few women could honestly claim, either.

"Ladies," Reid stated, reaching them first and dipping into a bow. "This is an unexpected pleasure. May I introduce Commander Winifred Davis, captain of the HMS *Dutiful*? Winnie, this is Miss Isabella Parsons and Miss Abigail Montrose."

"How'dya do?" Davis's bow was just as correct and certainly

better suited to waistcoat and breeches than a curtsy, but it had Bella wishing for her own vest and trousers. Especially since this new commander was nearly as tall as Reid himself, with good shoulders, a fine bust, and clean, handsome features. Not classically pretty, perhaps, but she had that air of health and ease that came from an active life out of doors and a quiet confidence no doubt borne of command.

Nor did Bella miss how easy she appeared to be with the man beside her!

"Commander." Bella did her best to keep the chill from her voice, for that would be uncivil, and look catty, besides. "I was unaware His Majesty allowed women to rise to such a rank. That's most impressive."

Reid chuckled. "Even he'd never dare stop Winnie getting what she wants!" She swatted him, and he explained, either not noticing or ignoring the way Bella was starting to seethe. "We were friends at the academy, if you can call the star pupil and the class clown friends. And now she's here to make me look bad. Again."

"Nonsense," Davis corrected, though there was a smile on her lips and laughter in her gray eyes. "I was sent to escort a merchant ship. And to assist you, nothing more. Two pirates, two Navy frigates. Simple as that. The command is still yours." She laughed, big and broad but with a surprising bite. "Of course, if I should happen to see either of those bloodthirsty savages first . . ."

Much to Bella's surprise, Abigail was nodding. "It does make sense," her friend stated. "A woman commander to chase down a woman pirate captain. Don't you think, Bella?"

"Indeed," Bella forced herself to say. "I wish you good hunting, Commander. Both of you. May our coastline be safe and secure once more."

Davis inclined her head, her dark braid swaying behind her. "Most kind of you, and let's hope your prediction comes true. But we won't do anyone any good standing around here." She slapped Reid on the arm as she turned and made her way back onto her ship, already shouting orders to raise sail and cast off.

"Was there something I could help you with?" Reid asked them after she'd gone, and though the words were aimed at them, both his eyes were squarely upon Bella. However, she was still too angry to entertain kind thoughts and raised her chin in response.

"Thank you, no, we were merely taking the air and thought we might stop by to see the ships." She saw him frown, but he smoothed that away an instant later.

"Of course. Well, it is always a pleasure, but I'm afraid Commander Davis is correct; we had best be off on patrol. If you'll excuse me?" He bowed and slipped past them, his long stride carrying him quickly down the dock and to the adjacent one, where his own ship waited.

"Hm," Abigail commented softly, watching him go. "That was unexpected, eh? A female commander! Striking, too. And they seem . . . chummy."

"Yes, thank you, I hadn't noticed," Bella snapped, turning on her heel and marching back toward the gig. "Come on, let's head back." There was little more to see or do here.

She was in a foul mood the entire way home, barely speaking a word. Abigail did her best to keep up a running stream of light conversation without her, filling the air with idle observations about the weather, the horses, the harvest, the other townsfolk, and anything else that came to mind.

Anything and everything except the two naval officers they had just left behind. Because, despite her seeming vacuousness, Abigail Montrose could be quite perceptive. And a true friend.

The part of Bella's mind that was not currently a mass of jealousy and outrage pointed out that they probably didn't deserve her.

Chapter Ten

NEITHER COMMANDER WAS IN ATTENDANCE AT services the following Sunday. This did not surprise Bella, whose sunroom had an excellent view of the ocean. She had noted the sails of both frigates circling in the distance like a pair of oddly crenellated shark fins. Clearly, the HMS *Dutiful* and its new partner the HMS *Diligent* were making good on their intent to heavily patrol this stretch of coastline, protecting it and its inhabitants from the depredations of pirates by sheer show of force.

Currently, their efforts were successful. Bella was keeping the *Deadshot* safely hidden away for the time being, despite her crews' displeasure at such inactivity, and she had not caught a single glimpse of the *Hunger*, either. Of course, the fact that there had been no new merchant ships in the past few days might also be contributing, since even sharks could not dine upon seawater alone.

Abigail had also pointed out to her that the twin naval vessels' vigorous patrols would no doubt account for Commander Reid's continued absence, along with the lack of any correspondence. "He has no need to write and inquire after your health, as he saw you mere days ago and can attest to that himself," Bella's friend had been quick to remind her. "Nor, since he knows you have no intent to travel and has already apprised you of his own plans, can he see a reason to waste good ink and paper on asking after such, or telling you that which you already know. Give him some credit, Isabella. He is an officer and thus has responsibilities to attend."

"As opposed to attending me, you mean," Bella had all but

snapped, then sighed and quickly hugged her friend. "I am sorry, Abigail. I am as prickly as a thornbush right now, and you are only trying to help."

"I am glad you can at least recognize that fact," Abigail replied, then chuckled. "But here, perhaps, is someone who will be better at raising your spirits—and no doubt recognizes that the loveliest of flowers are those that carry barbs." Her gaze was directed past them, farther onto the church lawn, when she said this, and Bella followed suit, twisting around in time to see a pair of gentlemen approaching. The one in the lead was familiar, and his handsome countenance and warm smile did indeed bring an answering expression to her own face.

"Ah, just the lovely ladies I was hoping to see!" Basil-White declared as he reached them, bowing quickly before bobbing upright once more. "May I introduce my good friend Hugh Fletcher, also recently arrived from London? Hugh, I present Miss Isabella Parsons and Miss Abigail Montrose."

"It is a pleasure to meet you both," the second gentleman stated, bowing over both their hands in turn. He was not as tall as his friend, nor as athletically formed, and his clothes, while good, were not of as fine a cut, but while his face was rounder and softer, it had a pleasing look and a friendly expression, and his blue eyes were warm beneath chestnut curls any woman might have envied. "Charles told me he had met two of the loveliest women in the world here in Hillington, and now I am forced to acknowledge that he is once again no less than truthful."

"That is very kind of you, sir," Bella answered, "though unless he has in fact traveled the whole world over, I wonder that he can make such a claim? There may be entire islands, nay, countries, filled with far prettier ladies than us two."

"Perhaps not the whole world," the gentleman in question demurred. "But a goodly portion of it, and enough to hold to my prior statement." Ah, that explained the accent she'd heard, then. He'd not grown up in England, Bella would wager.

Abigail thwacked her fan against Bella's arm. "Don't ruin a

perfectly good compliment with facts," she warned before grinning at Mr. Fletcher. "I, for one, am only too ready to accept such a grandiose statement in the spirit it was intended."

Both gentlemen were laughing as well, and Bella did feel much of her recent irritation lifting at the general merriment of their little group. "I can see already," Fletcher commented, "that you two are quite the balanced pair. The one quick to retort and the other happy to forgive. Wit and amiability." He beamed at Abigail. "Thank you for showing such kindness to a relative stranger."

Bella watched her friend flush with pleasure and decided to step in, giving Abigail time to recover her composure. "Recently arrived, Mr. Basil-White said? Was that your ship docked in Riverside the other day? When we were there I noticed a ship being unloaded."

"You've a sharp eye as well as a quick wit," Fletcher told her, dipping his head. "It was indeed. The *Safe Return* is her name, and she carries all of my hopes and dreams each time she sets sail. I have been lucky thus far to have her live up to her name."

"Hugh is more daring than I," Basil-White told them, lowering his voice and leaning in as if sharing a confidence. "I am not willing to stake all upon the waves nor even to venture onto them myself, especially not with pirates so close by."

"Yes, well, I was fortunate enough to have an escort on my voyage here," his friend admitted freely. "Though I cannot say that Commander Davis would be my first choice of companion, in this case, her presence was a welcome one, and I had no fears when setting forth."

"And do you intend to head back to London now that your cargo has been delivered?" Abigail asked him, fanning herself. "Or will you stay in Hillington awhile?"

He smiled at her. "In truth, I'd not made up my mind before this point, but now I find myself thinking I might linger for a time. It would be a shame to come upon such a fine town and such pleasant company, only to depart again so quickly."

Their conversation continued, interrupted here and there as

other residents stopped on their way past to greet Bella and Abigail and—especially in the case of the other young ladies present—to meet these two new eligible bachelors. But, while both men were perfectly friendly toward all, they soon discovered that at least one no longer qualified for such a title.

It was when Penelope Sinclair pointedly asked the men if they would be attending the ball being held that next Saturday. "If so," she stated, her tone as sharp has her features, "I hope you will deign to dance with as many of the young ladies present as possible, rather than giving all your attention to just a few." The glare that accompanied this plea made it clear which two she meant in particular, and Bella fought the urge to step forward and wipe that haughty little smirk from the other woman's face. As it was, something must have shown in her expression, for Penelope paled and took a step back.

"I would be only too happy to attend, and to dance," Mr. Fletcher responded with a bow. "I must warn that I am engaged, however. Still, my fiancé, Miss Emily Grove, waits for me back in London, and would not gainsay my offering my hand to any partner in need."

Abigail deflated slightly at this news, and Bella felt a pang for her friend. She had obviously taken an immediate liking to the man, whose relaxed and friendly nature seemed so well matched to her own. And now to find him already engaged! That was cruel indeed. Though she could hardly blame Mr. Fletcher for having found a match in London, nor for not proclaiming it the instant they met.

"Unlike Hugh, I have yet to fall under love's embrace," Basil-White stated, his eyes upon Bella as he spoke. "But, like him, I will happily join in the dance and whatever other merriment is offered."

His friend was not slow to accept the change in topic. "Yes, I have yet to see much of town, though what little I've noted has been highly pleasant. Perhaps you ladies would be willing to show us around and point out any areas of local interest?" That had been directed at Bella and Abigail specifically, though his gaze did shift to include Penelope, as it would have been rude not to. Before she could agree, however, her aunt called her away, the older woman reminding that Mr. Sinclair's gout was acting up and thus they had best head for home straightway. It was clear Penelope would rather have stayed and attempted to claim more of the two gentlemen's time and attention, but she could not refuse the summons and so made her good-byes, though not without securing the promise of a dance from each.

"Well, that returns us to even numbers," Basil-White noted, bowing to Bella. "Might I request the honor of your company in a stroll about town?"

Bella laughed and curtsied in return. "Yes, you might, and I might accept, if you did." He offered his arm and she laid her hand upon it. Beside them, Fletcher did the same to Abigail, who giggled but did not hesitate, and a moment later the four of them set out. It was a fine, brisk morning, and Bella felt her spirits lifting with every step. She enjoyed being out and about, and here she had not only the company of her closest friend but that of a charming and attentive gentleman—and one who was not afraid to tell her what he wanted, or to request her time and acquaintance.

Yes, the day was looking up indeed! She wished Reid well on his hunt, but while he was out there seeking foes, his true adversary was here on land, taking advantage of his absence. Bella looked forward to seeing how the commander responded to such news upon his eventual return.

Chapter Eleven

QUINCE NODDED AS HE LOWERED THE spyglass, squinting against the early morning sunlight. "Aye, she's a beaut, no doubt," Belle's first mate agreed, handing the brass tube back to her. "Spanish, by her flag. Not sure where she's hailing from or heading toward, though, not with that bearing." They'd spotted the ship and were studying it from the safety of the shore, where they'd blend in against the rock and sand and trees.

"It's odd," Belle agreed, accepting the device and using it to study their target again herself. "But I don't see how we can pass this up. We've had lean pickings since those two Navy types began stalking us." She tapped the spyglass against her leg, making her decision. "Ready the crew. We're taking her."

"Aye aye!" Quince turned away, shouting orders. But even as the men leapt into motion, bringing the *Deadshot* around and aiming her like an arrow at the Spanish freighter, Belle wondered. What was a ship like that doing out here all on its own? And why was it traveling north to south? Could it be coming from Edinburgh toward London? If so, why stay so close to the coast when there was ample room out at sea, with better sightlines and greater maneuverability?

In the end, though, none of that mattered. Only that what she'd told her second was true. They'd had precious little prey lately, and here was a nice fat ship just cruising along in easy reach, asking to be plucked.

How could they resist?

The *Deadshot*'s sails filled, propelling the ship out over the water, her prow slicing through the waves as she beat a course away from the shore and straight for her intended victim. It was a full frigate, so larger than their own ship, but with far fewer gunports than a Royal Navy version might possess. Belle was confident they could overpower any resistance, strip the ship clean, and be gone before either of the royal ships arrived. She hoped the crew didn't put up too much of a fight, though. Because her own men were spoiling for one, and even the smallest hint of defiance could lead to a conflict she could not easily abate.

They were still racing toward the merchant ship, which must have seen them by now. Instead of running, however, it angled its sails away from the sun, the wind pushing the ship toward shore. That killed its momentum, and soon, it was only being carried by the current. The move made no sense, and that had Belle worried. What was she missing here?

She examined the ship once more and could make out figures on its deck now, presumably captain and crew. Belle didn't see any rifles yet, however, and everyone seemed almost frozen in place. Were they already resigned to their fate, then? She'd have expected at least a little panic! She wished she could make out more, but they were mere silhouettes against the blinding sun, their shadows shifting and stirring behind them.

Wait, behind them?

"It's a trap!" Belle shouted, spinning around and racing over to where Gregor was steering them closer. "Take us away at once!"

"Cap'n?" That was from Luke, who'd been handing out cutlasses and pistols nearby. "Are ye sure? Seems safe enough."

"I'm sure," she replied quickly. "I don't know how yet, but it's a trap." Quince had returned, and she shifted her attention to him. "Shadows at their backs," she explained, the words spilling out in a rush. "But the sun's behind them. Shadows would be in front of them."

She could tell that he didn't fully understand, but he nodded nonetheless, his long blonde hair whipping about from the motion.

"We trust your gut, Cap'n," he promised, then raised his voice. "Full stop! Bring us about!"

Gregor was already spinning the wheel, and crew members rushed to obey the new orders, slackening sails and shifting booms so the *Deadshot* foundered, losing speed as it began to turn.

Which was when Belle heard the unmistakable sounds of cannon firing. Yet the merchant ship's ports remained closed.

Something flat and dark came whirring from that ship, but not down below where the cannons waited. No, this skipped across the deck, slicing through railing and rigging alike as it sped toward them over the water. Belle knew what it was at once, both from the hum and from the way it spun like a top. Nor was she the only one.

"Chainshot!" Quince bellowed. "Everybody down!"

Belle dove for the deck, landing hard on hands and knees and chest, jerking her head back just in time to keep from slamming her chin onto the planks. The impact had her gasping, but she forced herself to stay flat.

A second later, something sliced through the air only a foot above her back before hurtling across the deck and over the far railing, disappearing out over the waves toward shore.

That had been close!

Picking herself up, Belle surveyed the damage. The railing had been shattered in places, but most of their rigging looked intact, and their sails were undamaged. They'd been lucky. Chainshot, which consisted of two half cannonballs linked by a length of solid chain, could utterly destroy a ship, shearing through masts and ropes as easily as a blade through thin cotton. It wasn't used often, partially because such a weapon indiscriminately made a bloody mess of anyone who got in its path but mainly because it was only effective over short distances. Had they stayed the course as intended, those would have struck a good deal harder, instead of doing only superficial damage.

But she was sure the Spanish ship hadn't fired those at her. Which could only mean one thing.

"Someone else is on the far side—and they're firing through

the ship!" She stared hard at the offending vessel and past it, struggling to see in the glare.

And then she did. What she'd initially thought was just streaks of light was in fact sails. Sails behind those of the merchant, which had been raised for concealment. That's why there'd been shadows behind the ship's crew. The dark outlines weren't theirs.

They belonged to the crew of the second ship, the one using sail and sun to hide right behind this first vessel. The one that had been lying in wait for them.

The one that was evidently willing to destroy an innocent ship—and kill its crew, who'd done nothing wrong—just for a chance to take down Cannon Belle and the *Deadshot*.

And if she hadn't realized in time that something was amiss, they might have done just that. And still could, if she didn't think of something fast.

Bad news was, their attacker—Belle was almost certain it was the HMS *Dutiful*—was between them and open water. Try to escape that way, and the frigate would certainly run them down.

They could turn back toward shore, but they'd be sitting ducks with no room to maneuver. Not unless they returned to their mooring, and that would give away its location.

Meanwhile, she was sure the Navy was preparing for a second shot, most likely with conventional cannon balls this time. And since they clearly didn't care about harming the merchant ship, she was convinced they'd have no qualms about shooting through her again and holing both ships' hulls at once. She had to prevent them from taking such action. Which necessitated some drastic moves of her own.

"Archers!" Belle shouted. "Fire arrows! Aim past the Spanish ship!"

"Aye, captain!" Several of the men rushed forward, unlimbering long, strong bows. They had arrows at the ready, the tips already liberally coated in tar. Now they gathered around the covered brazier before the ship's wheel, dipping those same arrows in the fire until they caught. Then, not awaiting further orders, the pirates let loose a stream of arrows, arcing high and then falling like a rainstorm on the merchant ship's far side—and the second frigate hiding just past them.

Chainshot was only accurate for perhaps a hundred yards. A proper English longbow could fire three times that length. These weapons were not as grand, but their arrows still covered the distance easily. And, unlikely their still mostly concealed attackers, Belle's volley mostly bypassed the innocent ship between them.

A second later, she heard the telltale whoosh of fires catching, and it was music to her ears.

"Get us out of here, Gregor!" she yelled, and her pilot nodded, hauling on the wheel to complete their turn. Their sails billowed, catching the air, and the *Deadshot* ran like a startled hare back toward the safety of the shore.

Behind them, Belle heard another round of cannon fire, and more chainshot ripped through the merchant, seeking them. Evidently, the Navy hadn't had time to switch out their ammunition. But by then the *Deadshot* was too far away, and the linked cannonballs plummeted down into the intervening water well shy of their railings.

The Spanish ship was not so lucky.

Belle had done her best to block out the screams the first time around. She was not so lucky this time. Even as the *Deadshot* fled, she could hear the agonized cries of those men, killed by the very people sworn to protect them.

All in an attempt to get at her.

"Damn them!" she screamed, banging a fist on the railing. "Who's the bloodthirsty savage now?"

"Not us, and that's a fact," Quince agreed, stepping up to the rail at her side. "Good news is, they're too much a mess to come after us just now. Doubt they've got a single intact sail left." His smile faded away. "But I ain't never seen nothing like that afore, Cap'n. Hiding behind that ship, that was clever."

"It was," Belle forced herself to acknowledge. "That's why they were cutting south, so the ship's sails kept them concealed from this side. And the sun was in our eyes the whole time, too. Well planned. But that chainshot, and shooting through the ship to take us by surprise? That wasn't just crafty. It was downright vicious. The merchant's men had to know the plan, too. No wonder nobody was moving over there. They were scared stiff." And probably had been threatened if they didn't cooperate. Left with a choice of being a decoy and possibly surviving or refusing, being branded pirates themselves, and being summarily executed. It took someone with little regard for human life to come up with something so underhanded and so utterly ruthless.

Quince was rubbing his chin. "Don't think it was that one fella, either," he pointed out. "That one held off when we used the *Mère de Nacre* as cover, and didn't even blow us away when we were passing right behind him. No way he'd hurt innocents like that."

"No," Belle agreed. "It's got to be the new one. Davis." She recalled the light in the other woman's eyes when she'd talked about chasing down pirates. Chasing *her*. That hadn't just been eagerness, she realized now.

It had also been bloodlust. This was a woman who'd stop at nothing—including killing innocents—to take Belle down. And very nearly had, just now.

The problem was, short of fleeing the area altogether—or giving up her ship and her career as a pirate—Belle wasn't sure what she could do about it.

Chapter Twelve

A FEW DAYS LATER, BELLA WAS exiting Mister Keats' office—fortunately, nothing was currently amiss, her father had not yet had the time or the freedom to make any more lavish purchases that might strain their accounts, so this was merely a standard visit—when she all but bumped into a tall figure in blue. Luckily, it was the one she preferred, especially since she was not entirely sure she'd be able to remain civil to the other, should they meet in the guise of polite company.

Now, however, her smile was genuine as she curtsied. "Commander Reid. This is an unexpected pleasure." Daniel was already standing by the coach door, in plain view but just far enough back to allow a semblance of privacy as she faced the handsome officer.

"Miss Parsons. The pleasure is all mine." His bow was deep but his smile was tight and his eyes seemed less warm than usual. More troubled, perhaps? Certainly there were dark shadows beneath them which had not been present before. "I apologize that I have not had time to call upon you since you and your father so kindly had me to dinner," he went on, straightening. "I have, as you can no doubt guess, been exceedingly busy. This is only the first time since our last encounter that I've been back on dry land more than a few hours, and that only because we need supplies and I thought it quicker to find them here in Hillington than to wait for an order in Riverside."

"Of course." She did her best to be understanding. After all, he had a job, and an important one, even if it currently ran counter to her own interests. "I hope all is well, though? I'd have thought having a second frigate here would have eased your burden, rather than adding to it."

He nodded. "Yes, Winnie is a great help, to be sure. Far easier to patrol the area, now. As a result, I've yet to see even a hint of either pirate." He frowned. "But all is not entirely well, no, and as I do not think you the type who would prefer pleasant lies to honest truth I will allow myself to deliver the latter. It seems our presence has stirred up the hornet's nest, and both pirates are now behaving with equal depravity."

"Both?" That made Bella stand straighter, her own chin coming up. "Whatever do you mean? I know you'd mentioned before about the one attack by that new marauder . . ."

"Yes, and now there has been another, upon a Spanish ship, this one by Cannon Belle herself." Reid's face was taut with what she took to be barely restrained anger. "And, like her new ally, she has left no one alive to tell the tale."

Bella had to stop herself from speaking for a moment, until she had her own emotions firmly in check. "If no one was left alive," she finally managed to ask, "how can you be sure it was her and not this other ship? Since you already know them capable of such villainy, and had said you'd had firsthand experience of Captain Belle's civility?"

Unfortunately, he had a ready answer to that, and it was exactly the one she'd feared he might give: "Winnie saw the whole thing. She tried to stop the slaughter, but couldn't get there in time."

"I see." She saw his brow twitch at the bite in her words, but could not stop herself. "And she was close enough to say for certain which pirate was responsible?"

"Close enough to trade shots," he confirmed. "But of course Cannon Belle kept the hapless merchants between them as a living shield—a trick she used on me as well." He looked ready to bite through iron. "And then she fired through them, the poor Spanish devils. The *Dutiful* barely escaped going down with the other vessel, while the murderess sailed clean away."

Murderess? There *was* a murderess there, Bella wanted to snap back. Only she was garbed in navy and white, not black! And flying the Union Jack, not the Jolly Roger!

She could not say such a thing, of course. How could she, when Isabella Parsons would never have been in a position to know any of that? Instead she could only come up with, "Does it not strike you as odd that this pirate would be so vile now, so brutal, when you were so clear before on her almost noble conduct? If she had kept another ship between her and yourself previously, why did she not harm them then, only to do so in a similar encounter now?"

Reid shook his head. "Who knows why pirates do anything?" he replied, his own tone gruff. "Perhaps she was toying with me. Perhaps she knew she could get away clean then, but Winnie had her boxed in this time. Perhaps she was simply in a foul mood, and took it out on those hapless souls who merely had the misfortune to fall into her path. All I know is, that is what happened."

"Because Commander Davis has assured you it is so." Bella was struggling not to spit the words at him, and fanned herself in the hopes it would help conceal how red her face must be—but with anger, not shame. "And there is no possibility of her being mistaken? Or having somehow misinterpreted events?"

Now it was her companion's face that flushed. "I do not believe I like what you are implying, Miss Parsons, and so I will do you the courtesy of ignoring it. I can only assure you that I have known Winifred Davis since our school days, and that she is an exemplary officer and a fine woman who believes wholeheartedly in doing her duty and serving her country."

"I do not doubt that, and apologize if it sounded as if I might," Bella assured him, but could not stop herself from adding, "I only wonder if, in her zeal to fulfil such duties, she might not have seen what she wanted to see, or at least what she felt she *should* see when dealing with pirates, rather than something more unvarnished but perhaps less stirring and thus less motivating."

He was standing very straight and stiff now, and dipped his head barely at all, his tone clipped as he replied, "We are all of us guilty from time to time of seeing that which we wish rather than what is truly there. But I trust that, with time, we learn to distinguish between them. I know I prefer reality, harsh though it may be, and my friend and fellow commander is much the same. Good day, Miss Parsons."

"Good day, Commander Reid." Though her curtsy was less graceful than usual, she made sure it was at least proper rather than perfunctory. "I wish you well, and hope for a speedy resolution to your current difficulties."

He nodded and turned away, as sharply as if he were on parade. His stride was swifter than usual as it bore him off down the street, leaving Bella there with her eyes prickling and her throat sore from the shouts she had swallowed. She wanted to scream and curse now, but Daniel was watching and she spied Brian Fried and his sister Gertrude across the street, so she simply gritted her teeth and stepped up to the carriage instead. "Let's for home, Daniel," she said, the words coming out in almost a growl.

She said nothing more on the ride home, but once back at Crestmont Bella hurried upstairs to her parlor. She sent Sophie from the room, then screamed herself raw and hurled pillows every which way until she at least felt her rage was spent for the moment. She was furious with Commander Reid for believing such lies, but far more so with Commander Davis for spouting them—and, if she were being honest, with herself for not finding some way to fully refute them while still keeping herself and her crew safe. But what else could she have done?

Still, it galled her to think that Reid now considered her—even if only that other side of her—a wild and unrepentant killer. And how easily he had bought into that lie. "Winnie saw the whole thing," Bella repeated with a snarl, kicking over a chair and then another. "Yes, of course she did—because she was the one doing it!"

But why would Reid believe her? He and "Winnie" had been friends for years. Perhaps more than that, given the ease they had with one another, and the tales Bella had heard—and romances she'd read had repeated—about people being thrown together in close quarters on account of schooling. Whereas she had only known the commander for a few weeks, with a handful of encounters scattered throughout that interval. A single ball, a single dinner, a few brief meetings. Why should she expect him to take her word over that of a trusted friend and fellow officer? The fact that Davis was another woman, and a tall and attractive one at that, had nothing to do with it.

Nothing at all.

Only, now Bella had effectively run Reid off—and more or less driven him straight into the arms of that other woman. "Oh, well done, you," she muttered to herself, righting the chair only so she could shove it to the floor again. "Well done indeed."

Then, her energy spent, she sank down onto the couch and buried herself among the pillows scattered across it. Perhaps if she hid here long enough, the matter would simply right itself.

And perhaps the *Deadshot* would grow wings and take to the sky, where she could ransack bird's nests and flying castles alike.

Chapter Thirteen

As they exited the church that Sunday, Bella was surprised but pleased to spot a flash of Navy blue amongst the crowd. Once they'd paid their compliments to the Barnes, and received the like in return, she quickly handed her father off to the Commodore's attention and sought out her own friend and confidante.

Abigail's laughter was easy enough to discern from the general chatter, and Bella homed in on that, feeling much like a predator as she stalked through the milling residents to locate her friend. When at last she found her, Bella was not at all surprised to find Abigal in the presence of not only her family but the ever amiable Hugh Fletcher.

"Ah, Miss Parsons!" Fletcher bowed, his face split in a warm and welcoming smile. "Lovely to see you again. I trust you've been well?"

"I have, thank you, Mr. Fletcher," she replied, curtsying. "And yourself?"

"Tolerably, tolerably," he answered. "Far better today, when I can enjoy both fine weather and even finer company."

Abigail blushed at the compliment, inadequately hiding the fact behind her fan, and his smile broadened, though it did not seem mean, only teasing. Clearly the man was interested in her despite his engagement, and Bella was not sure how she felt about that. Happy for her friend to have won someone's attention, of course, and such a genial fellow at that. Concerned that it could never go anywhere, and a little worried what it said about him and his character that he would so openly display such partiality when he was already spoken for.

Then again, his would not be the first marriage arranged for convenience—and money—rather than affection. And as long as he did not make any untoward advances, he was well within the bounds of common decency.

Plus, she liked to see her dearest friend so happy.

This did, however, complicate Bella's own plans. "I had thought we might take a short stroll among our neighbors, greeting this one and that," she said now, resting a hand on her friend's arm.

Abigail started, clearly torn between wanting to agree and not wishing to give up her current activity. But, to his credit, Fletcher spotted that dilemma and solved it by offering them each an arm. "I would be delighted to accompany you both on a turn around the lawn, if it please you."

"Thank you, that is very kind," Bella told him, slipping her arm through his on the left and letting Abigail claim the right.

The three of them set off, threading their way through the throng, pausing here and there to nod to or speak to various other residents. Penelope Sinclair sniffed and turned away upon their approach, no doubt miffed that both of the gentleman's arms were taken and thus there was no place for her to attach herself. Constance and Beatrice had returned, and Bella was forced to pause several minutes with them, engaging in the usual civilities and ignoring the biting comments both sisters directed her way.

"I am sorry Charles could not be here today," Fletcher remarked as they finally broke free of the Tremont sisters, "else you could each have your own gentleman to squire you, rather than being forced to make do with only me." His eyes crinkled from the same smile that touched his lips. "Yet I cannot be too sorry, for his absence is my good fortune."

Abigail laughed. "Well, we appreciate your presence and your assistance," she assured the gentleman, her color high and her eyes bright. Yes, partiality indeed!

Yet Bella's attention was now firmly fixed upon the blue coat she had spied before and was rapidly approaching now.

She was surprised, as they neared and finally caught a better look, to see not one but two such jackets, and had a brief stab of concern. Were both commanders in attendance today? Yet neither bore a woman's shape. Nor, she realized with a sudden burst of disappointment as she caught a better glimpse, did either have the dark, glossy brown hair of Commander Reid.

The two men in question turned at their presence. Neither was familiar to Bella, though the one with the black hair bore the navy coat and white waistcoat of a commander. No, she corrected herself, for he had only a single epaulet, on his right shoulder. He was a lieutenant, then, no doubt serving under either Reid or his female counterpart. The other man, whose hair was short and blond above a tanned face, had a similar coat but no waistcoat or epaulet, marking him as some variety of warrant officer.

"I beg your pardon," Bella began curtsying as they stopped by the two Navy men. "We had thought you someone we knew."

Fletcher took over from there, as society dictated. "Hugh Fletcher, owner of the *Safe Return*," he stated, offering his hand. "I believe we were introduced at the start of our journey here together. And may I present Miss Abigail Montrose and Miss Isabella Parsons?"

"Martin Lovell," the blond man replied, shaking with Fletcher. "Master of the HMS *Dutiful*. This is our lieutenant, Roger Talbot." Talbot deigned to shake as well, though it was clear he did so only because manners demanded it. His eyes were focused on the ladies instead.

"You was looking for Reid, wasn't you?" he stated boldly, studying Bella with an unpleasant smirk on his narrow face. "Sorry, luv, but I doubt you'll see him round here again. Out to sea like a dog with its tail between its legs, he is. Set to task by our own commander, and that's a fact." His accent and manners spoke to a low upbringing, though he seemed the sort of man who might delight in playing that up to the discomfort of those better bred.

Bella had focused on his statement rather than his tone, however, and now she frowned. "Set to task by Commander Davis?" she repeated. "But I'd understood that the *Diligent* had charge of the area, with the *Dutiful* only providing an assist?"

Talbot laughed, an unpleasant sound. "Aye, that were how it began," he allowed. "Matters change, though, eh? After all, the *Diligent* had a run-in with pirates once and got not a single shot off. Whereas we traded blows and have the burns and scars to show for it." He grinned at them, though Bella did catch his subordinate's wince. So Lovell, at least, had a conscience, even if he could not publicly contradict a superior officer. "Navy felt it better to give the stronger ship the lead, as is only proper," Talbot continued, not noticing. "Can't have Reid half-arsing around, as is his wont, pardon my language."

"Whatever do you mean?" Abigail put in, sparing Bella the need to snap at the smarmy lieutenant. "Commander Reid always struck me as perfectly fit to lead. Very direct and in control."

But Talbot shook his head. "Aye, he comes off as such at first," he answered. "But it's all for show, ain't it? Man's got no follow-through. Never had, way I hear. Too much like his brother, dontcha know. That's why he's only got a frigate, right? Not a ship of the line. He follows orders well enough, but nothing more."

Bella was forced to admit, at least in her own head, that this matched what she'd seen thus far herself. The memory of their card game returned to her. Reid had been only too happy to follow her, and quick to respond when doing so, but when it had been his lead he had dithered, playing it safe rather than taking to the attack. He had seemed direct enough at the ball, but she had been the one to invite him in the first place, and Abigail had warned previously that he'd not yet attended any such event.

And what was this about a brother? Reid had never mentioned any family. In fact, Bella realized she knew very little about him beyond the immediate present.

Still, she felt the need to defend him. "Your own captain is likewise a commander, and in charge of a frigate," she pointed out, but knew the reason for that even as the words emerged.

It was Lovell who responded, and his tone was quieter, more thoughtful as he said, "Aye, but as a woman in the Navy she's had to prove herself twice as much. She'd have been full captain by now, were she a man with the same initiative." That much Bella could readily believe.

Fletcher chose to join the conversation. "I must confess, having been escorted by you chaps from London, that I am happy to put my faith in Commander Davis." He turned to Bella. "Not that Commander Reid does not seem an excellent fellow. Together, I am sure they will keep all of us well protected."

"Yet the *Dutiful* is not currently at sea, is it?" Abigail asked, and Bella wanted to hug her friend for sticking up for Reid, and thus her by proxy. "Else you gentlemen would not be here right now." She craned her neck, studying the crowd. "Though I take it your commander is not in attendance?" Oh, bravo, Abigail!

Talbot smirked again, but Lovell spoke first. "She is not," he agreed without any evident rancor or irritation. "Commander Davis is not much for church, but she does not prevent such of us as are from attending, when our duties allow. We are currently resupplying, which is why we are at liberty this morning. The *Diligent* did so earlier in the week, so that we might stagger our schedules and thus provide an overlap in our patrols." Well spoken, and without offense or scorn. Bella decided that not all members of the *Dutiful* were awful.

His companion, however, was all but leering at her and Abigail as he added, "Yeah, Martin here wished to attend services. I came along, more for the chance to see the town than anything else." His gaze made it clear that by "town" he meant "ogling any young ladies he could find," and Bella suppressed a shudder as his oily gaze swept over her—and fought back an urge to belt him and knock that smug look off his face.

"Well, it is a pleasure to meet you both," Abigail stated, curtsying, "and I wish you all the best on your continued mission to keep our waters safe. We must continue our rounds, but perhaps we will see you at services again in future."

"Oh, count on it," Talbot replied, giving a quick, almost mocking bow. Lovell's seemed more sincere, as did his smile and his words of parting. Fletcher shook hands with both of them again, and then offered Bella and Abigail his arms and led them away.

"A thoroughly unlikeable fellow," he murmured once they had gone out of earshot, other lingering residents shielding them from the two sailors' gazes. "I feel, as a gentleman, I must apologize for his behavior."

"You did nothing wrong, and are a credit to your sex," Abigail assured him warmly. She shuddered. "But Commander Davis must indeed be a strong leader, to maintain control over such a man."

On that Bella could agree—if Talbot had been aboard the *Deadshot* she'd have seen him overboard long since. Not that she didn't have her share of unpleasant crew members—John Wynn came to mind, as did Tom—but they were far less offensive than that, or at least knew to rein in their natures when she was about.

Still, she had to assume that what Talbot had told them was true, at least so far as the *Dutiful* now taking the lead over the *Diligent*. That had to be a blow to Reid. She remembered something he'd said before, when he'd first introduced them to Davis: "We were friends at the academy, if you can call the star pupil and the class clown friends. And now she's here to make me look bad. Again." The clear implication was that he had been the class clown, though she could hardly reconcile such a position with his serious and dutiful nature. But he was correct in one thing: Davis's arrival, and her now taking over, certainly made him look bad. And would no doubt be a mark against him in his naval career.

Only, Bella knew the truth. Davis was far from the noble captain she appeared. And, to be fair, part of that could be from what Lovell had said. As a woman, she would have had to work twice as hard to prove herself. Yet that did not excuse her actions. If anything, she should have been even more determined to do everything properly and honorably.

Clearly, Commander Davis was willing to use any method to succeed. No matter who got hurt in the process.

Chapter Fourteen

GREGOR SQUINTED OUT AT THE WATERS. "Touch a' the hoar today," he noted. And, indeed, there were already traces of fog curling up along the water, giving the overcast day an otherworldly feel as if their ship sped across clouds rather than waves.

Beside him, Quince laughed. "Yer Scots is showing," he warned the *Deadshot*'s pilot. "It's fret, down 'ere."

"Whatever it is called," Belle cut in, interrupting their banter, "it may bode well for us—or ill, should there be others hiding within it. So keep a weather eye out."

"Aye, Cap'n," her first mate was quick to assure her. "We've got both eyes peeled."

She nodded. "Good. Because with two hunters seeking us, I'd as soon not run afoul of either."

From up above, Isaac called out, "A ship! I see a ship!"

"Whither away, and what sort?" Belle shouted back.

"Hard to tell, with all this fog," their young lookout answered. "I don't think it's a frigate, though. Looks too small for that. More like a barque. It's ahead and three notches starboard."

"Out to sea, then," Belle mused. "With all that open water beyond it, and the fog to hide anyone providing escort. A nice bit of bait to lure us away from shore and snatch us up."

She frowned, considering as she leaned on the rail and stared out into the thickening mist, wishing she could see through it somehow. The crew were desperate for a catch and eager for a win, as was she. Not that Crestmont was at risk right now, but she'd gained the taste for adventure and for victory alongside the rest, and hated having to let easy targets escape. Yet could they afford to risk it, with both the *Diligent* and the *Dutiful* after them? Not to mention the *Hunger*, which she had no doubt would show no qualms at going through her to get at its prey.

But there was more to it than that. Belle had won the crew's loyalty over their time together in the Mediterranean, but she knew that, as a female, she had to work harder to maintain their respect. If she let too many ships pass unmolested, she would begin to lose them. Already she'd seen Tom and John Wynn muttering, though both were careful not to do so near enough for her to make out what they were saying. Yet even Quince and Gregor were look-ing longingly toward the horizon every time Isaac spotted any-thing. All of them were on edge, and anxious to be in motion. How many times could she pull back in the name of caution before they revolted?

"Take us to them with all speed, Mister Quince," she declared finally, straightening and spinning around to plant her back against the rail and face him and the rest of the crew. "Isaac, keep watch in case it's another trap. But"—she grinned—"it's time the *Deadshot* filled its hold once more."

The response was immediate, as if lightning had just shot through the men. "Yes, sir!" Quince replied with a matching smile, then glanced around him. "You heard the captain! Let's show them why we're the most feared pirates on the high seas!"

The crew cheered as one, and leapt to their tasks with a will. Belle smiled, basking in their enthusiasm. She just hoped it wouldn't return to bite them in the arse.

"Barque, all right," Quince agreed a short time later, studying their target through his spyglass. "British flag. And I'm not seeing any other ships." He shrugged, his long blond hair barely shifting in the mist. "Seems safe enough."

Belle nodded, watching the same thing. "Aye, for now. But let's not dawdle. We strike fast and cut away quick. I'd rather leave loot behind than get caught with our knickers down."

Her first mate laughed. "Right you are, cap'n. Don't worry, the trick'll be holding the boys back, not speeding 'em up."

Which was true. Everyone was eager to be about their business. Belle had not seen them this excited since their encounter with the *Mère de Nacre*—and the HMS *Dutiful*.

She wished the fog—fret or hoar or however one called it— would burn away, though. Give her a clear, crisp morning and clean sightlines any day. Still, if they did have to flee, having the mist to fade into could prove a lifesaver.

They were nearly upon the barque now, and she nodded to Quince. "Ready the cannon."

He called out the order, and together they stood at the prow. "Fire!" she called, and an instant later felt the faint rumble and heard the boom as the cannon ball sped away. Bill, their master of cannon, was an expert shot, and as Belle watched that first blow sliced through the other ship's railing, skidded across its deck low enough to leave a furrow in the planks, and then crashed through the railing on the far side, disappearing into the mist.

"Ahoy, the ship!" Belle shouted, keeping her voice deep. "Toss down your weapons and surrender, or the next one will go through you rather than across you!"

She could make out the figures there, though only as blurred shapes in the fog. No doubt they looked much the same, and the *Deadshot* had seemed to emerge from nowhere. But they were close enough for the other ship to make out their colors, and after a moment a cry came back over the fog-tipped waves.

"We surrender!" a man answered in clear, unaccented English. "Do not shoot!"

Belle nodded. "A wise choice!" she replied. "Stand down and prepare to be boarded!" She glanced back at Gregor, who was already spinning the wheel about. The *Deadshot* responded easily, crew adjusting her sails and killing her forward motion even as she turned, until her hull bumped gently against that of her prey. The merchant ship was larger than their own but not as agile or as fast, with a deeper hull built for cargo rather than chases. They carried only a handful of cannon, and had clearly chosen the safer course in surrendering rather than attempting to fight or flee.

"Ropes!" Belle ordered, and grapples were flung over the side, catching on the other ship's railing and tugging the two vessels even closer, holding them fast against the current. "Boarding party, away!" She already had hold of a rope, of course, and swung over with the first handful, landing on the other deck and drawing her sword as soon as her soles made contact with the heavily lacquered wood. "Who is in command here?"

A man stepped forward, tall and broad but with enough belly to suggest good fortune and rich food, thick hair graying but short beard still black. "I am. Captain Andrew Hodge of the *Sea's Midwife*, at your service." His bow was stiff but serviceable, and as he straightened he held out his unhooked belt, from which hung both pistol and sword.

Belle swept into a far grander bow, then sheathed her own weapon to accept his. "Cannon Belle, captain of the *Deadshot*, at your service. Cooperate and we'll be on our way with none harmed. Resist"—she gave him a tight, toothless smile, the kind she'd practiced in the mirror for just such occasions—"and matters will go poorly for you and yours."

Hodge nodded. "Understood. We want no trouble, and will offer none."

"Very good. Then we will be out of your hair soon enough," Belle promised.

They were still midway through transferring cargo—the *Sea's Midwife* had full holds, and they'd first needed to prioritize the richest items, as the *Deadshot* could not possibly take everything without floundering like a pregnant whale—when a cry came from Belle's own ship. At its very top.

"A ship!" Isaac shouted. "Just came out of the mist! Heading right for us!"

"Where away?" Belle yelled back, whirling to glare at Hodge, who held up both hands.

"I know nothing of this, I swear it," the merchant captain insisted. "We spied a frigate at some distance earlier, but have encountered naught but you."

Damn. Belle could guess what that meant, and it was exactly as she'd feared. The Navy had seen the *Sea's Midwife* and recognized it for the temptation it was, but had deliberately stayed back, using the fog to hide while the merchant drew the *Deadshot* in. And she'd fallen for it.

"Out to starboard, beyond," her lookout answered. "But there's a shape on the port side as well, I think it's a second ship!"

Damn and double damn. Both frigates, one from the sea and one from the shore. With them caught in between. "Cut the lines!" she shouted, turning back to her own ship. "Finish up and away before they can pin us!"

She heard a sound, then, something like wind but with an odd sizzle to it, coming from overhead. It took only a second to realize what it was.

Quince, who was on deck supervising, caught on a hair faster. "Fire arrows!" her first mate shouted. "Wet the decks! All else, take cover!" He suited action to word, diving behind a crate.

Belle did the same, arms going over her head as flaming arrows rained down upon them. Coming from starboard, she noted, with well more than half striking the *Sea's Midwife*. Clearly that way lay Davis and her customary disregard for innocents.

A few feet away, she heard a cry of pain. Glancing up, Belle saw that Hodge was down, an arrow in his leg. "Damn!"

Before she could even consider her actions she'd abandoned cover and rushed to his side. "Hold still!" With a swift tug she yanked the arrow free, tossing it away. "I need a cloth!"

The merchant captain tugged a kerchief from his pocket.

Belle took it and tied it around the wound, cinching it tight. "That should hold. Can you walk?"

"Aye." With her help, he rose to his feet, favoring the one leg. "But to where?" Tears streaked his cheeks, and not just from pain, she thought. "My ship is done for."

He was right, Belle saw. The *Deadshot* had been prepared for a fight, and had wetted her deck before accosting the merchant vessel, plus the mist itself had kept ropes and sails damp, preventing the fire from spreading. What little had caught, the crew had quickly doused with buckets. The *Sea's Midwife* had not been so lucky. Fires had caught on bales and bundles and crates, all of them kept dry belowdecks until her own crew had hauled them up. Now there were blazes going all across the barque, and the railings and riggings were starting to catch as well. Once it spread to decks and sails, the ship was doomed.

As was everyone still on it.

Belle turned away from him to face his ship and its occupants. "Everyone to the *Deadshot*!" she bellowed. "Mister Quince, have the men help them across! Hold the ropes till then!"

Her first mate came close and lowered his voice. "Are ye sure, cap'n?" he asked, too soft for anyone else to hear. "It'll slow us, and with those frigates closing fast . . ."

But Belle refused to yield. "I'll not leave anyone to die like this," she stated firmly. And after a moment, Quince nodded.

"Aye, it's hellish," he agreed. Then he winked at her. "And we be pirates, not monsters." Then he was away, shouting at the men to help the merchant crew across with all speed.

"Thank you, Captain," Hodge told her then, as she helped him to the railing. "Your kindness is unexpected, and thus doubly welcome."

She paused long enough to favor him with a smile. "We are pirates, sir, not savages. But you are most welcome." Luke O'Dell was waiting on the *Deadshot*, and she handed Hodge over to him before leaping across the gap herself. The *Sea's Midwife* was well ablaze now, great columns of smoke rising from it to mingle with the fog, and peering at it, Belle had an idea.

"Don't cut the ropes!" she hissed to Quince, who'd been hur-rying forward, knife in hand to do just that. "Not all of them! Leave one or two, but give it some slack. And get us moving." She explained her plan, and her first mate grinned.

"Aye, it's our best chance," he said. "And a bold one, at that. Not that I'd expect any less." He got to work on the ropes nearest them, calling Luke to loosen the two at the front but leave them connected, and to the rest to raise sail and make for shore as best they could in all this mist. They might not be able to land safely, but they could certainly move closer, and away from here.

Except that they'd be trailing the burning barque behind them.

Belle heard the thud of cannons, and a moment later felt the shudder from the adjoining ship as it was struck repeatedly. But for the moment only the ship on that side—the *Dutiful*, she was sure of it—was shooting, and the *Sea's Midwife* still provided a fiery shield. One stray shot did strike the *Deadshot*, inflicting some dam-age to the hull but not enough to disable them.

Then a new sound emerged, from their other side, still a bit distant but clear enough. A voice. One she knew all too well.

"This is the HMS *Diligent*!" Commander Reid called, his words carrying through the mist. "Surrender, stand down, and you shall not be harmed!"

Belle couldn't help it. She laughed. "A little late for that, Com-mander!" she shouted back. "When your fellow officer has already fired upon us and our target both, with neither warning nor con-cern. Perhaps we'll leave the two of you to discuss the matter?"

"You lie, blackguard!" That was from the starboard side, and though she'd only heard the woman once before Belle knew it to be Davis. "You attacked us first!"

"And set the ship beside us alight?" Belle replied. "While still tied tight to it? I must be a fool as well as a monster!"

"All pirates are fools," Davis responded. "No doubt you pan-icked when you saw you were trapped."

"She did no such thing!" The shout surprised Belle, for it came from beside her. From Hodge. "This is Captain Hodge of the *Sea's Midwife*. Captain Belle has been a perfect . . . well, gentleman, but you take my meaning. You fired upon us both, madam, with no warning and no regard for our safety! And she has rescued myself and my crew from the destruction you created! I will happily take oath on that."

Belle nodded her thanks to the merchant captain, who tipped his cap to her in return. So some good had come of her showing mercy, besides just saving people's lives!

Of course, that was assuming they all made it out of here alive.

They had been underway during this exchange, and now Belle caught Quince's eye. No words were exchanged, but he nodded and moved to the remaining ropes. A few quick cuts severed those. Then he whispered to Gregor, who angled the wheel slightly, turning the *Deadshot* a few degrees to port.

And separating her from the *Sea's Midwife*, which continued to sail on, a burning beacon in the mist.

Cannons fired again, and Belle had no doubt the barque was being bombarded once more. But they were now a full ship's length ahead of that target, as well as several spaces apart, and increasing the distance with each second, the fog serving to hide their diverging paths.

"Davis, stop shooting!" Reid called out. "You're as likely to hit us in this bloody fret!"

"Oh, grow a pair!" came the reply from his fellow commander. "You always lacked the guts to do what was necessary, Reid! I'll take her down, and damn the cost!"

The two naval officers continued to argue across the waters. Let them, Belle thought, as the *Deadshot* sailed silently away into the mist. Now Reid knew she had been right about Davis and her cavalier attitude toward harming others. Hopefully he would act on the matter.

Meanwhile, Belle would take her own ship well out of range.

By the time the fog burned off, they'd be out of sight. She'd set ashore somewhere, or close enough to let Hodge and his people off, then make for the cove. They might not have taken in as much treasure as they'd hoped, and the *Deadshot* would require some repairs, but it would still be a fair haul. And if the day had rid them of Davis, she'd have counted it a success even without the plunder.

Chapter Fifteen

A FAIR HAD COME TO HILLINGTON, and Abigail had little difficulty talking her best friend into inspecting the activities with her. For, in truth, Bella was glad for the chance to escape not only her home but her own thoughts.

The *Deadshot* had limped back to its cove, the damage it had sustained more serious than they'd realized during the conflict itself. "We'll get her patched good as new," Luke O'Dell had promised, eyeing the jagged hole in her hull. "But it'll not be quick, particularly since we cannot take her to a proper shipyard." Her ship steward had sighed, glancing around at the rough rock walls rising up on either side to form their shelter. "It's a fine hideout, captain, and no mistake, but we can hardly drydock her here." He must have seen the despair in her face, though, because he'd quickly rallied and added, "But we'll get 'er done, no fear. It'll just take a little longer, is all. No harm in that."

No, no harm—except that it meant the she and whichever crewmembers were not helping with repairs were at loose ends in the meantime. And Bella was quickly realizing that, while her old self might have had no problem idling away her time with nothing, she was no longer capable of that. Thus she'd welcomed the invitation to stroll the town and admire the rides and music and games laid out in and around the square.

They had not gone far before they'd been hailed by a pair of gentlemen near the ring toss. "Oh, this is good luck!" Basil-White declared as he and Fletcher approached. "Now, you must give us your blessing and your favor, so that we may win spectacular prizes in your honor."

"Spectacular?" Bella eyed the little rag dolls and carved animals on offer. But she also noted the look of the boy manning the booth, no older than Isaac and just as grimy, and the way he watched as she plucked a wooden horse from the display. "Yes, they are, aren't they?" She handed it back to the boy. "Beautifully done, as fine as any I've seen," she told him, and watched him puff up with pride. Her next words were directed at Basil-White. "Sir, if you have any regard for me, you will win me that treasure."

"Then win it I shall," he promised, handing the boy a shilling and receiving a set of three rings in return. His first toss missed one of the bottles by a hair. His second wobbled but caught on the rim and settled around its target. His third landed cleanly, not even touching the glass sides as it dropped to encircle its prey.

"As promised, milady," Basil-White stated after accepting the little statuette, sweeping into a grand bow and offering the wooden horse up to her. "A token of my great esteem." He straightened and grinned at her. "But perhaps you'd prefer something smaller, with a bit more sparkle to it?"

"Perhaps," Bella replied, admiring the little horse. The cuts were rough and the details crude, but there was a sense of energy and motion to it, almost as if the boy had carved it to show a horse in motion. "But for now, this will suffice."

He offered her his arm, Fletcher gave his to Abigail, and the four of them proceeded on, two by two.

"Did you hear of the recent troubles at sea?" Fletcher asked as they walked. "With the Navy and that pirate queen?"

Bella laughed. "A queen, is she? Last I'd heard, the woman was only a captain, so that is quite the promotion! And where exactly was she crowned?"

The young merchant shook his head. "Fair enough," he admitted, chuckling himself. "But the trouble, that was real enough. Saw a bit of it with my own eyes, or at least the aftermath."

"Oh? Do tell!" Abigail urged. Her eyes were bright with

excitement over the prospect of fresh gossip.

Fletcher glanced around them before continuing in a lower voice. "I was down at the docks, seeing to the *Safe Return*," he explained. "When both frigates returned. I couldn't see any scrapes or holes on either, but though the day'd grown bright now that the fog'd gone, the two commanders' faces were dark as any storm. No sooner'd they all moored and disembarked than they were in each other's faces.

" 'You let her escape!' the *Dutiful*'s captain, that woman Davis, shouted.

" 'You nearly got us all killed!' the *Diligent*'s Reid yelled back. 'And you set fire to that merchant's ship!'

"What?" Bella feigned shock. "No! You must have misheard, sir! Surely no officer would do such a thing!"

"That's what I'd have thought," their narrator agreed. "Only, as you might imagine, such a notion concerned me greatly, so I was listening hard to be sure I weren't mistaken.

" 'So what if I did?' Davis told him. No backing down, that one! 'That pirate would've done worse! And catching her would have been worth firing a dozen merchant ships!'

"But Reid wasn't having any of it. 'You've gone mad!' he insisted. 'You're a menace to the very people we're sworn to protect.' He drew himself up all straight and tall, and I must say, looking every inch the proper officer. Then he announced, 'Commander Winifred Davis, I am relieving you of command for wanton disregard of not only His Majesty's laws but the safety of his subjects. You are to be returned to London, where the Admiralty will decide your fate.'

Bella snorted, picturing the scene and the firebrand of a female commander. "I can't imagine she took *that* lying down!" At the same time, she felt a thrill. Reid had stood up to his old friend and comrade. And, whether he knew it or not, he'd sided with Bella. He'd believed her.

Fletcher laughed. "No, not likely. She reached for her pistol, and so did her second—that unpleasant fellow we met after church—and a few of the others. But Reid's gun was already drawn and leveled, and all his officers had theirs out as well. So did several of Davis's crew, but aimed at her and her sympathizers. That other chap, the one with the curly hair, was among those.

"They all stood there a moment, no one moving, and to be fair I scarcely dared breathe for fear I'd set them all off. But Davis was badly outnumbered, and still hadn't drawn. Finally she lifted her hands clear and Reid yanked her gun free, tossing it down and throwing her sword down after it. That was that. Her men surrendered as well, and the lot of them were marched out."

"No doubt with her spitting fire the whole way," Abigail remarked, shuddering. "She was terrifying enough when she was in a good mood!"

Her companion nodded, patting her hand. "Indeed, she was fit to burst, and cursing as they led her off," he confirmed. "Vowing revenge on Reid, on Cannon Belle, on all and sundry. But I don't expect that'll come to anything. She'll be drummed out of the service for her crimes, and even if she don't go to prison she won't have a command no more."

Bella nodded, breathing a little easier now that she'd heard the whole tale. "I'm just glad everyone is all right," she said, fanning herself. "That could easily have turned bad, if she'd drawn or any of her men had fired." And Reid had been right there in the thick of it, the obvious target for Davis and her supporters' ire. Bella's blood ran cold, thinking of how close her commander had just come to death, and on dry land of all places!

"Yes," Abigail said, nudging her with a hip, her eyes alight and a smirk on her lips. "I can see how you were worried for everyone involved, and no one person in particular."

"I can't imagine what you mean," Bella told her closest friend, elbowing her in return and eliciting a small squeal of protest, which only made her laugh. "But if Commander Davis was indeed so bloodthirsty, and so indiscriminate in her attacks, I am very glad she will trouble our neighborhood no longer."

Basil-White had been quiet throughout the recitation of events, but now he stirred. "That is indeed a comfort," he agreed. "And let us hope that the pirates do not take advantage of her absence, for where before there were two protectors, however dubious one may have been, now there is only the one."

"Yes, but one is enough, as long as it is the right one," Bella replied, unable to prevent a smile as she thought of Reid standing proud and tall. Was he the right one, though? Certainly he was the honorable one of the two commanders, and he had done well in calling Davis on her villainy. But there was still the question of his taking the initiative, both at sea and here at home.

"Quite," was all Basil-White replied for a moment. He looked troubled by something, but soon shook it off. "I am sorry I cannot be here to see the immediate result," he continued after a moment. "I had not planned to spoil the evening with unfortunate news but a short while ago I learned I must deal with some urgent business as soon as possible, and I'm afraid it has been weighing upon me more and more ever since, to the point that I can no longer resist its pull. I must beg you to excuse me."

Bella felt her cheeks flush. "I do hope nothing is too amiss," she told him, "and that you'll be able to return to us quickly." She managed a smile. "After all, there are still prizes to be won."

"Indeed there are, including the fairest of them all," Basil-White told her, bowing low over her hand and planting a gentle kiss upon its back, his eyes seeking hers as he did. "And I shall hope to win such upon my triumphant return, to the wonder and envy of all. Until then, however, I must bid you farewell." He bowed over Abigail's hand as well, and shook with Fletcher. Then he was gone, leaving Bella with a dull ache in her stomach, a stinging at her eyes, a hitch in her throat, and a small, rough wooden horse clutched in her hands.

Chapter Sixteen

BELLA WAS STILL A BIT NUMB the next day from the events at the town fair. Basil-White had been so attentive, so accommodating, so flattering! He had been charm and admiration itself! And that comment he'd made, about something with more sparkle—surely that had been a thinly veiled reference to a ring? She had felt as if he'd been on the verge of proposing, or at least formally requesting permission to court her, though thus far he'd hardly seemed the type who paused to ask others for the right to act. No, he was forceful, in the most appealing way, and acted upon his desires.

Why, then, had he left so suddenly?

She did not for a minute believe his claim that business had drawn him away. Indeed, for the first part of the evening he had seemed content to stay in Hillington—and at her side—forever. Something had changed, and his statement was merely a hasty excuse meant to cover the real reason.

Bella just had no idea what that might be. Was it something she'd said or done? Or something entirely separate from her? It had occurred right after Fletcher had told them about the events in Riverside—could it have been related to what had happened with Commander Davis?

She didn't know. Nor could she have said, in all truth, what her response would have been if he *had* proposed last night on the green. She certainly liked him well enough, and far more than any man she'd met before.

With one notable exception.

The question was, did she like Basil-White enough to marry him? And how did her feelings toward Reid play into that, if they did at all? Besides which, if she married anyone, what would that mean for her ship and her crew, for her entire other life as Cannon Belle? How could she possibly maintain that and still share a life with someone?

Her thoughts were interrupted by Sophie entering the room. Though the lady's maid had worked for her for several weeks now, she was still diffident about calling attention to herself. "Beg pardon, milady," she began now. "But you have a gentleman caller. One Commander Reid." The girl's face was carefully composed, but Bella thought she detected a gleam in her eye and color to her cheek. Yes, the good commander had that effect on women.

Nor was she herself immune, as she leaped to her feet, casting aside her dressing gown. "The blue silk, Sophie," she commanded. "At once!"

"Of course, milady!" To her credit, Sophie was quick and competent, and had the day dress out and ready in a moment. Bella did her best to stand still and let her lady's maid work, but she could not stop fidgeting. Reid, here at long last! And just when his erstwhile rival had departed! Could that be a sign?

She would soon find out.

"Commander Reid," Bella said as she swept into the drawing room. "What a pleasant surprise. I apologize for keeping you waiting, but I was not expecting visitors."

"I am sorry to have disturbed you, Miss Parsons," he replied, striding across the room and bowing over her hand. Was he slow to release it from his grip? It certainly felt that way. "I wished to see you, however. And to apologize."

"Oh?" She sat, and gestured him toward a nearby facing chair. "Whatever for?" *Perhaps for making my heart race like a horse at full gallop,* she thought, arranging her skirts.

He sat as well, resting his hat upon his lap, and she noticed that his leg was bouncing up and down. "I—" He cleared his throat and started again. "I spoke harshly to you when last we met. You had commented on recent events, and expressed concerns about certain statements that had been made and accusations that had been leveled. I grew impassioned in the defense of a friend, and we did not part amicably as a result."

Bella nodded, opening her fan and waving it before her face before shutting it with a snap. "Yes, I recall."

"Well . . ." Reid straightened, lifting his eyes from his own hands to her face. "You were correct in your concerns," he stated clearly. "As it turns out, I did not know my supposed friend half as well as I thought. She was no proper officer, being of low moral character and possessing a tendency toward wanton violence and even brutality." He shook his head. "I would not have believed it, had I not seen such with my own eyes, yet there is no denying it now. You were in the right, and I in the wrong. I am sorry to have doubted your judgement or your perceptiveness."

Leaning forward, Bella patted his hand. "Thank you," she told him, "but I am sorry, too. I would far rather there had simply been some mistake or miscommunication than that your friend prove so false."

He managed a small smile. "You are most kind, Miss Parsons. Thank you. I hope this means you accept my apology, and that this rift between us can now mend?"

"I see no rift," she answered with a smile. "And I am very pleased to see you again."

"And I you." He dipped his head. "I apologize for that as well. The German Ocean has become more dangerous of late, necessitating increased vigilance on my part. Those duties have kept me from shore and from socializing far more than I'd like."

She nodded. "I understand. And would never tell you to shirk your duty. Indeed, I would think far less of you if you had." Her lips quirked. "But perhaps a little more attentiveness might be in order."

"Indeed." He smiled back, but then his gaze darkened. "Though, as I hear tell, you have not been lacking for companionship in my absence."

Ah. "No, I have not," she admitted, since there was little point in lying and she disliked the practice anyway. Except where necessary, of course. "Mister Basil-White has been most attentive, and very agreeable." She laughed. "As a naval man, you must know that, if you leave your headquarters unsecured, you risk its invasion and capture. Constant vigilance is required."

"Even that is not enough, when the invader ignores all warnings and boldly enters uninvited." Reid's words emerged with more force and even some heat, enough to make Bella arch her brow.

"Uninvited?" she replied, snapping her fan open and shut again. "By you, perhaps, but it is not your place to forbid or allow. I keep my own counsel, and welcomed his presence, as I did not have anyone else to occupy my time or engage me in conversation."

"So, because my duties called me elsewhere, he took advantage of my absence and you allowed it out of loneliness?" Reid's cheeks flushed. "I admit, I had hoped for more partiality, or at least more constancy."

Bella stared at him, fan forgotten in her lap. "I beg your pardon? I showed you every partiality, and you did nothing with it! At least Basil-White made his intentions clear, and pursued them at every turn, albeit in a most gentlemanly manner."

"That is all well and good for such as him," Reid shot back, "who has no occupation and can spend the day at your side. I am a working man, Miss Parsons. I have a job to do. And those responsibilities must come first."

"I'm sure they must," she snapped. "And I do not dispute that. I only do not wish to come last."

They stared at each other a moment. Bella's heart was beating wildly in her chest. She felt nearly lightheaded, and knew her cheeks were red and hot, her breath coming in gasps.

Reid looked no better. Sweat beaded his brow, dripping into his eyes. He did not pant or gasp, but his nostrils were flared like those of a horse just after a race. His hair had partially pulled free of its braid, and strands were stuck to his forehead and cheeks.

Bella thought she had never seen him look better. He was a man possessed by passion, enflamed by it.

Now if he would just act on it, and damn the consequences!

After a moment, however, he shut his eyes, straightened, and drew in a deep breath. When he blinked, he was calm once more.

"I am afraid I must depart for London," he told her, rising to his feet and setting his cap back upon his head. "I have orders, and must follow them with all due haste."

"Oh." Bella stood also. So he was leaving as well?

He bowed, his dark gaze unreadable. "Good day, Miss Parsons. I hope you will remain in good health and good spirits."

Before she could reply, he had marched to the door and slipped through it, disappearing into the hall beyond.

Bella did not even clearly recall how she got from Crestmont to the Montroses', but next thing she knew, she was standing in their front parlor. The door creaked behind her, and she spun about just in time to see Abigail enter the room.

"Oh, Abbie!" Bella hurried over and hugged her friend.

"What is it?" Abigail asked at once, patting her back. "Is it your father? Is he all right?"

"Oh, Papa is fine—well, as fine as he ever can be, these days." Bella sniffed on her friend's shoulder a moment more before pulling back, daubing at her eyes as she laughed. "You must think me utterly ridiculous right now! And so unlike me, too, to have such an outburst!"

"Unlike you, yes," Abigail murmured. "Then again, what isn't, these days?"

Something about her tone made Bella look more closely at her friend. "Whatever do you mean, Abbie? Are *you* all right?"

"Me? Of course," Abigail replied. But instead of giggling as she normally would, she fixed Bella with a sharp gaze. "The question, my dear Isabella, is—are *you*?"

Bella started to reply, to laugh, to wave the comment off, but her friend stopped all that with a surprisingly imperious raised hand. "No," she warned, her tone far more serious than her usual wont. "Do not brush this aside. I would like a real answer for once, Bella. What is going on with you? Because I know something is."

Abigail began to pace about the room, her steps sharper and more forceful than usual. "You have not been yourself since you returned," she stated bluntly. "Oh, you traveled, you saw the world, you handled your family's affairs, I understand that can change a person. But this?" Stopping, she studied Bella. "Your hair is but the most outward sign. You are not the same person who went away, Isabella Parsons. Something happened on that trip. Something that changed you. I would like to know what it is." Her stern gaze crumpled just a little. "I would like to help. Please, let me help."

Bella's heart broke inside her chest, so violently she was surprised there was not a loud twang like a violin string snapping. Here was her oldest, dearest friend, the ever sweet and supportive Abigail Montrose, and somehow she *knew*. But not all of it. Never all of it.

And Bella could never tell her. For her own safety, and for Abigail's as well.

"I—" she began, not even sure what she would say, but a single look from her friend stopped the words cold. The look was not angry. It was not enraged. It was not even disbelieving.

It was disappointed. And that hurt far, far worse.

"I am sorry that, whatever it is, you feel you cannot trust me with it," Abigail stated flatly. "But if that is the case, then surely you can have no cause to be here. Good day, Isabella."

With that, Abigail Montrose turned and walked from the room. Not storming. Just determined.

Determined to turn her back on Bella.

And the worst part was, Bella thought as she dejectedly dragged herself back home, who could blame her?

Chapter Seventeen

QUINCE SCOWLING WAS NOTHING NEW, BUT this particular grimace of distaste and disbelief was gruesome, even for him. "Yer leaving?" he asked, hands on his hip. "Now?"

"Yes, now," Belle replied, refusing to back down. She couldn't, especially not with John Wynn watching and sneering from where he sawed boards. How that man had survived so long as a pirate she had no idea!

But her first mate was still staring incredulously at her, and he, at least, deserved some explanation. "The *Deadshot* is laid up," she reminded him, and they both glanced up at the ship whose shadow they currently stood within. "And it will be for a few weeks or more, I believe?" Luke O'Dell, standing beside them, nodded. "Which is why I gave the men liberty," she went on. "Those who are not involved in the repairs, that is."

"Aye, and we're rotating those, even," Luke put in. "That way no one's got a right to complain that they're being put to work while all else are living it up in the nearby towns."

"Indeed. But please make sure to remind them that it must be town*s*, rather than all in one town," Belle told them both. "A handful of strangers in a place like Mappelton or Tunstall can go unnoticed, provided they do not break the peace, and up to a dozen or so might mingle in a larger town like Hillington and not cause a stir. But two dozen, all carousing together, will draw attention anywhere outside Leeds. And attention is precisely what we don't want."

"I've told them," Quince answered. "Whether they listen or

not, that's on them." He rubbed at his chin. "And you've got as much right as any to enjoy your spoils, cap'n. Not saying you don't. It's just . . . what happens if we're caught out an' this fine little hideout of ours is discovered, with us unable to fight free or sail away? Or if there's an issue with the repairs? Or something else goes wrong and you ain't around?"

Belle laughed. "Then you will handle matters, Mister Quince," she assured him, resting a hand on his shoulder. "I have every confidence in you." She prevented herself from giving in, or sighing. "I will be back before she returns to the water," she promised, moving a few steps to pat her ship's side. An action she quickly regretted, since it was all slippery and slimy from soaking in the sea for so long. "But for at least a short while, I am leaving you in charge."

That made Quince puff up a little, as she'd known it would. "Well, I guess we can muddle along without you for the nonce," he agreed slowly.

Beside him, Luke nodded. "We'll have her ready to set sail when you get back," he promised, saluting. He'd been a Navy man before being captured by pirates and eventually becoming one of them, and at times that discipline still showed through.

Belle didn't mind. "Thank you both," she said, dipping her head. Then she turned and left the cove, keeping her back straight and her chin up the whole while. She was Captain Cannon Belle, Terror of the Mediterranean and now Scourge of the German Ocean.

Which is why she had to make sure she was alone before slumping, the spark fading from her eyes as tears threatened to fill them instead. Still, she'd meant what she'd said. It was time for her to go.

"Must you go?" Lord Roderick asked, his voice high and wavering like a small child's. "When will you return?"

"I don't know exactly, Papa," Bella replied, giving him a quick, careful hug. "But yes, I really must. I did promise, and I've put it off long enough."

He looked as dejected as she felt, but finally nodded. "Very well. Give your cousin my love, and her husband my regards."

"I will." Not wanting to prolong their good-byes, Bella let herself be handed up into the carriage.

As she settled back into the unfamiliar seat—she was not taking their own coach, so as to avoid depriving her father of Daniel's services in her absence—Bella considered how different this trip must be from her last extended time away. Then, she had been traveling on urgent business, seeking to address issues on their properties that threatened their financial security. Now, she was going to visit a beloved cousin for the first time since she had moved away.

And, if she were being honest with herself, to nurture what felt suspiciously like a broken heart.

She only prayed that this trip would end far better than the last one had.

Bella was not entirely sure what to expect, having only visited London a handful of times since childhood and always with her father. What she did know was that Hillington felt strangely empty with both Basil-White and Reid gone, and completely hollow without Abigail to lean upon for support. Thus, when she'd spotted that last letter of Nancy's, with its renewed request for her to visit, Bella had resolved to take her cousin and new husband up on their kind offer. Surely a change of scenery would do her good? The fact that the *Deadshot* was unable to sail only solidified her plans, for what better time for Cannon Belle to take some much-needed respite? She had answered the letter, agreeing to visit, and had received a quick response welcoming her to do so at once. That had only left purchasing the tickets, packing, and now she and Sophie were on the coach and headed south where, Bella fervently hoped, some welcome distraction awaited.

The trip to London was a full two days by coach, and they stopped overnight in the small village of Melton Mowbray, not far from Leicester. Sophie quietly expressed displeasure with the dark, cramped rooms at the inn there, and the plainness of the supper, but to Bella it was no worse than her cabin aboard the *Deadshot*, or the rough food from its galley. What she disliked far more was the coach ride itself, simply from being cooped up for all those long hours on end, with nowhere to go and no room to move. It was with a great deal of relief, then, that she peered out the window near sunset the second day as they drew up outside a house in London proper.

Stepping from the coach, Bella considered the establishment before her. The place was a modest one, she felt, but not unhandsome, with its brick exterior, three rows of windows, and cheery blue shutters that matched the front door. The fact that it was adjoined by a matching home, with another set to either side, threw her at first, but of course London was a good deal more crowded than Hillington and so she imagined homes were often built in such a way here. She did not recall such from previous visits, but she had always stayed either with family friends on their estates or at lavish hotels.

As the coachman was fetching down her and Sophie's bags, that same front door opened and a tall, dark-haired woman emerged, a bright smile upon her face. "Here you are at last!" Nancy Lilley proclaimed, rushing forward to give Bella a tremendous hug. "Oh, it is so good to see you!"

"And you," Bella replied honestly, happily returning the embrace. Nancy Egerton was Bella's closest friend after Abigail, and far and away the dearest of her relations after Papa himself. Though Nancy had been raised here in London, the two had seen each other regularly all through their childhoods, as Bella's father had brought her down to the city whenever he visited and his sister, Nancy's mother, had often taken Nancy and her little brother Patrick up to Crestmont to escape city life. The visits had grown less frequent after both girls had come out, though they had continued to correspond regularly. The last time they had seen each other had been at Nancy's wedding, well over a year ago.

Now Nancy pulled back, studying her cousin at arm's length.

"You look well," she said finally. "A little tired, no doubt from the ride, and perhaps a little sad? But in good health, and that cut suits you." She fondly linked her arm with Bella's. "Come, let me show you the house. Andrew is down for his nap at the moment, but you'll meet him once he wakes."

A butler held the door for them, and Nancy introduced him as Dennis. "Joshua will be home soon," she said as they entered the foyer, which was large and cheerful. "He'll be delighted to see you again." A charming staircase led upstairs, and Nancy took them that way, down the hall to a handsome room with a large window that must let in a great deal of light during the day. "This will be yours," Nancy explained. "Therese's is just there, through that door."

"Sophie," Bella corrected quickly but softly, glad her lady's maid was trailing far enough behind to not hear that exchange.

"Ah. Yes, of course. Sorry." They peeked into the nursery, where baby Andrew slept peacefully, watched over by his wet nurse, then traipsed back downstairs to a happy little sitting room off the main hall, centered around a broad fireplace with a delicately carved mantle. They were just settling in when the front door opened and a man's voice called out. Nancy was up again at once, replying, "We're in here!" and a moment later her husband entered the room.

Bella had only met Joshua Lilley a few times before, but seeing him now confirmed her earlier recollection of him as a good-looking man, more amiable than dashing, with fine brown hair and a broad forehead. His manners were so easygoing, his welcoming hug so unaffected, that Bella could not help but like him, and the joy on her cousin's face made her even more well-disposed toward the man who had captured Nancy's heart and her hand.

"We are very happy to finally get you here for a visit," Joshua assured her as the butler called them all in for dinner. "Nancy has been speaking of nothing else since your letter, and I am quite as glad myself. You must stay as long as you like, and do not stand on any ceremony, for we are family."

"Thank you," Bella replied, following the two of them into a cozy dining room. "You are most kind, and I shall do my best not to overstay my welcome or abuse your generosity." She smiled as they sat. "But I am very happy to see you both as well, and to spend some time with you."

Dinner was a pleasant affair. Joshua was a banker and, if not directed otherwise, would apparently spend all his time discussing the ins and outs of the financial world in general and his bank in particular. But he was easily led to other topics, and happy to speak on them instead, nor did he insist upon having the last word or upon claiming knowledge he did not truly possess. Nancy was as delightful as ever, possessing some of Bella's same wit but mixed with a lighter nature. She had only been mistress of her own house since their marriage, and thus one of her principal topics was the running of that household, the other being of course their infant son, who the nurse Tessa brought down as they were finishing dessert.

"Isn't he scrumptious?" Nancy asked, and Bella agreed that yes, her little cousin was indeed adorable, with his rosy cheeks, bright eyes, and dark curls. He cooed and gurgled at her, and grasped at her finger with his chubby little hands, and she found herself completely charmed. She had not been around small children much, aside from the occasional encounter in town, and had not expected one to be so engaging, especially when he did not yet speak or even walk.

After dinner, they all adjourned to the sitting room, Joshua bouncing Andrew on his knee as they chatted. It was a pleasant way to pass the time, and Bella was surprised to find, upon yawning and glancing at the mantle clock, that it was nearing ten.

"We've kept you up," Nancy said, rising to her feet, Andrew now curled up on her shoulder. "Let's put you to bed, then. We'll have plenty more time to talk tomorrow."

Bella suffered herself to be led up to her room, where Sophie helped her into her nightgown. The bed was thick and soft, the blankets warm, and she quickly fell asleep.

Chapter Eighteen

THE NEXT DAY DAWNED BRIGHT AND cold, and Bella was happy to accept the heavier gown and shawl Sophie offered. When she descended to the ground floor she found Nancy still at breakfast, cooing at little Andrew in her lap.

"Joshua has already gone in, I'm afraid," her cousin explained, "but he will be home for supper. In the meantime, it is just the three of us."

Bella smiled at her, and at the baby, who blew happy little bubbles in response. "I do not mind, truly. And do not let me keep you from anything you have planned or need to do. I'm happy to help, as well. You may put me to work."

Nancy laughed, then eyed her. "You are serious," she noted with that keen gaze of hers. "You were never standoffish, never afraid to handle matters yourself, but it's more than that now, isn't it? You desire to be active. To be useful. Is that because you do not wish to face whatever thoughts and feelings idleness might let seep in, or because you simply cannot bear to sit still?"

"You are as acute as ever, my dear," Bella told her, setting her tea cup back on its saucer and splaying her hands atop the tablecloth. "And as direct. Which I am glad of." She sighed. "If you must know, it is most likely both. I cannot bear to be idle, but there is also something to be said for keeping the mind occupied in the here and now."

Her cousin was still watching her, idly bouncing Andrew on her knee as she did. "I will not pry, but you know that you may tell me anything and I will not say a word of it, even to Joshua. I cannot promise to withhold my own thoughts and opinions, but whatever it may be, I could never not love you dearly."

Bella found that her eyes were moist, and dashed at them with the backs of her hands. "Nor I you," she acknowledged. "And perhaps I will tell you all soon. Not today, however." She managed a weak smile. "Today I would prefer to just settle in and spend time with you."

"That we can certainly do," Nancy promised. She chuckled, which made Andrew gurgle, and that made both ladies laugh. "How are you at balancing accounts?"

"Quite good, if I do say so myself," Bella replied. "Let me at the books and I will battle them into submission, no matter how tricky or treacherous they may be."

The rest of breakfast passed agreeably, with some small reminiscences of childhood events. Once they'd finished they adjourned to Joshua's study, where Nancy directed Bella to the household accounts. Those were in good order, in fact, with only a few errors here and there, and by lunch Bella had them all sorted, much to Nancy's relief.

"Joshua offered to handle such things himself, of course," she revealed as they sat to eat. "But that would never do. Still, as a banker, he is very keen on tidy numbers, so you have my thanks for making them so."

As they ate Bella filled her cousin in on her father's health and on the status of those Hillington residents Nancy might still know. Then Nancy caught her up on the people Bella knew here in London. That was a far quicker and simpler task.

"Mama is well, and delighted to have a grandson to dote on," she said. "We tried getting her to move in here with us but she insists on maintaining her own home. I'm sure you'll see her soon, not a week goes by that she's not over at least thrice."

"And what of Patrick?" Bella asked, nibbling a sandwich between sips of tea. "Is he still at Oxford?"

"Indeed he is," Nancy replied. "He swears that he is studying

law, but I suspect it is more drinking, smoking, and gambling."
They both laughed, and only a little meanly. Nancy had always had
a good relationship with her younger brother, one that had only
grown stronger after their father had died while Patrick was young.
Bella had no idea what he might be like now, but she remembered
her cousin as a mischievous, energetic but otherwise pleasant
enough little boy. She hoped she would see him during her stay
here, to see how he had turned out thus far.

After lunch, however, Bella decided she'd had enough of being stuck
indoors. "I should like to take a walk," she announced once her
cousin returned from putting Andrew down for his nap. "Shall we?"

"Oh, I would," Nancy answered, settling back into the rocking
chair Bella had already noted was clearly hers, "only, the grocer
will be by today, and Liza's afraid of him so I need to be on hand
in case he tries bullying her into taking inferior cuts again. Perhaps
later, though."

But Bella was not to be put off. "No need to trouble yourself,"
she replied. "I will simply walk on my own."

That had Nancy staring. "What? You cannot mean that, my
dear! A young lady such as yourself, walking without any company? What would people think?"

"I do not care what they think," Bella said with a laugh. "And,
as I do not know anyone but you here, I am none too worried that
it will affect my reputation."

"But the streets are not safe!" her cousin insisted. Then, in fair-
ness, was forced to amend, "That is to say, what if they should turn
out to be unsafe, though I've never heard of them being so. But if
they were, and you were by yourself . . ."

"I will be fine," Bella promised. "I shall bring an umbrella,
and should anyone attempt to harass me, they will get soundly
thwacked." And, moving quickly to avoid any additional protests,
she armed herself and made for the door.

She did not know this part of London, of course, but Bella

scarcely cared. The day was crisp and clear, and the cool air and stiff breeze felt glorious as she began to stroll down the street, nodding to anyone she passed. There were few enough of those, and the ones she did see stared a bit but nodded back politely enough. None of them were right by Nancy's home, and so she felt sure no one could associate her with that address or its occupants.

London was an impressive place. The buildings were far larger, far grander, and far closer together than in Hillington, and there were so many more of them! The streets were narrower and curved more, threading their way between homes and businesses, but at the same time seemed flatter, as if the city builders had been unwilling to let the ground lift or dip their paths. Bella kept track of her route by the simple expedient of going straight until she decided she'd gone far enough, then turning around and heading back. Nancy was visibly relieved when she returned unharmed, and made no mention of Bella's solo excursion to Joshua that night.

The next few days went much the same: Bella rose to breakfast with her cousin, helped her with household duties through the morning, lunched with her, then went for a walk by herself in the afternoon, returning in time to relax and change before supper. She found helping Nancy easy enough, as she handled much the same responsibilities at Crestmont and had for several years. Spending time with her cousin was always a delight, and Andrew was a dear, while Joshua was a kind man and quickly won a place in her heart as well. The servants were all very good, and the household in general was snug and sweet and welcoming.

But far and away her favorite time was those solitary walks. Each day, Bella chose a different direction. She crossed bridges over the Thames. She walked along its banks. She saw the Tower of London, and Buckingham Palace. She passed through the business quarter, with men bustling about in a great hurry.

And not a one of them knew who she was.

That was, she finally realized, the great attraction to these treks.

She appreciated the exercise, and the fresh air, and even the chance to be alone with her thoughts. But most of all, she was enjoying the anonymity. In Hillington, everyone knew Miss Isabella Parsons, daughter of Lord Roderick and mistress of Crestmont. Everything she said and did reflected upon her family and her own character. She could never truly relax, never just be Bella—even when she was with Abigail, those hints of her family remained.

Then there was her other self. Cannon Belle, the fearsome pirate captain. But that was a pose as well, and one she had to maintain at all times when aboard the *Deadshot*. The men expected certain behaviors from her, and would take advantage of any perceived weakness or hesitation as well.

Here in London, however, walking the streets with a shawl about her shoulders, a cap upon her head, and a sturdy umbrella in her hand, no one knew her. No one could hold her up to her position or reputation and measure her against it. No one could see her as a disappointment or as a fraud. She was only Bella, and those she passed did not even know that much. She could laugh or cry or swear or scowl all she liked, and it would not matter.

It was amazing. For those few hours each day, Bella could truly be herself and not have to care. She wondered that she'd ever be able to give that back up.

At the same time, spending the mornings with Nancy and little Andrew, Bella had discovered that there might be room in her heart for a child, at least someday. And, witnessing them with Joshua, she saw the appeal and value of a good match, one not for money but for real love and friendship. Watching her cousin laugh and flirt with her husband made Bella's heart both soar and ache. She had felt something similar with Reid at the ball, and with Basil-White at the fair, but more constrained, as they had been on display both times. Here, there was no one else. It was not for show, not even for her. This was simply how Nancy and Joshua were together.

Bella wondered if she would ever have that. And, for the first time, she started to think that perhaps she did want it after all.

Chapter Nineteen

NOT EVERY EVENING WAS SPENT SOLELY with Nancy, Joshua, and Andrew, however.

"You look lovely, milady," Sophie assured as she made one final adjustment to Bella's curls. "Once they see you, every woman there will want her hair done this way."

Bella snorted. "Quick, buy up all the scissors and shears, we'll make a fortune," she said, and her lady's maid smothered a smile. The girl was slowly opening up to her, but it was taking a while. Times like this, she particularly missed Therese, who had watched her grow up and was perfectly free with her when they were alone. But Bella quickly pushed those memories back, locking them safely away to concentrate on her appearance once more. "Thank you, Sophie," she said, studying herself in the mirror. "You've done a spectacular job, as always."

Sophie curtsied, her motions as elegant as any noblewoman. "I hope you have a wonderful time, milady."

"I'm sure I shall," Bella decided, rising to her feet in a flurry of silk and lace and ribbons. "And you enjoy your evening off. You've more than earned it." With her and the master and mistress of the house out, the only servants who'd still need to do anything were Tessa, minding little Andrew; Liza, preparing tomorrow's meals; Monica, finishing any extant chores; and Dennis, keeping an eye out for their return. Plus Martin, of course, who'd be driving the coach and then staying by it. And Annie, who most likely had clothes to wash. Well, at least Sophie would have some time to herself, anyway!

Heading downstairs, Bella found her cousins waiting. "Oh, don't you look beautiful!" Nancy gushed upon seeing her. "Doesn't she, Joshua?"

"I shall have the two loveliest women in London on my arms tonight," he agreed gallantly, earning him a quick kiss on the cheek from each. "Now, shall we?" And, offering the limbs in question, he led them to the door, and outside to where Martin waited.

"Oh, I am glad you came, Bella," Nancy told her as they climbed into the coach and settled onto the seats there. "I think the last time we attended a ball was well before Andrew was born."

Joshua looked somewhat chagrined. "I am sorry, my dear—" he started, but she shushed him with an affectionate pat on his hand.

"No no, you've done nothing wrong," she assured him. "We had the baby to care for, and then it just became so much easier to stay at home. I'm only telling Bella I appreciate her forcing us out of our sedentary habits for an evening. And Mama for arranging for us to receive the invitation, which was at least partially so her niece 'would not languish away by the fire.'"

He laughed. "Aye, thank you, and to her as well, though I hope it hasn't been as torturous as all that. I confess, though, I'm looking forward to this."

"So am I," Bella promised them both. Much of that was novelty, of course. She had never been to a ball here in London, or if she had she'd been a mere child spying on it from afar. Attending one now, she simply had no idea what to expect.

And at least if I hate it, she thought as Martin set the carriage into motion, *or if I make a fool of myself, there's no one to know.*

The ball was being hosted by Earl and Countess Prestwick, and their home was nearly as grand as Crestmont, though a bit smaller and with far more circumscribed grounds. A number of carriages were already pulled up by the front, and after a moment's wait Bella reached for the door.

"What are you doing?" Nancy whispered, though the three of them were quite alone.

"I see little point in sitting here when we are mere steps from the entrance," Bella replied. "We can disembark here and save ourselves a great deal of time." She saw the look on her cousin's face, however—half concerned and half mortified—and quickly relented, settling back in her seat with a sigh. "Fine. I shall wait." She flicked open her fan. "But I shall not be happy about it."

It took another twenty minutes before Martin could finally ease them up to the front and hop down to let them out, and Bella breathed a sigh of relief as she exited the confined space. At last! A short, stocky woman with a ruthlessly cheerful expression and jet black hair piled high was waiting to greet them. Judging by the extent of her jewelry, this must be the mistress of the house herself.

Accordingly, Bella hid her irritation and put on her best manners instead. "Your Ladyship," she stated, dipping into a low, smooth curtsy. "Miss Isabella Parsons. Thank you so much for inviting us. We are honored."

To her surprise, the woman laughed and raised her with one bejeweled hand. "Oh, none of that, please," the countess insisted merrily. "You can bow and scrape all you like inside, but out here we are all friends." She stepped back to study Bella, finally gracing her with a nod. "You are every bit as lovely as your mother, my dear. We were good friends, you know."

That left Bella stunned for a moment. She finally recovered her wits enough to say, "I did not, your Ladyship. But I am pleased to hear it, and thank you for the compliment." Nancy and Joshua had caught up to her by then, and it was a relief to turn and introduce them. Then, pleasantries exchanged, they took their leave, making their way into the house while the countess greeted her next guests.

The house was noble indeed, and built in a very different style from Crestmont, which for all its size and majesty did not have a single room that could host more than twenty. Here, however, the hallway led to a grand ballroom where several times that number already mingled, dancing or strolling or standing or sitting. The combined noise was enough to generate a steady din, and Bella wondered how anyone would hear anything. It was as if all of Hillington's high society had gathered for a ball, but in a space a third the size of Barrage Hall.

Still, everyone was dressed well, with proper comportment, and Bella received many polite and even vaguely friendly nods as she passed through. She led Nancy and Joshua across the room to the refreshments, then to a small grouping of chairs she'd spotted nearby, in front of one of the room's many stone fireplaces. Here, at least, they could sit and watch people and gossip in comfort.

"I had no idea Uncle and Auntie Roderick knew them," Nancy confided once they were well ensconced, glasses of punch in hand. "Though I suppose I am not surprised, since Mama was able to secure us an invite. Besides which, your parents were well and widely liked." She smiled at Bella. "As are you, of course."

Bella laughed. "I am not," she corrected primly. "There are those who like me, certainly, but a good many others think I am too forward, too aggressive, not ladylike enough. While to still others I am too distant and too cool to be of any interest." She smiled. "But *you* like me, and so you fancy others have such discerning taste."

They were still giggling when a gentleman approached. "Ladies, sir," he began, bowing to each of them in turn. "I am Viscount Newsom. You have met my mother, Countess Prestwick."

"Yes, how do you do, sir?" Joshua replied, offering his hand. "Joshua Lilley. This is my wife, Nancy Lilley. And her cousin, Mis Isabella Parsons, who is in from Hillington."

"Indeed." Newsom shook hands, glancing again at Bella. "Welcome to London, Miss Parsons. I wonder if I might claim a dance with you?"

Bella smiled. "Of course, sir. It would be my pleasure." Setting her cup down, she accepted his hand, allowing him to help her to her feet.

The viscount was not a tall man, nor a particularly handsome one, but he shared his mother's exceedingly dark, thick hair and her good cheer. He also proved to be a perfectly adequate dance partner, not terribly graceful but smooth enough to not embarrass himself or her and practiced enough to maintain conversation while going through the motions. "My mother was very pleased when she heard you were in town, and more so when you accepted the invitation for tonight," he told Bella as they circled one another, backs of their upraised hands almost but not quite touching. "And I confess, I was intrigued. I have heard tales of your parents, and I suspect we have met in the past, when we were both much younger, but of course not since."

"Of course," Bella agreed. "It is my first trip to London in many years, after all." She offered him a smile. "And have I at least matched your expectations and satisfied your curiosity?"

That drew a laugh from him. "Oh, exceedingly. Your mother was evidently a great beauty, and you clearly take after her. And you are charming. Nor nearly as stiff as most of those in my usual circle."

His compliments, and the ease with which he delivered them—and gently derided the normal court manner—improved his own charms immeasurably. "I confess, I did not know what to expect," Bella said as they marched several steps together, then waited until they had circled those beside them and reconnected before continuing, "Hillington is very small compared to this, and I'm sure quite provincial. Yet it is where I am most comfortable." *That and on the deck of my ship,* she added privately. That, however, was hardly a topic of polite conversation for a well-bred young lady.

"There is a certain appeal to such places, though, is there not?" Newsom asked. "Some may call them rough, even crude, but I disagree. I think them unfeigned, or at least less mired in politics and games." He shook his head. "You must forgive me, Miss Parsons. You will think quite ill of London if you listen only to my complaints. It is, in truth, a wonderful city, full of so much life and activity. And even court is not entirely bad. Just do not be surprised if you spy duplicity, and please do not think that all we are capable of."

The dance ended, and they faced one another as the music faded. "I will not," she promised. "And you have already shown me that there can be genuine warmth and welcome here."

His smile widened and his bow deepened. "Then I am well pleased, and will leave you to the many admirers already queuing up, just as I must dance with many others who expect it of me. But I am very happy we have met, Miss Parsons, and I hope this shall not be our last encounter."

"Nor I, milord," Bella told him, curtsying. "Thank you."

She made her way back toward Nancy and Joshua, and indeed Newsom had been correct, for she had not even reached them when another young man asked her to dance. So different from Barrage Hall, where there was always a shortage of dance partners! Though Bella knew some of her appeal was her newness. Some was also the mystery surrounding her, as no one of her generation would even know her father. And then there was his title, and property. All powerful lures.

She did enjoy herself, however. Not all of the men were graceful. Not all of them were eloquent. And several of them were downright mercenary, painfully so, in their inquiries about her dowry. But others were nice enough, and it was lovely to be able to spend the entire evening on the dance floor if she wished.

During one break from whirling about, Bella found herself approached by the host and hostess themselves. "I trust you are enjoying yourself, my dear," the countess said. "Darling, this is Roderick's girl, Isabella."

"Ah, a pleasure, Miss Parsons!" The Earl Prestwick was taller than his wife, though not by a great deal, and slimmer, also not by vast amounts. His hair was a milder reddish brown, now liberally streaked with white, and his face sagged, but his eyes were blue and bright as he kissed her hand. "And how is the old boy? Still getting up to trouble?"

"My father is well, thank you, sir," Bella replied. "And the very picture of respectability."

"Oh, well, that's a shame," the earl said, laughing. "When we were younger he was a regular scoundrel! Always chasing after the ladies—or causing other mischief. Why, I remember a time when we stole all the lanterns by the bridge, causing many a cart to miss the entrance and founder onto the banks instead."

Bella laughed. "I admit, I cannot see my father behaving so," she commented. "And, at the same time, I absolutely can. You two were close, then?"

"Oh, we were inseparable at Oxford," her host told her. "I often visited him at Crestmont over breaks. Lovely house, lovely countryside. He had this one old friend, even more of a scamp than he was, went into the Navy. Ayers, I believe."

"Do you mean Nathaniel Ayers?" Bella smiled. "He is a commodore now, and long since forced to retire from a bad leg. But he is a dear man, and he and Father are still close." She dared to rest a hand on the earl's arm. "You should visit, if you can, your Lordship. I know that he would be thrilled to see you, and I'm afraid his own health is no longer strong enough to endure the travel here."

"Ah." He patted her hand, and his eyes were genuinely sad. "That I am distressed to hear. You are quite right, and thank you for the suggestion. It would be wonderful to see him again."

His wife nodded, and that drew Bella's attention, and reminded her of the woman's previous comment. "Did you all four know each other, then?" she asked. "The both of you and my mother and father?" She glanced down. "It is only, she died when I was still quite young, and I have few memories of her."

The countess took her hands. "She was a wonderful woman," she said softly, her own eyes bright. "And yes, we were close. Your father and Prestwick were already friends, and Deborah and I had grown up in the same circles. When I met Prestwick, that caused them to meet as well. It was love at first sight, I do believe." Her smile was sweet and kind, deeply rooted in the past. "Certainly

Roderick could not take his eyes off her, and she seemed equally taken by his roguish charm."

Bella could not picture her father as a rogue—and yet, there were moments when he got that twinkle in his eye and that grin on his lips and she knew he was up to something, usually amusing himself at someone else's expense. So perhaps it was still there, just hidden now by age, infirmity, responsibility—and loss.

"When your mother died, we were all devastated," the countess was saying. "But your father most of all. I am only glad he had you for comfort. Deborah lives on in you." She raised a hand to Bella's cheek, and it came away wet, though Bella had not even realized she was crying. "I am so happy to make your acquaintance at long last."

"We both are," the earl agreed. He chuckled. "But we are upsetting you, and this is a party. You should dance again, whirl about the floor with some handsome young man, and enjoy yourself. We can discuss ancient history some other day. I am only sorry the king is not currently in residence, or we could arrange to have you presented to His Majesty."

"I appreciate the offer, and the kind thought that accompanies it," Bella told him, "but, if you'll forgive me, I'm just as glad His Majesty is not. I came only to visit my cousins, and do not know that I would be prepared to handle a royal audience."

Their hostess smiled. "I am sure you would charm him, as you have everyone else," she assured her. "But we shall have to put that to the test some other day."

She and the earl nodded and took their leave, resuming their tour of the room and visitation with other guests, and Bella accepted Joshua's handkerchief to dab at her eyes. "They are lovely," she commented to her cousins after making herself presentable again. "And not at all what I expected."

"No, nor I," Nancy agreed. "And I take it from your smiles after that Viscount Newsom also acquitted himself well. Though I understand their daughters, Lady Charlotte and Lady Elaine, are a bit more . . . aloof. And their younger son, Adam Kirkland, a bit wild."

"Well, perhaps I should dance with him, then," Bella said with a laugh. "I could do with a little more wildness right now."

She did not find it, for her next few dance partners were all sober men, thoughtful and subdued. After the last of those, Bella took herself to the refreshment table, where several other younger people were lingering.

"Hello," one of them said with a bow. "I don't believe we've met. Baron Ashborough." He was tall and thin, with a long nose and straw-colored hair, and his motions reminded Bella of a jointed wooden marionette. He turned to the young lady at his side. "And this is Miss Emily Grove."

"Oh? How do you do? Miss Isabella Parsons." Bella curtsied, then studied the other woman, who was small and neat and moderately pretty. "I believe I know your intended, Miss Grove. A Mister Hugh Fletcher."

Miss Grove looked alarmed. "I am not engaged, Miss Parsons," she corrected primly, with a quick glance at the gangly baron beside her. "I do know Mister Fletcher, as he once called upon my father, Sir Desmond Grove, regarding a business proposition, and I may have danced with him once or twice, but that is all."

"Oh. I'm very sorry. I must have misunderstood." But Bella knew she had not. Fletcher had said he was engaged, and she doubted there was a second Emily Grove here in London, or that he'd be acquainted with two ladies by that precise name. She exchanged small talk with the pair a moment longer, then made her way back to her cousins, deep in thought.

"Is everything all right?" Nancy asked upon her return. "You seem distracted, and not happily so."

"I am fine, thank you," Bella answered. "It is only . . . it seems a gentleman I met back home was untruthful." She frowned. "A good friend of mine was very taken with him, and I fear I must apprise her of his deception once I return." Assuming Abigail was speaking to her again, of course. But she would need to know. Not that Fletcher was the first man to claim a connection where there was none, and perhaps he had only done so in order to avoid risking any new entanglements. At least he had not done the opposite, concealing a real engagement to entrap someone else. But the falsehood spoke to his character, and not well.

This news and its implications had quite put Bella off from any more dancing. Fortunately, it was growing late, and Nancy and Joshua both appeared to be fading. Thus Bella felt safe in suggesting it might be time to return home.

They sought out the host and hostess to make their good-byes. "Thank you so very much," Bella told them both, and meant it. "I have had a lovely time, and all the more for meeting you both."

"You are a sweet girl, like your mother, though I think I see some of your father's fire in there as well," the earl replied. "It has been our pleasure. I hope we will speak again while you are here, and I am determined to visit your father before too much more time has passed."

It was past midnight by the time they returned home, and Bella felt worn out, both by all the activity and by the many revelations. Still, it had been a good night, and a pleasant change. She took comfort in those thoughts, and quickly fell sound asleep.

Chapter Twenty

Two days later, Bella was surprised to receive a visitor at her cousins' home. She and Nancy were sitting and chatting over their embroidery, Andrew being at his afternoon nap and Joshua not yet home, when Dennis entered the sitting room. "A Commander Reid for Miss Parsons," the butler announced.

"Oh?" Nancy, who had heard only a very vague account of there being a Navy commander in Hillington recently, glanced over at Bella, her own curiosity abundantly evident. "Why, show him in, Dennis. Unless you'd prefer some privacy?" she asked with a smirk.

Bella wasn't sure if she wanted that or not, but the only answer she could give here was, "No, of course not." It was Nancy's house, after all. Not to mention it would be improper for her and Reid to be alone together. If he even wanted to be near her.

Still, he had come calling. Which also meant he had sought information on her whereabouts. She took that as a good sign that perhaps he was not as fed up with her as he had appeared last time they'd met.

Commander Reid entered, and Bella couldn't help it. Her heart leapt at the sight of him. He had not changed, still as tall and broad-shouldered and handsome as ever, his hair tidy and his uniform neat but both with those faint, telltale signs that this was a working man rather than an idle officer, with the weathered skin and callused hands to prove it.

"Miss Parsons." He bowed. "I apologize for calling so abruptly."

"Not at all." Bella frowned at her own voice, which came out in a breathy rush. She took a deep breath to steady herself. "Commander, may I present my cousin, Mrs. Nancy Lilley. Nancy, this is Commander Nicholas Reid, master of the HMS *Diligent*."

"Madam, it is an honor," Reid stated, bowing to Nancy. "You have a lovely home."

"Thank you, Commander," Nancy replied with a smile. "You and your crew have been stationed at Riverside, I take it? Please, have a seat."

"Thank you." He came and sat on one of the chairs facing the couch they both occupied. Fortunately it was a pleasant enough day to have the windows open, with no need for a fire, else he might have roasted. "Yes, we have been at Riverside, though I was called down to London to deal with certain . . . administrative matters." He glanced at Bella. "When I told you, last we met, that I was required urgently here, that was no lie."

She nodded. "Nor did I expect it to be, for I both know and value your honesty." She leaned forward. "If I may ask, to what did that summons pertain? Was it the recent events involving the *Dutiful*?" To her cousin she explained, "That ship was also tasked with patrolling the German Ocean, but its captain proved as much a danger to citizens as the pirates she chased. Commander Reid was forced to remove her from her duties."

"I was, and she was to be delivered to London for a military tribunal to decide her fate," Reid agreed. "But she slipped the net, I'm afraid. With the aid of her second, a Lieutenant Talbot. The two of them have gone to ground somewhere. They will never serve again, but that does not mean they can be allowed to escape justice." He sighed. "When I return to Riverside, I will organize additional searches, in case they are foolish enough to remain in the area."

"I am sure everyone will feel safer knowing you are doing so," Bella assured him. "I certainly will." Especially since Davis had vowed revenge on Cannon Belle!

Reid was glancing down at his hat, clasped in his hands, and his face was slightly flushed. "There were other reasons I was summoned," he confessed. "The first, to no surprise, was to be told off for not having caught either of the pirates plaguing the area."

"You have done your best," Bella insisted. "I fail to see how anyone could think you were shirking your duties."

That coaxed a small, rueful smile from him, if only for a moment. "And yet, the admiralty does. Or at least, they feel that my efforts have as yet yielded no success. Nor are they entirely wrong. Even with the *Dutiful*'s aid, regardless of her captain's excesses, both the *Deadshot* and the *Hunger* continue to roam free, and both have been sighted—and actively plundering—in my absence."

"Have they? Both of them?" Bella felt a scowl of her own coming on, and fought to prevent it from surfacing. What was Quince thinking? Even if the *Deadshot* was already fully restored and seaworthy, he and Luke O'Dell had assured her they would wait until her return to put the ship back in the water. Why had they disobeyed? That was something she would have to see to upon her own return, whenever that might be.

Though at least, if the *Deadshot* was sailing about, it would further prevent anyone from making the connection between Isabella Parsons and Cannon Belle Pearcy.

"Yes, both," Reid confirmed. He frowned down at his hat. "And because of their recent activity, I have been given a temporary reprieve, with an accompanying warning. I must correct that matter, and quickly, or another will be assigned to the task in my stead."

Bella did not like the sound of that. At all. "Meaning you would be sent elsewhere, or that another captain would take charge and your ship would be tasked to assist?"

"The former, I'm afraid. I depart for Hillington with the noon tide tomorrow." He sighed deeply. "The other reason pertains to their increasing lack of faith in me as well. And to you."

"To me?" Oh, that *definitely* did not sound good!

"Indeed." Now Reid finally forced himself to meet her eyes, and his own gaze was tortured. "I have been informed that my behavior at Barrage Hall was inappropriate for a Naval officer, and cast the entire service in a bad light."

Bella could not decide whether to be mortified, disappointed, or furious. She went with the third option. "How dare they? We merely danced together! There was nothing inappropriate in that!"

"I would agree," he said quickly. "And it was an excellent dance." He smiled at her, but that faded quickly. "Yet other attendees apparently felt we lacked the proper decorum. And word of that reached the Admiralty. There are very particular rules officers must follow, a rigid code of conduct. I have been informed that I have skirted dangerously close to violating those codes, and will need to be more circumspect in future."

Now her blood was boiling indeed. "And do I have any say in how I, and those I am with, shall behave? Or does the Navy feel it can dictate conduct to me as well? I am a baron's daughter!"

"Yes, and that may be the only thing that has saved my commission thus far," Reid replied. "If I had behaved in such a way with anyone less, they would have simply assumed I had taken the lead in such actions. But with your rank and title, and a certain . . . reputation, the Admiralty acknowledged that I may have been following your lead."

"Which you were, and I will happily inform them of such!" Bella declared. "Can they blame you for accommodating a lady's wishes, when there was nothing untoward about them?"

Reid laughed, though it was not the sound of his genuine humor. "They can, and they do," he told her. "Hence the reprimand." He sighed again. "I am sorry, Miss Parsons. Please know this does not mean I have any less interest, but I will need to be a good deal more careful in future. And it would probably be best if I not approach you when we are back in Hillington, at least until my superiors have had time to relax their strictures and their attention."

"I see." So he had been ordered to steer clear of her, and was here to let her know he would follow those orders. Just as he always followed. Bella had to bite her tongue to stop from saying any of that aloud, for doing so would surely drive him away again, and this time for good. But could she truly love a man who would put orders over her? Who would let himself be told not to see her?

Evidently her anguish showed on her face, for Reid rose at once. "I have distressed you," he said, "and that was farthest from my intentions. I am sorry. I will leave you, to avoid further upset, and bid you both a good day." Restoring his hat to his head and bowing to them both, he quickly saw himself out.

"Well!" Nancy said once the door had closed behind him. "I do not know entirely what that was about—you have been keeping things from me, Bella—but one thing is clear. He did upset you, and I can only assume from it that you will deeply regret the loss of his attentions."

"I—" Bella started to say something, to retort, to argue, but could not get the words out.

Because, with dawning horror, she realized her cousin was right.

She hated the idea of Reid staying away from her. And not just because he would be doing so not out of disinterest but because he had been ordered to. No, she hated it because she didn't want him to stay away. At all.

Ever.

Damn it all, how had she not noticed him stealing her heart away? Yet he had evidently done just that, because here she was, on the verge of weeping or cursing at the thought of losing him.

When Basil-White had said he was leaving, she had been upset. But part of that, she knew, had been mere vanity, annoyance at the thought that her charms were not enough to keep him in attendance. When Reid had left right after, she had been crushed. And she'd told herself it was because both suitors had gone, one right after the other, compounded with the fact that she no longer had Abigail to confide in and seek solace from. That last still stung, and Bella knew she would need to find some way to rectify that once she returned. But, looking at all this now, after more than a week away, she saw clearly enough.

Basil-White meant nothing to her. Oh, he was charming, certainly. Handsome. Charismatic. And assertive.

He was not a certain Naval commander, however. And, for all his faults, Nicholas Reid was the man she wanted.

Now that she had finally admitted such to herself, Bella felt her heart sing and her blood race. Yes, she wanted him! Reid could be difficult, but so could she. He was reticent, but she was bold, so they balanced one another. But he listened to her, truly. He saw her. He cared what she thought. And he was not afraid to keep pace with her.

Yes, Reid would obey his orders. He was an officer, and an honorable man. He believed in keeping his word and fulfilling his responsibilities. She could hardly fault him for that, even if it hurt her personally.

So. She was determined now. She knew her heart's goal.

The question was, was she too late to obtain it? Could she find a way to overcome Reid's orders, or his need to follow them so utterly? Or would she never again have the pleasure of his company, just as she realized his was the only company she wanted?

Chapter Twenty-one

OF COURSE, AFTER THAT NOTHING COULD be done but that Nancy must hear the entire story. And so Bella told her.

Nearly all of it.

"Well, your commander certainly presents himself as a very respectable, honorable, even noble man, whatever his origins," Nancy decided after hearing about Reid, Basil-White, Fletcher, Davis, and even Abigail. "And his circumspection not only does him credit, I believe it would be an excellent counterbalance to your own more impetuous nature. Yes," she declared, folding her hands over her needlework. "I believe I like him very much—but not half so much as you do."

Bella sighed. "I do like him very much indeed," she agreed heavily. "But you heard him. He is no longer my commander at all. How can he be, when he will have nothing to do with me?" She held up a hand to forestall the criticism about to emerge from her cousin's mouth. "Yes, I am aware that he has his orders, and that he is doing the honorable thing by obeying them. I am not even arguing that. I am merely saying that, regardless of my feelings for him or his for me, surely if he cannot be around me, that is a clear preventative to the very notion of courting."

There was little Nancy could say to contradict that, and it was with a heavy heart that Bella excused herself to go lay down. She chose not to dine with the family that night, pleading a headache when it was the heart that hurt, and took some soup in her room before attempting to sleep. Eventually exhaustion won out, and she did slumber, if fitfully.

The next morning found Bella still in her doldrums. Her melancholy was disturbed, however, by a polite knock on the door shortly after dawn.

"There is a letter for you, miss," Dennis reported through the door. "Just arrived. Shall I slip it under the door?"

Bella was up and in her dressing gown, so she nodded at Sophie to accept it from the butler. Her curiosity was aroused. Who knew that she was even in town? The Countess Prestwick was her first thought, followed by Miss Emily Grove. Her heart dared hope it might be from Commander Reid, professing his love, though she did not think that likely.

When the maid handed over the missive, however, Bella found herself abruptly short of breath, gasping to draw in air. Because the stamp was not from London but from Hillington. And the return address read "Solomon Keats, Esquire." The fact that their family solicitor had felt the need to contact her all the way in London filled Bella with dread, and she quickly tore open the envelope.

Inside was a single sheet of folded paper, little more than a notecard. Which indeed sufficed, as Keats had only written:

> *My dear Miss Parsons,*
> *I am very sorry to report that certain matters necessitate your immediate return. Please arrive with all due haste.*
> *Yours sincerely,*
> *Solomon Keats, Esquire*

Bella was on her feet and out the door at once. "Nancy!" she called. "Joshua!" For it was Saturday, and both of them should be home.

Nancy emerged at the bottom of the stairs. "Bella? Whatever's wrong?"

"I need to leave at once," Bella explained breathlessly once she'd reached her cousin, who she caught in a fierce hug. "I'm sorry." And she thrust the letter at Nancy in explanation.

Nancy was still reading the short missive when Joshua emerged to join them. "What's all the fuss about?" he asked, and his wife handed him the letter as well. "Oh," was all he had to say at first. Followed by, "I see." And then, "I will call a coach for you at once."

"A coach?" Bella cried. "They only leave at dawn, do they not? And it is already past that hour. Which means the soonest I could depart would be on the morrow, and it would be the day after before I could reach home. This letter is already at least two days old! Who knows what could have happened since then?" Her mind was racing. Her father's health was weak at best, his grasp on reality tenuous. What if one or the other of those had fled? Every minute counted!

Which was why she turned and shouted up the stairs, "Sophie, pack as quick as you can! We leave for the Naval Yard at once!" She was halfway to the front door before Nancy caught her by the arm.

"What do you mean to do?" she asked.

It was only out of love that Bella did not shake off her grip—or punch her full in the face to get loose. "I am going home," she managed instead. "By the quickest way possible."

Assuming, of course, she could talk him into it.

"Miss Parsons." Commander Reid regarded her from the prow of the HMS *Diligent*. "This seems to me the exact opposite of 'we must keep our distance.'"

Nancy was elbowing her in the side, but Bella ignored her cousin, focusing all her attention—and whatever charms she might still possess—upon the handsome officer. "I am aware, sir, and I apologize profusely," she called up, the distance necessitating shouting that did not allow for niceties in tone. "But I have urgent need to be back in Hillington, and so I must rely upon your kindness and your mercy to see me home at once."

He scowled down at her. "The coach will take you there swiftly enough," he began, "and—"

But she cut him off. "No, it is urgent, truly." And she held up the letter she'd retrieved from Joshua. "This is from my family solicitor, urging me home as soon as possible." She felt her lower lip quaver, and forced herself to remain composed. "I fear something terrible has happened."

Reid was studying her, and though he still frowned it was more thoughtful than annoyed, at least. He glanced at Nancy and Joshua, both by Bella's side, as once they'd realized they couldn't talk her out of this notion they had promptly accompanied her and Sophie instead. Bella could have kissed them when they both nodded gravely.

"Please, Commander," she said. "I am begging you. You said you were leaving on the noon tide, and is half past eleven now. You can be in Hillington by mid-afternoon."

When he sighed and glanced away, she knew she had won. "You must steer clear of the crew," he instructed. "I will not have you in their way."

As if I did not know how to captain a ship at least as well as you, she thought but wisely did not say. Instead she merely nodded.

"Very well," he said at last. "You and your lady's maid may come aboard, with your luggage. We will place you in the prow. I myself will keep to the helm and the stern. I trust you will respect my wishes as previously stated, and confine yourself to that area for the duration of the trip."

She hated that, the idea that he would be so near and yet so far away and so unreachable, but right now romance was the farthest thing from her mind so she nodded again.

"Lower the gangplank!" Reid shouted to one of his men, who hurried to obey. "And make ready to depart as soon as Miss Parsons and her maid and their bags are safely stowed!"

With that settled, Bella had time to turn to Nancy and Joshua. "I am so sorry to leave so abruptly," she told them both. "Thank you so much for allowing me to visit and to stay with you. I love you both. And give my love to little Andrew. I promise to come back again sometime soon, and with far less drama."

Nancy hugged her. "I love you too," she said as they embraced. "Write once you know what's happened, to put us at ease. And be safe."

After a hug and more statements of affection and exhortations to take care from Joshua, Bella led the way up onto the ship. She had to force herself not to run ahead but instead let herself be guided to the prow as if she did not know where it was. A cozy little bench was nestled in there behind the bowsprit, and Bella sat there, making room for Sophie to sit beside her. The girl's eyes were wide and a little wild, and Bella remembered that her maid did not much care for sea travel.

"It will be all right," she assured Sophie. "These men are in the Royal Navy. They know their craft. Besides which, the day is fair, the wind strong and steady, and the waters smooth. We should have clear sailing."

The girl gulped but nodded, and Bella turned her attention to watching the preparations. The crew did indeed know their stuff, and moved quickly and competently, each man to his task. Within minutes, everything was tucked away, the lines were cast off, and the small sails were raised. They filled with wind, pushing the ship away from the dock. Then she was turning, still backing off, until her prow was pointing north. Toward Hillington.

"Raise the main sail!" Reid shouted, and sailors rushed to comply. The large sails rose and promptly belled out, propelling the ship away from the city and toward the German Ocean.

And home.

Chapter Twenty-two

NORMALLY, BELLA FELT AT HOME ON a ship.

This time was different.

Typically now when she was at sea, she was the captain, roaming freely across the deck, calling out orders, or stationing herself just behind the helmsman where she could watch everything and everyone.

Here, she was confined to the bench at the prow, along with Sophie and their luggage. She was forced to play the role of a lady, sitting straight and still.

It reminded her of her first sea voyage, the one that took her to the Mediterranean. And of the first part of her return voyage, on the ill-fated *Bold Fortune*.

She did not enjoy being reminded of that.

Of course, she also had Sophie to think about. The poor girl did not enjoy being at sea. She had looked dreadful when she'd first arrived at Crestmont, and had admitted tearfully that she'd been woefully sick on the voyage over from France. She'd actually been terrified that Bella would take one look at her and sack her on the spot, leaving her to either find new employment somehow or make her way back to her homeland. Needless to say, Bella had taken pity on the girl and kept her on, and time had since confirmed the wisdom of that choice, as Sophie was an excellent lady's maid and a kind, sweet girl in general.

But in her haste to return home Bella had forgotten her maid's aversion to the water.

"Are you quite all right?" she asked Sophie now. "Shall I have them bring you anything? Even though it is the Navy, I am sure they can at least rustle up a cup of tea."

Her lady's maid shook her head. "Non, thank you, milady. I will be fine." She lifted her chin resolutely and took big gulps of air. "I will be fine," she repeated, as if she could will it so.

Which perhaps she could. "Turn your face toward the open water," Bella instructed. "Close your eyes if you like, but the breeze will be invigorating. Also, calm your breathing. Do not gulp, just breathe normally. And relax your body. Let it sway with the ship, rather than fighting the motion."

The girl did as she was told, and Bella could see her relax somewhat and even manage a wan smile. "Yes, you are right, milady. That is better. Thank you."

A man cleared his throat close by, and Bella turned to discover that, during her distraction, an officer had approached. He was young, not much more than a few years older than her, she guessed, though already tanned from constant exposure to sea and sun, and had a friendly face fringed by blond whiskers. His single epaulet proclaimed him a lieutenant.

"You are clearly no stranger to sea travel, miss," the newcomer commented, his smile warm. "Very commendable. Lieutenant Alex Hatcher, at your service." He saluted, but quickly returned to a more casual posture and tone. "The captain sent me to make sure you're comfortable and have everything you need. I heard you say something about tea. I can certainly have cups brought for you both."

"Thank you, Lieutenant, that would very kind." Bella studied him thoughtfully. He seemed quiet and capable, and she liked him immediately. While not as dashing as his commanding officer, Hatcher had a very approachable air. "Miss Isabella Parsons, a pleasure to meet you. And this is Sophie, my lady's maid." The girl managed a smile and a seated bob.

"A pleasure for me as well, miss." Hatcher glanced around, then shifted a little closer and lowered his voice. "The commander has mentioned you to me more than a few times, and I can see why he is so taken with you."

That warmed Bella more than a thousand cups of tea could, and she knew her smile brightened in response. "Did he, now? I am sure you should not be telling me so, Lieutenant."

He laughed, as she'd hoped he would. "No, I should not. But Reid is not just my commanding officer; he is my friend. And when he speaks of you—" Hatcher shrugged. "It's good to see him happy, and thinking on things other than his duties."

Yes, Bella decided, she did indeed like this Lieutenant Hatcher. "I agree with both parts of your statement," she replied. "And I am very glad to see he has such a friend, who looks out for him and hopes for his happiness."

Hatcher's own smile was warm. "Indeed, miss. I can see that we both do, and I'm well pleased about that. I'll see about that tea, and if you've a need for anything else, just tell one of the men. I'll check in on you as I'm able." With that he bowed and retreated toward the galley.

Unfortunately, his parting words reminded Bella why the ship's captain was not checking on her himself, which dampened her mood again. However, the sun was out, the breeze was pleasant, the waves were calm, and the *Diligent* was speeding along, all things that helped cheer her.

When a sailor returned a few minutes later bearing two cups of tea, that was even better.

The voyage home was completely uneventful, beyond leers from a few of the sailors—which quickly disappeared whenever Hatcher was nearby, the men straightening and suddenly remembering tasks they needed to be about. That only confirmed Bella's opinion of the man, and of course of Reid, since it spoke well of his character to have such a decent man for a friend. Not that Bella didn't already know and admire his character, barring that one unfortunate tendency to hesitate before acting. Still, she would have been very happy to speak with him during their trip, or at least see him. That was not possible, however. He evidently did not stray from the helm the entire time they were at sea, and Bella obeyed his request and remained at the prow. There was no sign of him until they had pulled into Riverside, and then only because once they were docked Bella felt it was safe to break his stricture and seek him out.

She found him by the helmsman, as expected. "Thank you for your great kindness in conveying us home so quickly, Commander," she told him, dipping into a curtsy. "I am in your debt."

"I am happy to have been of service, Miss Parsons," he replied, very properly. "I will have one of my men fetch a carriage and drive you home."

"That is very considerate." She smiled at him. "I wish you good fortune, sir, and hope that circumstances will soon allow us to encounter one another again."

His answering smile was fleeting, but lasted long enough for her to be sure she'd seen it. "That would be my wish as well, and I hope whatever concerns brought you home in such haste are easily and speedily resolved."

There was little more to be said after that, and Bella allowed Lieutenant Hatcher to help her and Sophie down the gangplank. Her maid sighed loudly in relief once she was standing on the rough timbers of the dock once more. Whereas for Bella, being off the *Diligent* only served to remind her that something dire awaited her at home.

A sailor rode up on a wagon. "Sorry, miss, this is all I could find on short notice. If it won't do, we'll have to send to a stables for better."

Bella eyed the conveyance, but it appeared sturdy and the bench seat was easily wide enough for the three of them. "That is fine, thank you," she answered. The man nodded and reached down to haul her up onto the seat beside him, then did the same for Sophie, who Bella placed in the middle so the girl would not be at risk of falling. Other sailors loaded their luggage into the cart, and then the driver shook the reins and they were off.

The ride home was silent, the driver clearly not feeling comfortable speaking to them and Sophie being equally shy, while Bella herself was lost in thought. But soon enough they were pulling up at Crestmont, where Daniel greeted them with obvious surprise.

"Miss Parsons!" her footman exclaimed, hurrying over to help her and Sophie down and then collect their bags from the back. "What are you doing home, and with no notice?"

"Thank you, sir," Bella told the sailor, who nodded and clucked the horses into motion once more. Then she turned to Daniel. "Is my father all right?"

"Lord Roderick was fine last I saw him, and nobody's said otherwise," was the answer, which while not entirely satisfactory at least was encouraging. With a nod, Bella stepped up to the front door, even as Geoffrey tugged it open from within.

"Welcome home, miss," the tall butler stated, appearing unfazed at her sudden return. "I hope your time away was a pleasant one."

She was eyeing him, but if there was anything amiss she saw no hint of that on his lined face. "Thank you, Geoffrey. Is my father well?"

"He is, miss. I believe he is in the solar just now, having a short rest after luncheon."

"Hm." Bella followed the aged butler into the house, Sophie coming in after her and then Daniel with the bags. "I received a letter from Mister Keats, requesting that I return home immediately. It sounded rather portentous. Do you have any idea what that might be about?"

But Geoffrey shook his head. "Mister Keats did stop by a few days ago," he recalled, "and spoke to his Lordship, but I did not hear what was said. He left soon after, and we have received nothing from him since."

"Very well." Bella considered her traveling gown, which was damp in places from the sea spray and wrinkled from sitting on that bench the last few hours, but there was nothing for it. "Daniel, please ready the coach. I will visit Mister Keats at once."

As the footman nodded and hurried off, she focused on Sophie. "Air everything out," she instructed, "and then take some time to relax and recover. I know you do not enjoy going by boat, and I appreciate your braving that with me." The girl nodded, looking both relieved and grateful as she headed upstairs to her rooms. Bella, on the other hand, sighed and retraced her steps, to wait outside for her coach.

Mister Keats was at his desk, and glanced up when Bella entered, staring. "Miss Parsons!" He quickly rose and came around to give her a quick embrace and a kiss on the cheek, and the fact that he did not linger made her worry all the more. "I admit, I am gratified by your quick action," their family lawyer told her as she chose a chair in front of his desk and he returned to his own seat. "But I had not expected you to manage that feat so quickly."

"You said 'all due haste,'" Bella reminded him. "So I made haste. And here I am. Now, what exactly are these matters?"

He took a moment to settle himself, and to fidget with the ink-well and quill and other tools on his desk, but eventually he nodded. "Quite simply," he began, "it is this. A new creditor has come forward. It seems that your father borrowed money from the man, for what purpose I do not know, but the debt has now come due. I tried to speak with your father about it, but he waved me off. Thus I was forced to contact you in his stead. I apologize for causing you to cut your holiday short."

Bella sighed. "I am glad you did reach out. Thank you. And how much is the bill?"

Mister Keats met her gaze. "Five thousand pounds."

For a moment, she was too stunned to speak. "Five thousand pounds!" she repeated once she regained control of her voice. "That is insane! What would he possibly have needed such money for?" There had been recent periods where they had been stretched thin, but certainly nothing that could have required a loan of such size!

Nor had her father, for all his vagaries and impulses, made any random purchases of that magnitude.

But her lawyer looked grimly certain. "I do not know, but they have made their claim, which appears to be above board, and are prepared to pursue it as far as necessary, I'm told." He steepled his fingers together. "We are both aware that you do not have such funds as that. If you were to sell the house . . ."

"Sell Crestmont? Absolutely not!" Bella rose to her feet. "What is the name of this man who says we owe him such an amount?"

"Elias Crawford," Keats replied. "He is a merchant out of Leeds."

Bella frowned. "I have never heard of him, nor have I seen his name on any receipts or bills of sale." But given her father's fogginess, and her own recent absence, it was not impossible that some purchase had not been properly recorded. Still, five thousand pounds?

"I will find out the truth of this," she promised the solicitor. "And, if the claim is legitimate, we will find a way to pay it. Without selling Crestmont."

Keats nodded. "As you say. It is good to have you home, Miss Parsons. I knew I could rely upon you for swift and decisive action."

Yes, Bella thought as she swept from the room. *I can certainly be counted upon for that.*

Chapter Twenty-three

UPON RETURNING HOME, BELLA WAS SURPRISED to learn that she had a guest waiting for her in the sitting room.

Abigail has forgiven me! was her first thought. But of course Geoffrey would have mentioned her by name, and Margaret would probably already be hard at work preparing those sandwiches. Abbie was a great favorite among all the staff, both because she was Bella's closest friend and because she was a kind soul who always thanked them warmly.

Perhaps it was Commander Reid? Bella's heart quickened at the thought, but she quickly squashed that notion before it could take root. If he was half the man she knew him to be, there was no way the good commander could have broken his vow so quickly. One of his men, perhaps, sent to deliver a message? It could not be Mister Keats, as she had just left him and no one had passed their coach on the way. Who, then?

Entering the room herself, she immediately received her answer, in the form of a certain tall, handsome man with auburn hair and impeccable attire.

"Ah, Miss Parsons!" Charles Basil-White stated, sweeping into a grand bow. "I apologize for calling upon you so abruptly! But I am returned from the business that took me away so precipitously, and simply could not wait to see you again."

"Mister Basil-White, how lovely to see you safely back with us," Bella replied, dipping into a smooth curtsy. She tugged off her gloves and untied the ribbon holding her hat in place, removing that as well and handing them both to Sophie, who had materialized behind her. The girl also took her coat, allowing Bella to sink gracefully onto the couch and motion her caller to take a seat as well. He chose the one nearest her, and leaned forward eagerly, as if planning to drink in her every word.

With exquisite timing, Geoffrey chose exactly that moment to arrive with the tea service. "Shall I pour, milady?" he asked in that deep voice of his, the pot swallowed up in his colossal hands. Many a man would have quailed at such a sight, and such sepulchral tones. Basil-White hardly seemed to notice.

"Yes, thank you, Geoffrey," she answered. "Will you take tea?" she asked her guest politely.

He seemed inclined to refuse, then thought better of it. "Yes, thank you. Milk, no sugar." All of that was directed at her and not at the butler, but then Basil-White's eyes had not left her since she'd entered.

Once they had their tea in hand, Geoffrey withdrew as far as the door, providing that silent but crucial bulwark to a lady's sanctity and reputation. There were times when Bella might have despaired at his presence while a man came calling. Right now she felt an odd relief.

"I hope that your business went well?" she asked once they'd each had a chance to sip their tea.

He nodded, then shrugged, offering a lopsided smile she had found charming before but which had lost some of its luster now, at least to her eye. "It did, it did. Or at least, it is well started, and I believe will bear ample fruit in short order. There was an initial outlay, of course, but money is of little concern to me if it gets me what I want. And I certainly have enough of it, though I suppose that is rude of me to say."

Perhaps a bit, yes, Bella thought. What she said, however, was, "Well, I am glad to hear it. And I hope you will not have to run off so suddenly again any time soon. Hillington was quite too dull without you."

He was studying her over his cup, his hazel eyes as bright as ever—only now she realized how much she preferred a darker gaze. "Have no fear of that. I believe all of my current interests are safely bound up right here, and will have my full attention from this time forward."

She nodded, smiled, and sipped her tea. Strange how, before, his boldness had always seemed so enticing. Now she saw it as a more grasping version of her own nature, quick to act but driven by darker impulses, she suspected.

"Miss Parsons." Her gentleman caller set his cup aside, leaning forward once more, and reached out for her free hand, capturing it in both of his own. "You will forgive me if I dispense with idle pleasantries and come straight to the point. You are the very object of my attention, and of my affections. I can no longer conceal them and must therefore profess my love for you. I hope that you also have warm feelings for me, and I ask that you consent to be my wife."

"Oh." That was all she could think to say at first. Flustered, she set her cup down, the motion forcing him to release her hand lest she overbalance and fall from her seat. "That is . . . very sudden, sir. I am flattered, certainly. But I . . ."

He was already holding up his hand. "Do not give me an answer yet," he insisted, drawing a calling card from his waistcoat pocket and setting it upon the table between them. "I would not have you make your decision in haste and regret it later. Think upon it, upon what we could mean for each other, and what we could do for each other in terms of not only love and friendship but also support and comfort. I have done very well for myself, and if we marry that wealth would be at your disposal for the maintenance of this house and all within it."

With that, Basil-White rose to his feet. "I hope you will consider it, and I admit that I flatter myself to think one answer is the obvious choice. But I will not rush you, and so until you have made up your mind, I bid you a good day." He bowed and turned, heading straight for the exit at a brisk enough pace that Geoffrey had to quickly stand aside and pull the doors open for him.

Bella was left alone on the couch, the remains of her tea cooling before her. Her mind was all awhirl, and she could barely focus enough to think clearly. A proposal! And from Charles Basil-White!

He was handsome, certainly. And charming. And knew what he wanted, as his proposal demonstrated. No hesitation there!

He was also rich. Rich enough, she realized, that he could pay off this strange new debt her father had somehow accrued. A timely intervention indeed!

Yes, it was the obvious choice. But her heart cried out at the very thought of it. Because, for all that he was, Charles Basil-White was no Commander Nicholas Reid. And matched up side by side in her mind, that was starkly evident. Basil-White was assertive, yes—but bordering on pushy. He was attentive—but only when it suited his own interests. He was successful—but somewhat of a braggart. Nor had she missed the way he'd ignored Sophie and Geoffrey. "Watch how someone treats their servants, or yours," her mother had told her once when she'd grown old enough to at least remember it. "You will see their true character then, not the one they put on for guests." Basil-White treated the staff as disposable. That was unkind, and countered all of his smiles and compliments to her and Abigail and other young ladies out in public.

Still, it was a proposal. And she certainly had no others. In fact, the man she'd like to receive had made a point of telling her he could not call upon her.

But did one accept a man simply because he'd offered himself? A man she suspected was far less pleasant under the skin?

Perhaps before, she might have. But Bella was no shrinking flower. She did not need a man to complete her, and certainly did not require or even want one to tell her what to do. If she could not have Reid, that did not mean she had to take someone who would not make her happy in his stead.

The problem, of course, was this bloody debt. Five thousand pounds! If not for that, Bella could easily refuse Basil-White and think no more of it. That was a great deal of money, however. Far more than she had from her misadventures. Could she afford to risk her home and the livelihood of her servants, much less the safety and security of her father, when such a ready answer had presented itself?

Thinking of the servants made her glance up. Geoffrey had returned to his place before the door, now protecting her privacy. "What do you think, Geoffrey?" she asked.

"Milady?" Of course, as a good servant, he pretended not to have heard any of the conversation which had taken place before him.

He was not fooling anyone, however, and Bella had known him her entire life. "What is your impression of Mister Basil-White and his proposal?" she asked clearly and definitively.

The tall butler frowned, his gaze finally straying from some distant point to fix upon her. He cleared his throat. "Milady, it is not my place—"

"I know, but I am asking. Please."

He nodded. "I do not like him, milady. He is cruel to his horse and mean to the staff. He is demanding and arrogant. I do not think him anywhere near worthy of you." The stooped old man looked almost aghast at having said such a thing, but Bella smiled and rose to cross the room and hug him.

"Thank you," she told him. "I have always valued your loyalty and your steadfastness. Now I also value your judgement."

With a sigh, she stepped toward the door, which he opened for her with a nod, though his blush had not yet faded. No, she would not accept Basil-White's proposal, she decided. Were she a normal lady of her class, she might feel constrained to do so, if only to rescue them from this latest dilemma.

Fortunately for her, Bella had other means of obtaining a great deal of money in short order.

It was time to return to the sea.

Chapter Twenty-four

OF COURSE, SETTING BACK OUT IN the *Deadshot* meant dealing with its recent—and, by her, unsanctioned—activity. Belle had some suspicions on that, and prepared accordingly.

The morning after Basil-White called on her, she exited Crestmont by the French doors off the dining room, which looked out on the ocean beyond. Taking care to cross the lawn quickly so as not to dampen her house coat too much, Belle hurried to the gazebo perched just before the cliff's edge.

Once there, after making sure no one else was out and about—not that any should be, since Walter tended to be a late riser and they deliberately left much of this back area natural rather than fully cultivated or trimmed—Belle stripped off her coat, revealing the black velvet pants, white silk shirt, red vest, and high black boots she wore beneath it. Folding the coat, she placed it on one of the gazebo's built-in benches, then lifted the next seat over and extracted a bundle from within. Unfolding that, she took up the black wig, setting it carefully atop her head and using the small hand mirror to make sure it was on correctly. Next came sword and pistol, both hanging from the wide leather belt. Finally, she donned her long velvet coat and tri-corner black hat.

The transformation was now complete. Where before had been only Isabella Parsons, now there stood Cannon Belle Pearcy, Terror of the Aegean. Mistress of the *Deadshot*—or so she hoped.

To aid with that last part, Belle took something she'd prepared earlier from her house coat's pocket. She set the coat itself in the now-empty storage space, closing the seat again to conceal it. Once that was done, there was nothing for it but to slip around the back of the gazebo and locate the stones that marked the start of the hidden stairs down toward the water far below.

The way was narrow and slippery, and Belle moved carefully. It would not do to slip and break her neck, nor would it preserve her image or her authority to arrive with torn breeches and skinned knees if she fell. Eventually she reached the bottom, and made sure she was still presentable before emerging from the narrow split in the cliff wall. That opened out onto a thin strip of beach here, and she had to trek only a handful of paces before the wall receded, this time forming a rough natural arch. The entrance was almost impossible to see unless you were right upon it, and the cove curved back and away, allowing those within it to hide entirely out of view. Even a full-sized schooner could be so concealed, as the *Deadshot* had proven.

Belle had known about the cove since childhood, and had early memories of venturing down to picnic here by the water with both her parents. After her mother's death her father had refused to go anywhere near the place, and she was sure he'd long since forgotten it even existed. Meanwhile, it did not appear on any official maps. It was the perfect hideout for a lord's secret stash—or a pirate's treasure.

She had been half afraid her ship might still be out to sea. Fortunately, as she traipsed around the bend, using the slender path up against the cliff wall, the *Deadshot*'s gilded stern came into view. She also heard noise as she approached, the casual mutterings of conversation among men who did not worry overmuch about being discovered.

That was about to change.

A hush fell over the crew as Belle emerged. Many of them were sitting on the rough sand and rock, or perched on barrels and crates, but all of them rose to their feet as she stalked forward, looking for one head of long blonde hair in particular.

Spotting it, she made straight for him, coming to a stop only feet from her first mate. "Mister Quince," she stated, coat sides pushed back and hands hooked into her belt. "The *Deadshot* looks to be fully restored. Good work."

His expression was more glum than sour, and he did not meet her eyes as he muttered, "Thanks, cap'n."

Her own gaze narrowed. "But I have heard," she declared, her words ringing through the sheltered space, "that there have been sightings of her on the German Ocean. While I was away. Despite my explicit instructions not to take her out until I returned." She sharpened her tone. "Am I mistaken?"

He looked miserable as he shook his head. "No, cap'n. We've taken her out twice."

"Aye, and found rich booty both times," another, oilier voice cut in. John Wynn pushed his way forward, customary sneer well in place. "No Navy to stop us—and no woman holding us back, neither."

Belle refused to back down, even though he was close enough for her to feel his hot, onion- and rum-laced breath on her face. "Is that what you think?" she asked, voice low and hard. "That I've somehow held you back? That you would have fared better without me? Or perhaps that you can now, when I've brought you here, back to England, and to this hideout no one else knows? When I've gotten us out of scrape after scrape, and found us prey after prey? You think you can do better?"

There were mutterings and rumblings all around from that, and many of the men—who had been glaring and sneering during Wynn's announcement—were now glancing away and shuffling their feet. Good, they were as yet undecided. Which meant there was still a chance to turn this around.

Her chief antagonist was not so easily swayed, however. "Aye, I'd say we can do better," John Wynn stated loudly, arms across his broad chest. He topped her by a good handspan or more. "Quince claimed we were just testing the waters, checking that the repairs held, but I knew better. We were seeing what it was like to be our own men again. And we liked it."

"You mean *you* liked it," Belle countered, meeting his glare head-on with one of her own. "You've always chafed under my command, Wynn. Can't stomach taking orders from a woman, hey? Well then, you know the way out." She gave him her best imperious look. "Walk now, and I'll not pursue you, nor seek redress for your betrayal."

"Betrayal?" he barked out a laugh, as abrasive as the man himself. "The word you're looking for, missy, is 'mutiny.' And you're the one who'll be walking—if you're lucky."

Belle nodded. "Fine. Enough talk." And, before he could react, she yanked free the shortened Sea Service pistol hooked onto her belt, cocked it the rest of the way, aimed at his left knee, and fired.

From this range, she couldn't miss. The explosion was almost deafening in the space, the flare blinding, but of course she had been prepared for it. No one else had, and everyone flinched and yelped, many of them toppling to the ground as they backpedaled furiously.

Wynn, meanwhile, screamed in pain, falling hard as he clutched his bloody knee. "You bitch!" he bellowed up at her, tears in his eyes.

"Aye, I am that," she agreed, tossing the spent pistol aside and drawing the second from her belt. "I'm Cannon Belle Pearcy, Terror of the Mediterranean and Scourge of the German Ocean, don't ya know?" She leaned in close, and poked his wounded leg with the gun barrel. "How's the knee?"

He only glared at her, but his attempt at stoicism was ruined by the whimper he made when the hard metal and wood pressed on torn skin and blood and bone.

She had to laugh at that. "You'll live from it," she told him, and the rest of her audience, lifting her head so they could hear. "I used half powder for that one. Consider it a warning shot." Then she cocked the second gun and leveled it at his head. "This one's full strength, though. So, what'll it be, Wynn? Still think you can replace me?"

He blustered for a second—then hung his head. His reply was

almost inaudible, but no one could miss the defeat in his tone and his posture. "No."

"Good." She kept the pistol there, though her arm ached from the weight of it. "Will I have any more trouble out of you?"

He shook his head, or started to, but froze as the barrel scraped his temple. "No."

"Fine." Rising to her feet, she uncocked the pistol and hung it back at her side. Thank God for the Commodore's training! "Mister Quince, have a few of the men escort John Wynn to the nearest town." Pulling a guinea from her pocket, she tossed the gold coin into his lap. "Consider that your severance, along with whatever shares you already took from recent spoils." She leaned in again. "But if you ever cross me, or make trouble for me, know that I will finish what I started."

Turning to the rest of her crew, Belle placed both hands on her hips. "What about the rest of you?" she demanded. "Anyone else think me too weak to lead?"

Several of them mumbled "no" and shook their head, but Belle tapped her foot.

"What was that?" she asked. "I said, am I too weak to lead?"

This time, the men shouted back, "No!" And Quince was loudest among them.

"Am I too soft?"

"No!"

"Am I holding you back?"

"NO!" Their answer shook the cove.

"Good." She smiled. "Because I've returned, and it's time for us to do the same. Time to hit the waters and take some treasure, boys!"

That had them whooping and hollering, and though she maintained an erect posture and a relaxed, confident smile, inside Belle nearly melted with relief. The crew was hers again.

"Sorry about all that, cap'n," Quince said to her as the crowd dispersed, several of the men moving to ready the ship and a few helping John Wynn to his feet and toward the exit. "They was restless once the work was done, so I figured if we went out they'd cool down. But Wynn, he's always stirring the pot, and he started grumbling about how much better off we'd be without you." He looked her dead in the eye. "I told him no, as did many of the others, but he just got louder, and it was safer not to bring it to a boil in case they cut us all down and took the *Deadshot* with them."

Belle nodded and rested a hand on his shoulder. "Thank you, Mister Quince. I never doubted your loyalty, and you did the right thing." She saw the relief in his eyes, and the pride beneath that sour visage. No, she hadn't doubted him. He had been one of her first supporters, and her staunchest.

Luke approached next, and she stopped him before he could even speak. "I know, Mister O'Dell," she assured her steward. "I never doubted you, either."

He grinned and saluted. "Thank you, cap'n. Quince and me, we did our best, but we knew you'd set things to rights once you returned. And we followed the course you'd set, treated our victims fair, did no more harm than needed to back them down."

Belle laughed at that. "I'm glad you have such faith in me!" She smiled at the two men. "And thank you for sticking to your principles. Now, let's go prove you right. Let's find a big fat ship to capture!"

"Aye aye, cap'n!" They both hurried away to oversee preparations, and Bell took a moment to savor the victory. Now they just needed loot, and lots of it.

After all, she had five thousand pounds to pay back.

Chapter Twenty-five

Several hours later, despite the heavy fog that clung to the water, obscuring everything as far as the eye could see, the *Deadshot* had located its next target.

"Looks like the perfect prize," Quince confirmed, studying it through his spyglass. Beside him, Belle agreed. The merchant ship emerging from the hoar ahead was a barque, big and slow, and riding low in the water so clearly stuffed full of something. The Dutch flag flew proudly from its mast. The sea was eerily quiet today, which at least allowed them to confirm that the ship sailed alone and that no other vessels lurked nearby, not unless those were capable of making no sound whatsoever as they sailed. That didn't mean one couldn't creep into range and out of the fog at any moment, though, so they needed to work fast.

"Fire the warning shot," Belle ordered as soon as they were in range and visible. Old Bill quickly set a match to the first cannon, expertly carving a furrow across the other ship's deck. "Ahoy, the ship!" Belle shouted, standing proud and tall with hands on hips, black braid swaying behind her in the breeze. "Throw down your arms and surrender, and live to tell the tale! Resist, and they'll tell tales *of* you instead!"

Unfortunately, what the barque lacked in speed and maneuverability, it made up in sheer size—and number of guns. Its captain must have decided those would be enough, because a moment later they fired an answering volley. None of those cannonballs hit the *Deadshot*, but two passed close enough on either side to potentially scrape against the hull.

"Close the distance fast!" Belle ordered, and her crew piled on all available sail. They shot toward the barque like a dark arrow, and a moment later they were scraping up against the other ship's side—too fast for its men to reload their cannons.

"Fire!" she shouted as the *Deadshot* heeled to, sliding up along the barque, flank to flank. Their cannon was already prepared, and shot directly into the merchant ship's gun ports, causing explosions all along that length. There, that should keep them from continuing to resist!

"Prepare to board!" she commanded, and her crew roared in response. They were still all fired up from her little speech back at the cove, and boiled over both railings to swarm the barque's deck, with both Belle and Quince at their head. Luke stayed behind with Gregor to keep the *Deadshot* ready, in case they needed to hightail it.

The explosions belowdecks had thrown many of the sailors off their feet, but others were still able and spoiling for a fight. Belle met a man's sword thrust with her pistol, using the gun's heavy wooden shaft to block the blade. She drew her blade and thrust while her attacker was still off balance, and managed to bite back her cry as her blow struck home and he collapsed with a long, low gurgle. God, she hated this part!

Several others were waiting to engage, almost like men lining up to dance with her at a ball. Despite the danger, Belle laughed. Good to know she was such an enticing partner! She used pistol and sword with verve, and carved her way through the crowd, exulting in her victories even as she grieved over the loss of life. She could hardly fault the merchant's crew for resisting. This was their livelihood, after all. And they outnumbered her own men. But hers were all hardened fighters, and chafing from recent idleness. The combat was bloody, but her crew slowly fought its way across the deck.

Belle herself slid between foes, dispatching several with ease. At last she found herself facing a big, burly man, his hair grizzled but his arm steady as he leveled a heavy cutlass at her. His hat and coat declared him captain. Just the man she'd been seeking. "Surrender, and end this needless carnage," she warned, flicking her own blade forward to gauge his response.

He snarled in reply. "Never!" His sword clanged against hers, shoving it aside. Then he swung for her head.

He had strength, and reach. But Belle had speed. She ducked the blow and lashed out in response. Her blade's tip cut across his chest, leaving a bloody trail.

"Damn you!" His cry was laced with pain. "Fight like a man!" He swung again.

She laughed. "What, slow and stupid? No thank you!" This time she cut him across his sword arm. Then along one leg. "Surrender!"

But he refused. His wounds only seemed to fuel his rage, even as they sapped his strength. His blows grew more frantic but weaker and less accurate. He began to huff with each attempt. At last, bleeding from a dozen places, he dropped to his knees, sword falling from his hand. Belle kicked it away.

"Yield," she demanded, laying her blade across his throat. He tried to glare up at her, but lacked the strength. His head drooped, and then he was sprawled out upon the deck.

"It is over!" Belle wasted no time declaring. "Lay down your arms!"

All around, the merchant crew turned. Seeing their captain defeated, most of them yielded at once. The few who didn't were disarmed—and the handful who insisted on fighting still, dispatched. Belle hated that, the unnecessary deaths turning her stomach, but refused to show her discomfort. There was nothing she could do for them now, and she had a reputation to uphold.

"Mister Quince!" she called, and her first mate approached. He bore a few cuts, but was otherwise unharmed. "Tie them up and have the men search the ship."

"Aye, cap'n." He called out orders of his own and soon some of their men were shepherding the merchant's crew to one side, some collecting weapons, and the rest checking out the cargo holds.

"Tobacco, tea, and spices, looks like," Quince reported as he clambered back topside, where Belle waited. "Should fetch a pretty penny."

She nodded. "Good. Let's load up and move out while the seas are quiet. This has taken too long already." She was keeping an eye out all around, wishing for a moment the fog would clear as she stayed alert for either of the two threats she knew sailed these waters.

Sure enough, a shout rang out from the *Deadshot*'s top mast as they were transferring cargo. "Captain, a ship!" Isaac called. "Coming up ahead of us, across the sea!"

Belle moved to the merchant ship's far side, up near its prow, and pulled out her spyglass. Yes, there it was, its masts barely visible amid the fog. Young Isaac had sharp eyes. She couldn't tell which ship it was, not from this distance through the mist, but it had clearly seen them or their prey and was heading toward them in haste.

"Finish up!" she ordered. "Whatever we can't get in the next few minutes, we leave behind! Go!" For herself, she hurried to the captain's quarters. There on his desk was a small coffer filled with gold and jewels, payments for recent services. Hefting the heavy container, she lugged it back across. That alone would make a handsome reward to be shared among her crew.

"Can you tell which ship?" she called up as she returned to the *Deadshot*, handing her prize off to Luke O'Dell to be stowed away.

"It's the Navy frigate!" he answered after a moment.

Ah. Belle breathed a little easier. Reid was a tenacious foe, which she respected, but at least he was both rational and honorable. In fact, she could use that against him now. "Quick," she said to Quince, who was at her side. "Back across and reverse their flag."

It took him only a second to understand, and then his usual scowl stretched into a grin. "Aye, cap'n!" Quick as a wink, he leaped back over to the barque and hurried to their forward mast, where their flag waved. While he worked, Belle ordered her crew to stow their newfound treasure and prepare to raise all sail. The second Quince returned, she nodded and the *Deadshot* took off like its namesake, flying from the scene of its recent plunder.

Belle kept an eye out behind her as they raced across the waves, headed at an angle toward the shore. She could see the *Diligent* with the naked eye now, despite the hoar. It was approaching rapidly, but the merchant ship was still between them—and then she saw the frigate's sails slacken. Yes!

"It worked!" Quince declared. "Nice one, cap'n!"

Yes, it had worked. As she'd known it must. Reid was too honorable, too decent, to leave even an enemy ship in need. And that's exactly what the reversed flag had signaled. He'd had no choice but to stop and render aid as needed, even if it meant letting her get away. Again.

Knowing he was probably watching and near enough to do so, she doffed her hat and swept into an elaborate bow. She could almost picture him gnashing his teeth in frustration.

"Richest prize yet," Luke offered, and the men around them cheered. "Here's to Cannon Belle!"

Everyone was in high spirits, even those who'd been wounded in taking the barque. But then a cry from above cut through their merriment.

"Captain!" Isaac yelled, his high, clear voice carrying easily over the din. "There's another ship!"

"What?" Grabbing the rigging, Belle hauled herself up onto the railing, scanning the water all around. "Where away?"

"Out to sea ahead of the barque," came the answer. "I think—I think it's the *Hunger*."

The *Hunger*! Belle felt a chill shudder through her. Still, if it was so distant that only her lookout could spot it, even a ship that size couldn't catch them before they disappeared back into the fog and made for their cove. They were safe.

"Is it after us?" she asked nonetheless.

There was a moment's pause before her young lookout replied. "No, captain. It's turning—I think it's headed for the barque!"

The barque, whose captain she'd downed and whose crew were already injured and defeated, their holds more than half empty. She didn't envy them their fate if they couldn't escape in time.

But then another shudder hit her as she realized something else. It wasn't the merchant ship the *Hunger* would be after. It was the Navy frigate even now tying up against it.

A frigate focused on providing aid to the wounded craft. One all too aware of the pirate ship fleeing toward shore. And thus not paying proper attention behind it, where a second, much larger, much meaner pirate was now swooping in from behind, all but invisible in the mist.

The *Diligent* would be caught unawares. And the *Hunger* would claim another victim.

Unless she did something about it.

Chapter Twenty-six

WITH A GRIMACE, BELLE TURNED TO face her crew. "We need to go back."

"What?" That came from Gregor, who never questioned anything except the cook's choices. "Captain, we just escaped! Got away clean, and with the booty, too! Why in all the hell'd we go back?"

She knew it wasn't what they wanted to hear, but it had to be said anyway: "We need to rescue the *Diligent*."

For a moment, there was nothing but silence against the flap of sailcloth in the breeze and the groan of ropes pulled taut. Then one of the men shuffled and cleared his throat. It was Luke O'Dell.

"Uh, Cap'n?" he began, resolutely raising his eyes to meet her own. "We trust you, an' all. You know we do. But I gotta ask: why? They'd be cheering our destruction, roles were reversed. And one fewer Navy ship after us, that's gotta be a good thing, right?"

She cast a nervous glance across the water, struggling to peer through the fog to where that very frigate was nestled up against the barque—and still unaware of the vicious predator gliding toward it. Then she forced herself to focus all her attention upon her men.

"Listen to me," she started. "Yes, the Navy is after us. Yes, they'd capture us if they could. But this isn't about that." *Or the fact that the man I want is on that ship.* "This is about the *Hunger*." Several of the men shuddered, and she felt the same cold rip through her as well. "That ship is a menace," she pointed out. "And not just to merchants, but to everyone. Including us. It's a shark. It's going to gobble up everyone and everything in its path. If we don't stop it, it'll come for us, too. And we won't stand a chance against it."

"So why would we go head-on toward it now, then?" One of the sailors, Tom, asked. Belle had never cared much for the man, but right now he sounded genuinely curious rather than merely belligerent, and she appreciated that.

"Because," she answered him honestly, "This may be our only chance to take it down. We can't do it alone, no question. But us and the *Diligent* together? We'd have a shot."

The men stirred, turning over this unfamiliar notion. "Us and the Navy, together?" Bill asked. "Don't seem they'd be willing any more'n we would." A few others made grumbles of agreement.

"Aye, maybe we should just sit back and watch the fight," another man, Gareth, suggested. "Whoever's still standing at the end, we go after them instead. That way we only gotta face one, and they're already wounded." That got more sounds of assent.

But Belle was quick to cut that off. "Even wounded, the *Hunger* would swallow us whole." No one could argue that. "And if it's just the two of them, they'd wipe out the frigate with hardly a sweat, especially if they got in the first volley. No, we need the *Diligent*— and, like it or not, they need us. They just don't know it yet."

Tom crossed his arms. "I'm with Gareth," he stated. "Let the *Hunger* chew on the Navy for a bit."

Belle shut down any further ruminations with a glare. "Don't you get it?" she asked them all. "The *Diligent* is a Navy ship, yes. And its captain is an honorable man. He plays by the rules. He's chivalrous and fair." She grinned. "Which is why I beat him, every single time." That wrung a laugh out of her audience, and a few cheers and foot stomps. "He's an enemy we know, and one we can handle. But the *Hunger*?" She didn't have to fake her shudder. "It's a monster. No rules and no mercy. Ever. We need it gone, and this is our best, maybe our only, chance."

"Cap'n's right." That was Quince, who'd been silent up till now. "Like always. *Hunger's* gonna give us all a bad name, draw too much attention, plus chase away all the loot. Can't have that. And then what, when it decides we're next? Nobody'd shed a tear on our passing, and it'd barely notice as it took us down. We need to take it out afore that happens, and best bet is to do it now, while it still don't pay us no mind."

The men grumbled a bit, but no one argued further. And, after a moment, Gareth spoke up, asking, "So, what's the plan, captain?"

Belle smiled and, knowing her crew was with her once more, she glanced back, studying the scene as much in her head as on the fog-shrouded water. Two on one, those were better odds but still not great against a behemoth like the *Hunger*. They'd need an edge—and she suddenly knew what it was.

"Here's what we're gonna do," she explained.

When she was done, Quince stroked his chin as she waited, scarcely able to breathe. "Could work," he finally opined. "Lots a' little fiddly bits, and you've still gotta convince the Navy and all to side with us, but yeah. Pull that off and this just might do the trick."

She grinned and clapped him on the shoulder. "Leave the convincing to me, Mister Quince," she assured him. "Gregor, take us toward the *Diligent* with all speed. Get us as close as you can."

"Aye, Captain!" Hesitation now banished, he nodded and returned to his post, calling out orders to the men in the riggings as he yanked hard on the wheel. The *Deadshot* heeled about, nearly capsizing, but then righted herself. Now she was heading away from the shore, back into the fog and out toward the two linked ships, but not aiming for their prows. That was for honorable discourse among upright travelers. Her own credentials were less than sterling, nor could she risk presenting the *Diligent* with so tempting a view as her ship's unprotected flank. No, they would play it safe, as much as one could while attempting such a foolhardy maneuver.

As they approached, Belle grabbed up a boat hook, the long ash rod comforting in her hand. Gripping it near the upper end, she pulled a handkerchief from her coat pocket. Utterly unadorned and unembroidered, it was nothing more than a square of white linen.

Which, in this case, was exactly what she needed.

Tying that around the brass hook, she stepped to the *Deadshot*'s prow and began waving the makeshift flag before her. With all the fog, she was hoping the *Hunger* wouldn't even notice her ship's return, much less what she was doing. Meanwhile, Quince gave orders to slacken the sails, the waves serving to slow their headlong rush into a gentle drift.

"Parley!" She called out as they neared. "I wish to parley with the master of the *Diligent*!" The hoar swallowed her words, but she thought they were close enough now for the shout to still reach the frigate.

Sure enough, as its stern appeared out of the mist and fog, several Navy sailors rushed to the aft deck, guns in hand but not raised to fire. "Parley!" Belle called again, as her ship slowed further. Gregor, genius that he was, had shifted the wheel slightly, so that they were angled across the *Diligent*'s rear, their bowsprit jutting out past its side—and their gunports more or less facing it.

A familiar figure in a dark blue coat strode forward to join his men. "What do you want?" Reid shouted.

You, Belle wanted to reply. Instead she handed the boat hook back to Quince behind her and got right to it. "The *Hunger*'s creeping up on you," she informed her commander, turning to point across her own deck and into the fog. "There. You were too intent upon us and the merchant to notice."

He frowned, and nodded to one of his men, who hurried away. No doubt shouting up at their own lookout to confirm. "Even if that's the case, why tell us about it?" Reid asked. "We're sworn enemies, you and I."

The very thought made her quail, but Belle forced herself to stand firm, and to reply with what she hoped was a confident, even carefree laugh. "Sworn enemies? I prefer to think of us as two sides of the same coin, Commander. Balanced opposites." She dropped the gaiety. "In all truth, I respect you and your mission. And the *Hunger* is a threat to us all. It has to be stopped. But you can't do it alone."

Now it was his turn to laugh. "And, what, you want to ally with us for common cause? Why would I possibly trust you?"

She gave him her best resolute glare. "Because, though I have tricked you, yes, I have never taken advantage of you. Like now." She gestured along her ship's flank, where the gunports were open and cannons ready. "I could have snuck up and destroyed you before you even realized we were here. Instead, I am speaking with you openly. And before, I withheld a similar volley, did I not? Plus I rescued the crew of the *Sea's Midwife* when your own fellow commander fired upon them." She set her hands on her hips. "You may not like me, Commander, but you must admit that I have played surprisingly fair with you."

Reid stroked his chin. "Aye," he acknowledged with a nod. "That you have." The man he'd dispatched returned and whispered something to him, which made him scowl. "And you are correct, the *Hunger* approaches, using this fret for cover. Very well, madam. Clearly you have something specific in mind. I will hear you out." His lips twitched. "Perhaps you'd care to come aboard, where we could converse more easily?"

She laughed. "I thank you for your kind invitation, sir, but I believe I will remain within the safety of my own ship. No sense tempting fate, hey? And right now, I think we can all agree on the greater threat."

Quickly, she outlined her plan. Reid did not interrupt, but stood with his arms folded, listening intently, his dark eyes fixed upon her the entire time. When she'd finished, he shook his head.

"You are either brilliant or mad," he commented. "Or perhaps both in equal measure." Turning, he addressed the lighter-haired junior officer beside him. "What say you, Lieutenant? Does her plan have merit?"

Lieutenant Hatcher, the same who'd offered Bella and her maid support and succor on the journey from London, nodded. "It could work," he agreed. "If we're quick about it."

Fortunately, once Reid made up his mind he didn't hesitate. "Very well. We shall put aside our differences for now, madam, and attempt this bold, mad plan of yours. Let us all hope it works."

She nodded and offered him a grand bow, which he returned in more restrained fashion. "Thank you, Commander. And good luck." Stepping back, she nodded to Quince, who called out orders. The *Deadshot*'s sails tightened once more, the wind belling them and driving them forward, across and past the *Diligent*'s rear and back out into open water.

Now it was time to see if her plan worked.

Chapter Twenty-seven

THE *Deadshot* LEAPT ACROSS THE WAVES, the fog quickly closing back in around them and swallowing both the *Diligent* and the Dutch barque from view. The sea was strangely quiet, the hoar muffling sound as well. Their own progress was almost silent, and it was equally impossible to see how fast they were going with the waves themselves hidden from sight. It was as if they were alone on the ocean, and for an instant Belle had the mad thought to just keep going, to strike out for the Netherlands or even farther, to leave all of it and everything and everyone behind. But of course she couldn't do that. She wouldn't. So instead she glanced back over her shoulder. "Prepare to come about!"

That order was relayed, and when Belle shouted, "Now!" the *Deadshot* heeled once more, pivoting and heading back more or less the way it had come. "Silent running!" Belle commanded, and all along the ship lanterns were furled and all weapons and other implements stowed and wrapped. The *Deadshot* became a ghost, flying over the ocean without a sound.

The trick here was, they couldn't see where they were going, or what else was out there. In this particular case, where the other ships were. Belle had a fairly good idea where the *Diligent* was, and the barque beside it. What she didn't know was the exact location of the *Hunger*. They could make an educated guess based upon its previous speed and the position of its sails, but without visual confirmation they couldn't know for certain.

They just had to hope they were right.

Belle peered into the fog to her left. She couldn't see anything, but in her mind's eye she could picture the scene:

The HMS *Diligent* had disengaged from the barque beside it. Raising its sails, the Navy frigate began to pull away, angling toward the sea as it went. Its back was still to the *Hunger*, which was approaching like the predator it was, moving forward without a sound in order to take a bite out of the *Diligent*'s rear before it even knew it'd been struck.

Except that wasn't how things were about to turn out.

Quince sidled up beside her. "*Hunger* ahead and maybe two boat lengths to port," her first mate reported quietly. Belle nodded. They continued to sail on, and after a minute she could hear the noise of many men scuffling about, whispering and stomping and no doubt handling all the tasks required on a ship that size.

For their part, the *Deadshot* was an utter ghost.

A dark figure loomed up out of the fog, and Belle suspected she wasn't the only one biting back a shout of surprise. It had seemed to come from nowhere, and it was huge, easily the biggest ship she'd ever seen. Belle held her breath as it sailed past. Between the fog and their darker sails, no one should have even noticed them. Still, she breathed a sigh of relief when that piratical behemoth had disappeared.

"Come about again," she told Qunce softly. "But carefully." The last thing they needed was for the other pirate ship to hear them making a racket across the water. But Luke and the others knew their business, and the *Deadshot* was perfectly silent as it dropped anchor in order to make another, much sharper turn.

The hoar was beginning to break up as the sun rose higher overhead. That meant Belle could now see the tall, dark shape before them—and the slightly smaller, lower shapes beyond that. Again she imagined what had just happened:

The *Hunger* raced in, putting on all speed to keep the *Diligent* from escaping as the frigate began to glide away. The pirate ship would completely ignore the motionless barque, knowing the merchant would still be easy pickings later.

Except that, suddenly, the *Diligent* was no longer running away. Instead the Navy vessel had dropped anchor, using the weight as a pivot to both halt its forward motion and allow it to turn in place. Thus the pirate ship suddenly found itself running straight at the *Diligent*'s side—a side with gun ports open and all cannons ready and aimed.

The *Hunger* would slow—the *Diligent* being big enough that even a monster its size couldn't risk just running into the other ship—but not turn away. After all, it still outmatched the Navy vessel. And face-on was the safest way to approach an array of cannon, anyway, presenting the smallest possible target.

Only, now there was a second ship in range. This one was even smaller, but still formidable, and its cannons were targeting the *Hunger*'s rear—because that was where the *Deadshot* was now, having turned and sailed back up behind them, bracketing the larger pirate ship between them, with the barque off to its starboard side as well. The *Hunger* was thoroughly boxed in, with only its port side unencumbered.

Even with all that, the big pirate ship wasn't trying to run. It was too sure of its own superiority to be frightened, just annoyed. Which was why, as Belle brought the *Deadshot* to a halt behind it, she saw a tall, lean figure in a long, dark red coat and matching tricorn stride to the starboard rail, glancing fore and aft, taking in the situation. That had to be the *Hunger*'s captain.

"So," he declared, his voice bellowing out across the water. "Trapped, am I? We'll see about that!"

The words sent a chill through Belle, and not just because of the confidence in them, or the cruel tone.

She knew that voice.

But it couldn't be! Surely he was dead!

"Surrender, sir!" another, equally familiar but far more welcome voice replied. Reid's. "Lay down your arms and face justice for your crimes!"

The heavy, booming laugh that answered made her shudder, as

it confirmed her worst fears. She'd heard that laughter too many times before to be mistaken.

"Don't try reasoning with him!" she burst out before she could stop herself. "Finish him off now, before he does the same to you!"

"What?" The man on the *Hunger*'s deck straightened, turning her way. "It can't be!" Long strides took him to his own aft deck, to peer down at her from high above but only a few yards distance, close enough to see all too clearly, right down to the glossy black beard he sported. "It is! You!"

Belle struck a pose and bowed, burying her own fear beneath desperate bravado. "Me. Cannon Belle Pearcy. At your service."

He laughed again, derisively, looking down on her in more ways than one. "Aye, I'd heard that's what you were calling yourself now. How apropos."

The distance was too small and the waters too still for Reid not to have heard the entire exchange. "You two know each other, I take it?" he asked from his place at his own railing.

"Know each other? Oh, aye," the *Hunger*'s captain replied. "This saucy little wench stole my ship from me! 'Tis the very vessel she stands upon now!" He glared at her. "And she nicked more'n just the ship, come to that."

Belle smirked back at him. "The *Deadshot* was mine for the taking. You never treated it, or your crew, well enough. As for the rest, well—" She flipped her black braid over her shoulder. "I'd say it suits me, wouldn't you?"

Beside her, Quince laughed, drawing the other captain's eye and ire. "Hello, Quince," he called down. "I see you're still lapping at this bitch's heels, eh?"

"I serve my captain," her first mate snapped back. "And she's a better one than you ever were."

Reid cleared his throat. "I feel as if I've entered a party where everyone else knows each other, and I have yet to be introduced," he stated loudly. "Commander Nicholas Reid of the HMS *Diligent*, at your service. And you are?"

The other captain twisted back toward the Navy frigate and

executed a sharp bow. "You can call me Ravenous, sir. Captain of the *Hunger*, as you can see."

Now it was Belle's turn to laugh. "Is that what you're calling yourself now?" she shouted, echoing his own earlier words. "Commander, allow me to introduce you properly. Meet Argus Carlyle, former master of the *Deadeye*. Also known, once upon a time, as Raven Mane." She grinned. "A nice play on words, that new moniker. And at least it suits you better, hm?" She arched her brow, staring at him, or more precisely at his forehead, which gleamed beneath his hat.

"Damn you, woman!" Carlyle yanked the hat off his head, revealing his bald pate. "Give me back my famous locks!"

"Why would I, when they look so much better on me?" she shot back, toying with her braid once more.

Reid was clearly struggling to keep up. "That's . . . not your real hair," he finally managed, and even from this distance Belle could see that he was starting to put certain pieces together. Uh oh.

Carlyle, however, took an instant delight in the Naval officer's obvious distress and, his own anger forgotten, roared with mirth. "No, it's not!" he agreed, stroking his beard. "Not her right hair, not her own ship, not even her true name!" It was now his turn to favor her with a nasty grin as he waved a hand in her direction and uttered the words that froze Belle's heart:

"Commander, allow me to introduce Miss Isabella Parsons, only daughter of Lord Roderick of Crestmont—also known as Cannon Belle!"

Chapter Twenty-eight

REID STARED AT HER, FACE GONE pale, eyes wide, jaw slack. "What?" he managed after a moment, his voice almost too weak to reach her where she stood, unable to move. "Miss Parsons?"

"Oh, you know each other?" Carlyle's tone was sickly sweet. He was so clearly enjoying this. "I suppose you have been holed up in this region of late, have you not? And small wonder that she would return to her home territory after tricking me out of my ship, the little minx. Not that I didn't wind up with one far better, thanks to a generous friend."

That reference to the past, at least, enraged Bella enough to respond. "You took me captive!" she hotly reminded the old pirate. "You were going to ransom me back to my father—assuming you did not take villainous liberties first!" Her voice caught. "You murdered my maid!"

Poor, poor Therese. The woman had been with Bella since her mother had died, a constant support, and had been fiercely loyal. So much so that she'd actually stood up to the infamous Captain Raven Mane when he'd overtaken their ship home, the *Bold Fortune*, and had attempted to take the two women hostage.

Once he'd ascertained that the lady's maid was worth nothing in and of herself, the villain had run her through without a second thought.

"She brought that on herself," the fiend had the audacity to claim now. "Had she not put up such a fight, she'd have been returned home with you . . . only a little the worse for wear."

Reid was glaring at the man now, so that at least was something. "You are a scoundrel of the first order, and I look forward to seeing you swing from the yard arm," he declared. Then his gaze strayed back to Bella, and he once more looked stricken. "But I still . . . I don't . . . how . . ."

Refusing to beg forgiveness, Bella instead faced him, lifting her chin. "What choice did I have?" she stated, hands on her hips. "I was taken by pirates, held on their ship, and set to be sold back, if my father had even been aware enough to pay or had the funds to do so." Which he hadn't. That had been why she'd been forced to travel to Turkey in the first place. So much of the family fortunes had been foolishly tied up in investments there, and those had been so poorly managed since her father's worsening health that they'd been at risk of losing it all. At least she'd been able to correct that, firing the corrupt manager who'd been running their interests there and promoting one of the junior members who was both more effective and more trustworthy. She'd set sail home in triumph, only to see her own safety and virtue put at risk when the *Deadeye* had come bearing down on them.

"So you turned pirate yourself?" Reid's tone suggested that was barely better than the fate Carlyle had had in store for her. Bella disagreed.

"I did," she answered proudly. "Captive though I was, unarmed and alone, I convinced certain members of his crew that their captain thought of no one but himself, cared for no one, and would gladly desert any and all of them at a moment's notice if it would save or somehow serve himself." She glanced at Quince and Luke, both of whom nodded.

"Aye," Quince agreed, raising his voice so it carried to the other ships as well. "An' she were right. Raven Mane would leave any of us behind in a heartbeat. We was just cannon fodder to him. She promised us better, an' she's delivered every day since."

Now Belle grinned up at the rangy old pirate, remembering those heady times. "With their help, I staged a mutiny. Tossed you right off your own ship, even stole the wig from your very head. Served you right for what you did to me, and especially poor Therese." She'd renamed the ship the *Deadshot*, transformed Carlyle's luxurious black hair into a tidy braid, and gave herself a brand-new name to suit her new persona: Cannon Belle Pearcy.

"But . . ." Poor Reid was still struggling to comprehend. "I can understand winning free of them, and applaud you for it. But why continue the charade? Why become a pirate at all, when you could have simply escaped and left them to chart their own course?"

Belle shook her head. How to make him understand? "You are a man," she pointed out. "You have no idea what it is like to be constrained so. Society deems me fit for one thing and one only, and that is marrying a man I will then serve and obey like the meanest servant." She tossed her head, her stolen braid streaming out behind her. "I am not content to be so limited. When I took this ship, I suddenly saw a new option. As Isabella Parsons, I must obey society's rules, and my father's whims. As Cannon Belle, I answer to no one. I go where I will, do what I will. I am captain of this ship! These men obey me, not the other way round!" She planted her hands on her hips and glared at him across the water. "As Cannon Belle, I am free!"

"Free to rob and plunder," he shot back. "Free to do violence on innocents! How is that something anyone with a clear mind and a soul could embrace?"

A guffaw cut off Bella's next reply, and she shifted to regard Carlyle, who was clutching his belly and all but convulsed with laughter. "Perhaps," she told Reid sharply, "we might table this discussion until we have dealt with the matter at hand?"

He opened his mouth, then snapped it shut. "Fine," he agreed a second later, his own voice taut, face set in displeasure.

"Oho, such a lover's quarrel!" Carlyle said, still laughing. "I'm only sorry I won't get to see how it ends." He wiped at his eyes. "But since I'd hate to be the cause of any more tragedy, I'll make this offer once and once only—jump overboard now and I'll not scoop you up. Your ships I'll take, of course, but you might yet live yourselves." He grinned, all humor gone. "Refuse, and you'll not be so lucky."

Bella raised her voice to reply. "How ironic," she told him. "We were about to offer you much the same thing."

Her old foe smirked down at her. "The *Deadeye*, or whatever you call it now, is a fine ship, as I know only too well," he reminded her. "After all, you've had it only these past six months. It was mine for many years afore that. But that also means I know its guns. They'd barely chip the paint of this beauty." He pounded on the *Hunger*'s rail.

"I believe *I* can mar your finish," Reid answered, focusing at last on the old pirate captain.

Carlyle responded with a dismissive sniff. "Mayhap," he agreed. "But not much beyond, I'll wager. And then what? I'll sail over and through you, and pick the splinters of your pretty little frigate from between my teeth." That was a clear exaggeration, of course—the *Diligent* was no slouch, and ramming her would damage the *Hunger* as well. But the bigger ship could probably still survive such an encounter, and the *Diligent*'s broadside would catch it head on, many of the shots landing harmlessly to either side.

Reid did not waver, however. "Shall we test your theory?" was all he said, and raised a hand. Bella could see the sparks flare from his ship's gunports as sailors there readied torches to light the cannons.

"Prepare to fire!" she shouted as loud as she could. Quince nodded, and the *Deadshot*'s cannons were also readied.

In response, Carlyle glanced over his shoulder at his own men. "Raise the mainsail!" he ordered. "We go through them!"

"This is your last chance," Reid warned. "Surrender now or face the consequences."

"I'll take my chances," Carlyle—Captain Ravenous—replied. He stepped back from the rail as his ship's red-tinted sails began to catch the wind once more.

Reid sighed, then met Bella's gaze and nodded. "Fire!" he shouted, and the *Diligent* opened fire on the *Hunger* from the front.

"Fire!" Bella echoed, and the *Deadshot* struck from the rear.

And then the Dutch barque's gunports slid open all along its port side. The side facing the *Hunger*'s own starboard flank.

"What?" she heard Carlyle cry. "How—?"

That ship, too, fired upon the big pirate vessel, its broadside striking the *Hunger*'s side full on.

"NO!" Carlyle screamed, but anything else he said was lost in the sounds of cannons and explosions—and the horrible splintering of wood as much of the *Hunger*'s hull shattered. The big ship foundered, already taking on water. A few of its own cannons returned fire, but most had been damaged in those blasts, and the ship was dipping and tilting too precipitously to allow decent aim anyway.

The *Hunger* was clearly done for.

"We surrender!" someone called from its deck, and several men stepped to the railing, hands held high. Carlyle was not among them. "Don't shoot!"

"Into longboats and over the side, then," Reid commanded. "We'll pick you up and ship you back for sentencing, but at least you'll have a fair trial." It was a slim chance, but still something. Which, they all knew, was better than going down with their sinking ship.

Bella watched, ready to step in, as the *Hunger*'s surviving crew made it safely off. But one tall, bald figure in red was noticeably absent. "Where is he?" she muttered, watching. Finally, she could wait no longer. Grabbing a rope, she swung across, up onto the dying ship's aft deck. The damaged vessel looked deserted, but she wasn't fooled. "Carlyle!" she shouted. "Come out and let's finish this once and for all!"

As she'd suspected, the old villain couldn't resist such a challenge. "Fine by me," he responded, emerging from his cabin and already drawing his sword. "I'll carve that hair back off your head, girl!"

She freed her sword and blocked his first strike. "This time I have a blade of my own," she reminded him. "Not used to someone who can fight back, are you?" Her thrust almost took him in the chest. Almost.

"Oh, I like it when they put up a fight," he replied, leering at her over their crossed blades. "Seasoning for the meal, dontcha know?"

"You're disgusting." She lunged, and pinked him in the upper arm.

The pinprick, and the sight of blood blossoming on his sleeve, enraged Carlyle. He threw himself at her with a cry, swinging and stabbing with everything he had.

Fortunately, the Commodore had trained her well. Bella kept her cool, parrying or blocking or simply dodging each of her nemesis' attacks. Then she struck back. Nothing too flashy, just a good solid lunge. Carlyle leaped back, but still took a shallow slice across the ribs. Bella remembered how much that stung.

"Give up," she advised, batting away a flimsy riposte. "You can't win."

Her opponent was clearly used to letting his reputation do much of the work for him. That and his crew. Now forced to rely only upon his own skill, he insisted on lunging again, and this time received a stab through the arm for his trouble. Another weak attack earned him a cut across his upper leg. Another had him bleeding from a shoulder stab. His sword tip was drooping now, his blade wavering. Bella knocked it aside and set her own sword tip in the hollow of his throat.

"Surrender," she demanded.

He glared up at her, but fatigue and blood loss brought him to his knees, sword dropping onto the deck, and at last he bowed his head, crimson hat obscuring his features. "Fine," he all but spat out, along with some blood. "I surrender."

"Very good." Bella waved to the *Diligent*, and a moment later Lieutenant Hatcher was leaping across to secure the defeated pirate captain. As soon as he was there Bella sheathed her blade and hurried back to the safety of her own ship.

"Time to depart," she told Quince softly as she reached the *Deadshot*. "Before anyone else decides to visit another ship—like ours."

He nodded and set to work. "Miss Parsons!" Reid called out a moment later, and it was both thrilling and dreadful to hear him use her proper name in such a context. "Please do not run—that will only make things worse. Surrender and I will argue for clemency."

She had to laugh. "So I'd have a nicer cell, maybe even one with a window? I think not."

"You cannot escape," he pointed out, even as the divide between their two ships began to grow. "I now know your true identity, as well as where you live."

"I shall await you there," she replied, tipping her hat.

Then the *Deadshot* had gained enough momentum to carry it away and back to shore.

Bella waited until they were several lengths away, out of the fog and starting to gather up speed, before letting herself slump in relief.

Well, she thought, four ships involved and only one had taken insurmountable damage.

And that one was the *Hunger*, which more than deserved it.

Thank God their own strike on the barque had been on its starboard side! And that Reid had been able to convince the Dutch to help, and to do so by firing upon the pirates. It had been a bold plan, as most of hers were, but it had worked. The *Hunger*—and its bloodthirsty captain—were a threat no more.

Even so, she was not looking forward to what she knew must come next.

Chapter Twenty-nine

THEY WERE NEARLY BACK TO THE cove when a few of her crew finally gathered enough courage to shuffle forward.

"So," old Bill started. "You really a lady?"

Turning from her position by the rail, Belle faced them head on, as she did most perils. "I am," she acknowledged. "But I am also your captain. Nothing has changed."

"'Cept that Navy captain knows who you are, now," Tom pointed out. "He's gonna arrest you. And where's that leave us?" Several of the others behind him nodded, but Bella noted that they looked more concerned than angry. Good. Concern she could work with.

"He means to try," she agreed. "Though we've all seen how his previous attempts have gone." Several of the men laughed. "I assure you, I can run circles around him just as well in dress and shawl as I can in breeches and vest." She smiled at them, then turned serious. "Even if he does capture me, he will not find you. The cove is still safe. I will return home and face him. Should the worst happen, you will still have your freedom, and the *Deadshot*." She looked to Quince, who stood nearby, as always. "Mister Quince will be in charge during my absence."

Her first mate scowled at her. "We could free you," he offered, though his tone indicated he already knew her answer. And, indeed, Bella shook her head.

"No. I'll not risk the rest of you that way. Don't worry, I can handle myself."

Luke O'Dell, also close by, nodded. "Aye, that's the truth." He turned to face the men. "Three cheers for Cannon Belle, the best captain in the world!"

The responding cheers shook the boat, and Belle smiled through her tears. They might not be the noblest, or the kindest, or the most refined, but despite their profession they were all good, solid men, and knowing she had their loyalty meant more than she could put into words.

Sadly, that same loyalty might seal their fates.

It was with a heavy heart that she stepped off the gangplank and onto the cove's rocky ground a short while later. Then, with only a single glance back, and a nod to Quince and Luke and the others, Bella exited the sheltered hideout. Sliding around the side of the cliff, she found the entrance to the hidden stair and slowly began her ascent.

A part of her considered returning home in full garb, letting Reid find her there as Cannon Belle, but the disconnect was too great. The pirate captain had never been seen within Crestmont, and Bella decided not to change that now. So she stowed her gear in the gazebo once more, trading wig and pistol and coat for her housecoat. Then she traversed the lawn she had crossed just a few hours before. Yet so much had changed in such a short time, and would never be the same again.

Reaching the French doors, Bella eased them open and slipped inside. The house was quiet, which was odd, as it was already late afternoon. Surely her father was up by now, and the servants should be in full preparation for dinner. Where was everyone?

"Geoffrey?" She called, crossing the room and pushing open the door onto the main hall. "Ruth? Grace?"

A faint sound reached her ears from the drawing room. Bella shifted in that direction—and froze.

The front door was open.

Not just open but hanging from its hinges, with a large, jagged

hole where the doorplate should have been. Someone had fired a
pistol at it, from close range.

"Papa!" Bella could hear the panic in her voice, and did not
care as she raced for the drawing room. "Papa!"

But, upon yanking open the door, she found only a single figure
there, one far taller than her father and with much larger hands.
"Geoffrey!" Kneeling at his side, Bella at once noted the blood on
the aged butler's face and side. "What happened?"

"Milady . . ." Geoffrey's usually powerful voice was weak, his
face creased with pain. "I am . . . sorry. I tried . . . to stop . . . them."

"Who?" She almost shook the poor man as he seemed to lapse
into unconsciousness, but restrained herself, glancing about and
quickly rising to collect a glass of water instead. "Here," she said,
placing a hand behind his back and easing him into a sitting position. "Drink this." The blood at his side did not seem to be a great
deal, more from the cut on his cheek and his bloody lip than any
direct wound there, she thought. He would live.

"Thank you." He drank, ignoring any impropriety for doing so
in front of her, and his voice had some of its old strength back when
he continued speaking.

"There were two of them," he told Bella. "A man and a woman.
She was in charge, I'd say. They had a military bearing, though
they wore no uniform." He sighed. "They came looking for you,
milady."

Bella all but growled at the mental picture he'd painted. Davis
and Talbot, it had to be. But why come here?

Unless—Davis had sworn vengeance against several when Reid
had arrested her. Including Bella's own alter ego. Had the renegade
commander somehow figured out her secret?

"Is my father . . . did they hurt him?" she asked, focusing on
the present. The rest would no doubt reveal itself in time.

She uncoiled slightly when the butler shook his head. "Your
father is still in his study, I believe. At least, he had ensconced himself there with a book on horticulture after breaking his fast. It is
possible he emerged while I was incapacitated, but if so it was of his

own accord. The intruders never made it that far into the house."
He glanced down at his hands, then over at the divan. "They found
someone else to satisfy their evil intent."

Following his gaze, Bella saw nothing at first. Then her eye
caught on a splash of color. Crossing to the sofa, she picked up
an all too familiar fan, the ivory and silk and wood even more
mangled than when she'd grabbed it at Barrage Hall, though now
it had dark smudges and a smoky odor about it as well. Her heart
sank. "Abigail? What was she doing here?"

"She came to see you, milady," Geoffrey answered. "She seemed
anxious but determined."

The part of her that was not already leaden with despair and
worry soared. Abigail had come to mend the rift between them! It
was the only reason. Of course her best friend would not have been
able to stay angry at her! But Abigail's sweet nature had now put
her in danger—and Bella was to blame.

Her butler was still speaking. "They arrived at the front door
and demanded to speak with you at once. I refused—you were not
home, but even if you had been, I did not care for their look or their
tone." He shook his head. "They responded by drawing pistols. I
slammed the door in their faces, and they shot the lock off it." One
big hand went gingerly to the side of his head. "When I grabbed at
the man's gun, the woman clubbed me. I admit, milady, I did not
expect that from one of your sex." He sighed. "They shoved past me
into the drawing room, and found Miss Montrose there, waiting
for you. The man, he looked pleased. 'Well, if ain't her bosom companion,' he declared. The woman agreed. 'Aye, I met them together
as well. Grab her, and Miss Parsons will be forced to come to us at
a time and place of our choosing.' I attempted to block their path,
and received several punches and blows for my troubles. I am afraid
I may have passed out, milady, but not before I saw them exit,
dragging the protesting Miss Montrose between them. I am sorry.
I have failed you."

Bella grabbed him by the shoulders, but gently. "You did nothing of the sort, Geoffrey," she assured the aged servant. "You did

your best, but it was two against one and they were armed. Yet you kept my father safe, and have related what happened, which is more than most would have managed. Now you need to rest and recover." She rose to her feet, stripping off her housecoat and tossing it onto the nearest chair.

Geoffrey peered up at her, wincing from the motion. If he was surprised at her unusual attire, he did not indicate it. "And what will you do, milady?"

She smiled, though it was not a happy expression, nor, she suspected, a pleasant one. "I? I am going to go get Abigail back."

And, she added, *I am going to make them pay for what they've done to you and to her.*

Chapter Thirty

BEFORE SHE COULD MOVE, HOWEVER, BELLA heard the front door open, its bent hinges protesting the treatment. "Miss Parsons?" a familiar and normally quite welcome voice called out, its tone urgent. "Hello? Isabella?"

The sound of her name from those lips sent a thrill through her, as did the obvious concern embedded within it. Yet Bella knew she had no time for such distractions. She strode to the drawing room door and out into the hall, after a glance at Geoffrey and his nod that he was now well enough to tend to himself.

"I am here, and unharmed," she told Reid, who stood now just within the hallway, pistol in hand. "The same cannot be said for my front door, however."

He had crossed to her in an instant, and raised a hand as if to embrace her or touch her cheek, she knew not what. But he controlled himself, and lowered both that limb and the one holding the weapon, contenting himself for now with asking, "What has happened here?" His eyes flicked to her garb, and his brow furrowed further.

"It was Davis and Talbot," she answered. "They came looking for me, and found Abigail waiting for me. They have taken her in my stead." She grimaced, baring her teeth. "I mean to see her safely returned."

Now Reid appeared dumbfounded, though his scowl had only deepened. "Davis and Talbot! So they did not quit the area, as any sane person might have. And they sought *you* out—why? What were you to them?" His eyes widened, and he gazed at her anew, this time truly seeing her attire and what it signified. "Not you as Miss Parsons," he corrected himself. "But you as Cannon Belle. They knew!" The tone was almost accusing, and she was quick to shake her head.

"They must have deduced it somehow, for certainly I would not have told him, and there are none else who know that truth beyond the few members of my own crew I rescued from Raven Mane's employ." She sighed. "But both of them have seen me on the *Deadeye*, and met me in person, so perhaps my disguise was not so clever as I'd always thought."

"It fooled me," Reid remarked bitterly. "Though perhaps that is more a comment on my own perceptiveness or lack thereof, if they were able to see through it so easily where I, who have spent more time with you in both guises, could not."

Bella dared to reach out and rest a hand on his cheek, and felt a flutter when his eyes slid shut in response. "You did not see it because you were disposed to think only the best of me, for which I thank you. They had no such kindness, and so were undistracted."

He reached up, resting his hand against hers, cupping it to his face for a moment as he gazed upon her. "I still wish only to think that," he admitted softly. "And those desires war against the harsher realities now thrust upon me."

"I know. And I am sorry. I wish . . . well, many things." She gently extracted her hand from his grip. "But right now, my concern is for Abigail."

She could see the shift in his thoughts, from tender to practical, as he blinked and straightened. "Yes. Of course. Miss Montrose must be retrieved safely. What can I do to help?"

Bella smiled, letting him know how much she appreciated both the offer and the willingness to focus upon that first. She glanced past him, toward the courtyard beyond. "I do not suppose you brought any of your men with you?"

"I did not." He gave her a wry smile. "I thought it kinder to come for you alone, where it would not make so notable a scene."

She nodded. "That was thoughtful, thank you. But now there is no time to go retrieve them. It will be just the two of us. Against the two of them." She set her hands to her hips. "But at least they will not be expecting us." And she related what Geoffrey had told her.

Reid considered that, once she was done. "So they will be sending a note at some point," he ascertained. "Setting the time and the place. But you mean to take them unawares before that. Which means you already know where they are."

Bella couldn't stop herself from smiling at him again. How could this man possibly think himself slow-witted? "I do." She raised Abigail's fan, holding it close to his face. "What do you smell?"

Taking the delicate accessory from her, he sniffed it carefully. "A floral perfume of some sort," he replied after a moment. "I believe I remember Miss Montrose wearing one much the same. And . . . smoke?"

"Yes." She accepted the fan back, tucking it into her belt for safekeeping. "Smoke. The Grants' flour mill suffered a fire recently, and is closed for repairs."

He caught on at once. "The perfect place for a pair of fugitives to hide. And right on the water, so offering an easy escape route if cornered. Very well, what is your plan? Because I know now that you always have one, however outlandish." Was that the hint of a smile on his lips? Perhaps so.

"I will have one by the time we get close," Bella agreed. "But first, I need to retrieve my pistols and sword. And the rest of my garb. No sense going as anything less than my full pirate self."

Now Reid did grin at her. "If nothing else, it will make an impression," he agreed.

The flour mill was at the opposite edge of town, perched along an offshoot of the main river, its waterwheel continuously turned by the swift current. The building was a sturdy, squared structure made of weathered old bricks, and Bella and Reid regarded it from the shelter of a nearby tree.

"The front door is there," Bella indicated, pointing to the wide dirt path leading up to the building. "And there is a smaller door along the back, next to the waterwheel. I do not believe there are any others."

"Those windows are easily big enough to enter through," Reid mused beside her. "Yet reaching them unseen might prove difficult, depending upon where the pair is holed up. Davis is cany, she will have them alternating watch. I'd wager from up there." He indicated a single window up just below the eaves. "From that vantage one could watch the road."

Bella nodded. "So we do not take the road. We enter from the water. The gap is narrow enough we can jump it, get hold of the wheel, and let it pull us up to the service door. They will not expect that."

He chuckled. "Not expect that we risk breaking our necks in such a way? No, I'd imagine not!" But he held up both hands in surrender when she started to turn. "No, it is a good plan. Just a bold one. As I'd expected."

She sketched a quick bow to hide her blush. "Then shall we, Commander?"

"Indeed we shall, Captain." He returned the bow. Then followed her back into the trees and around to the mill's far side, as close to the water as the foliage could take them.

The bank was solid here—it was why the mill had been built in this spot, instead of even closer to homes or along the larger river—but overrun with tall, thick grass. There was no room to mow it down with her blade, so Bella simply grimaced and stomped forward. At least her tall boots and trousers protected her legs from scratches! Reid was right behind her, and steadied her when she tripped at one point, hand going protectively to her elbow. Oh, how nice it was, having him this close, and the two of them bent upon the same end! Bella knew it could not last, but she relished it in the moment.

They reached a point, as she'd known they must, where the bank petered out, disappearing beneath the building's sturdy foundation. The waterwheel was directly ahead, the small rear hatch just above its peak, but there was a good yard or two between the structure and where she stood.

"Well, nothing for it," she said finally. She flexed her hands in their gloves, but froze as a hand came to rest on her shoulder.

"Allow me," Reid offered. "I will have the longer reach." She nodded, and held her breath as he eased past her. There was no room, and she suppressed a groan as the buttons of his coat caught on her own, feeling the heat of his body separated from hers by mere layers of cloth. If he had paused there, with their lips nearly brushing, she might have tossed aside all propriety and kissed him—and, by the way his eyes drank hers in, she thought he might well have responded in kind. But he kept moving, and she eased back to give him space, until he was at the bank's edge before her.

"Ready, then?" His voice was gruff, nearly hoarse, and she did not trust herself to do more than nod, knowing he could feel the motion through his broad back. "Right."

And he leapt.

It was a good, strong jump, and well-timed. His hands latched onto one of the waterwheel's flanges, his left boot landing solidly on another—

—but the flanges were slick and treacherous, and his foot slipped, even as his hands scrabbled for purchase!

Bella tensed. Reid was grasping desperately, but his fingers kept sliding from the worn, wet wood. He was going to fall, and if he did not get dragged under and drowned by the wheel itself he'd crack his skull against the rocks below. She could not let that happen!

Taking her own leap of faith, she jumped—and slammed into him, the impact shoving him against the wheel. Thus propelled, his left hand finally latched onto the juncture of two flanges, and his feet wedged themselves into the one lower down. At the same time, he wrapped his right arm around Bella's waist, holding her tight to him as she found her own footing.

For an instant they just hung there, breathing heavily, their faces mere inches apart, their breath warm on each other's faces, their eyelashes almost touching each other's cheeks.

"Thank you," he managed finally, his voice husky. "You saved me."

"And you me," she replied, her own words equally hoarse from emotion. "We are well matched."

He smiled, and it was like the sun bursting from behind the clouds. "Indeed we are." For another second they stood as if frozen, drinking in the sight of each other, in perfect accord. But the wheel was still carrying them upward, its motion unimpeded by their weight, and finally he sighed, pulling back enough to glance up.

"Nearly there. I will hoist you up, then follow." Before she could argue, she felt his arm come loose and then both of his hands settle at her waist. Coiling herself, she nodded and propelled herself upward, arms outstretched—

—and her hands gripped the crossbeams of the door.

Pulling herself up to it, she twisted the knob and shoved the door open, tumbling inside and rolling to her feet, already reaching for pistol and sword. No one was in this room, which held the grinding wheels, and Bella immediately understood why, as the sound was loud and grating. But at least that meant it was clear for her to turn and offer Reid a hand as he stepped up beside her, and shut the door carefully behind him.

"Right," he said once that was done, drawing sword and pistol as he glanced around. "Where, do you think?"

"The office," Bella answered at once, hauling out her own weapons. "It will be the only place with any furniture, and it has a good view of the road as well. The stairs up will be right beside it."

"So one of us should venture up to deal with the lookout?" He suggested, but was already shaking his own head. "No, that grants them the higher ground. Better to draw them out and take them on the stairs, when they are off balance."

She smiled at him. "My thoughts exactly." Her gaze settled on a pile of heavy wooden buckets against the far wall. "And I believe that will do nicely." Striding over to them, she returned her half-cocked pistol to its place at her belt and hefted a bucket instead. It was good and solid. "Yes, perfect." Then she moved carefully to the room's arched inner door. "I will toss this out onto the road. The commotion will distract whoever is in the office, and draw the lookout down as well. We will be waiting for them."

Reid nodded. "Agreed." He was right behind her, again offering a distracting heat at her back, as she slipped out into the mill's main storage room.

This area was where the fire had been, she saw at once. The walls were badly blackened, soot staining even the high ceiling, and whatever tables and trestles had been here were nothing more than charred remains. The windows along the front had also been blown out, leaving only jagged bits of glass, which made Bella's task simpler.

"Wait," Reid told her as she went to the window and prepared to heave the bucket through. "Give me a moment to place myself beneath the stairs." She nodded, watching as he exited through this room's side door, presumably into the hall.

After what she judged to be sufficient time, Bella lifted the bucket and, cocking her arms back, threw it as hard as she could through the broken window. It landed outside with a satisfyingly loud crash, and she distinctly heard two separate yelps from somewhere nearby—one of them much more ladylike. Abigail!

"What was that?" A man's voice called out from above. So Talbot was on lookout, then. Which left Davis to her. Bella was pleased with that.

"I don't know," Davis replied, and yes, she was where Bella had heard the two cries, closer and on her own level. They were in the mill manager's office, as she'd guessed. "Check it out."

"On it." There was a clatter from above, and then quick treads hurrying down the stairs—followed by a sudden scream and then a much louder series of impacts, ending in a heavy thud. Bella moved to the door and eased it open. She was now gazing into the mill's narrow hall, with the stairs off to her left, the front door to her right, and the office door directly across from her. She readied her pistol.

"Talbot?" The sounds of someone approaching, and then the office door was yanked open, a woman silhouetted against the light beyond.

Bella raised her gun and fired.

"Damn it!" Davis ducked back, splinters showering her where Bella's bullet had struck the frame inches from her head. "You bitch!" But rather than fire back, the former commander ducked back into the room. Where Abigail presumably lay captive. Davis meant to use her for cover, leverage, or both.

Bella charged after her. "Oh, no, you don't!" She dropped the spent pistol as she crossed the hall, drawing and cocking her second but leading into the room with her raised sword.

That saved her life.

A flicker of motion caught her eye and she blocked instinctively, her blade catching Davis's as it came down hard. The blow would have cleaved her in two, had it landed. As it was, Bella could not entirely stop the force of the larger woman's blow but was able to angle it aside.

Then she slammed her shoulder into Davis's chest, knocking her assailant back into the wall behind her, though the impact cost her the pistol, as the weapon was jarred from her hand and went spinning away.

"Captain Belle. Or should I say Miss Parsons?" Davis taunted, lurching forward and swinging wildly to give herself space to recover. She grinned at Bella from her greater height. "Think you're so clever, do you? Parading around in plain sight?"

"Better than claiming to be a Navy officer while behaving worse than any pirate," Bella countered. Davis's face twisted into an ugly snarl and she launched herself with a series of nasty swear words. Her attack was fast and furious, but it lacked finesse, just like the woman herself. Bella blocked what she could, ducked the rest, and feinted a kick, then used the distraction to slice the other woman's upper arm.

"You cost me my career!" Davis screamed at her, swinging again.

"No, you did that all on your own," Bella countered, biding her time and then striking swiftly. She scored another cut. "Your own bloodlust did you in."

The woman was certainly showing that same propensity for violence now. She was all fury and power, with no skill and no aim. Bella, meanwhile, tucked her own anger away, leaving her icy cold, utterly calm and collected. She struck Davis several times in rapid succession, drawing blood each time.

"Surrender," she suggested coolly. "At least you will have your life."

"I don't have a life anymore!" Davis shouted back, face red and sweaty from her exertions, arms and legs and side streaked with blood. "You took that from me! Now I'll take yours—one precious piece at a time!"

She turned away—and for the first time, Bella registered Abigail sitting tied to a chair behind the desk, white-faced with fear. And Davis was now advancing on the helpless young woman.

"No!' Bella leaped, and lunged as she did. Her sword slid clean through Davis' exposed back, the tip emerging between her breasts. The former officer gurgled, a horrible, rattling sound, and slumped, her body sliding from the bloody blade to hit the floor. She twitched once, then lay still.

Bella allowed only enough time to be sure the woman was not feigning. Then she'd dropped her sword and was rushing to free her friend. "Are you hurt?" she asked, kneeling to saw at the ropes with her knife.

"No," Abigail replied softly. "Beyond being unable to feel my legs, or my backside." She rubbed at her wrists once the ropes were gone, then suddenly grabbed Bella in a fierce hug. "Oh, I am so happy to see you!"

"And I you," Bella promised, returning the embrace. "I am so sorry, Abbie."

"Sorry they took me to get to you, or sorry you did not tell me you were an infamous pirate captain?" her friend asked, but there was laughter in her voice. "I understand," she said once they pulled back enough to breathe and to eye each other. "But you will tell me all about it now, yes?"

"Yes," Bella promised. "All of it. No more secrets."

That earned her a smile from her friend, and she found her eyes tearing at the sight. "Good. Now, perhaps we can leave this dreary place? We simply must get Mr. Grant some curtains to brighten it up. And perhaps some flowers?"

Bella laughed, helping Abigail to her feet. They were met at the door by Reid, who took one look at the dead Davis and then bowed to them both. "Miss Montrose, I am very pleased to see you unharmed," he stated. "And allow me to apologize. If the Navy had kept hold of these two, you never would have been placed in such danger."

"Thank you, Commander," Abigail told him, much of her usual composure already restored. "I do not hold you or the Navy to blame, but I do appreciate the timely rescue." Her eyes went from him to Bella and back again. "Perhaps we might retreat somewhere we can all discuss what has occurred?"

Bella nodded, but first arched a brow at Reid. "Talbot?" she asked. When he shook his head, she nodded. She'd hoped they might take one or both of the renegades captive, in order to return them for their intended punishment, but such was not to be. At least they would never trouble her or those close to her—or anyone else—ever again. "Then might I suggest we return to Crestmont? As Abigail said, there are still matters to discuss, and situations to unpack."

She held her breath for a second. Would Reid acquiesce? Or would he insist upon taking her into custody this very moment?

But, after an instant, he nodded. "Yes, I believe that might be best for the moment. After you." And he bowed them both out of the room and the mill. A cart sat waiting just outside, and moments later they were all three seated on its bench, with Reid handling the reins. Bella could only imagine the sight they must make: a Navy commander, a pirate captain, and a young lady, all disheveled and all squeezed in close together. They would be the talk of the town, she was sure.

Chapter Thirty-one

WHEN THEY REACHED CRESTMONT—HAVING SEEN SURPRISINGLY few people out and about, for which Bella was grateful—Abigail declared that she must have a bath before they could do anything else. "I have been tied to a chair in a burnt-out old mill," she pointed out when Reid frowned, opening his mouth as if to argue. "Perhaps you are accustomed to such depravities, but I assure you I am not. I will think all the clearer for having soaked off this soot and ash. I trust you have something I may borrow?" That last was directed at Bella, who knew better than to protest. Sweet as she was, when Abigail set her mind to something there was no stopping her.

"Of course," she answered instead. "I will return in a moment," she promised Reid, then took her friend in hand to guide her upstairs to her own rooms, where she directed Sophie to draw a bath. The lady's maid gawked a moment at Bella's attire, but quickly recovered herself and got to work with the water.

"Go back down," Abigail urged quietly when the two of them were alone. "Now is your chance to speak with him in private. Get all of this settled while he is inclined to be merciful."

Bella laughed and hugged her, soot and all. "You little schemer!" But she was smiling as she said it, as was Abigail. "No wonder you were so insistent!"

"Well, I do want to rid myself of this smell," her friend insisted. "Now go. I will dawdle as long as I dare."

With another quick hug, Bella let herself from the room and retreated downstairs. Now that Abigail was back safely and the two of them were reconciled, she felt stones lighter. And the sight that greeted her as she entered the drawing room only added to her warm feelings, for she found Reid there, along with her father, the two of them chatting amiably together.

"Ah, there you are, my dear," Lord Roderick said, approaching and giving her a kiss on the cheek. He didn't seem to register her unusual clothing at all. "The Commander here was just telling me that two renegades were responsible for the damage to our front door, did you see? But that they will not trouble us again."

"No, they will not," she agreed, patting him on the shoulder. He smiled, but she noted how his eyes were already looking past her, seeing some distant past or chasing some random dream. "Would you like your tea in the solar, Father?" she asked, signaling Geoffrey, who was waiting by the door. The old butler, now looking none the worse for wear beyond a plaster at his temple and another on his cheek, came forward to take his master in hand and guide him from the room.

"Your care for him is admirable," Reid noted once they were alone, offering her a cup of tea, which she accepted gratefully. "And your love for him obvious." His expression was somber.

"Thank you." She settled onto the couch and took a sip. "My mother's death was a massive blow to him. He's never fully recovered, though on good days he is merely weak and limited in mobility. On bad days, he is so disconnected he does not even recognize me, only the Commodore and Geoffrey, who both knew him for many years before he was even wed." She sighed. "It is not always easy, and those times are the worst—it is terrible to look at someone you love and have them look back with no knowledge of you— but it is not his fault, and when he is lucid I know he loves me." She shrugged. "What more can one do but care for those they love as best they can?"

The commander took the chair nearest her, nodding as he did. "That is all one can do," he agreed. He sipped his tea, cleared his throat, and sipped again before setting the cup down. "My own father passed away several years ago," he stated, staring at his hands. "My mother, like your father, did not handle it well. It did not help that he died of fever, and she suffered the same. But while she survived it, her lungs were badly damaged, and her constitution in general. Before that, she was strong as an ox." A smile flitted across his face. "She used to carry my brother and I about like we were nothing, one tucked under each arm. Now"—he sighed, and she knew the grief in that sound all too well— "it is all she can do to drag herself from her bed most days. I visit when I can, and she has a live-in nurse, but still." He met her eyes. "As you said, what more can one do?"

"I am so sorry," Bella told him. "Truly. I know you are a dutiful and loving son, and I am sure she knows it as well."

"Thank you." He frowned. "You have taken on most of the job of running your household, then?" She knew, by his expression, that he was remembering what he'd recently overheard between her and Carlyle.

She saw no reason to lie, not any more. "I have. I do not mind, though at times it has been difficult. Before I set aside any worries of propriety and took the reins, however, my father, in some of his weaker moments, let himself be taken advantage of by unscrupulous business partners. Much of our estate was tied up in Turkey, and being badly mismanaged there. Writing did nothing, and so I was forced to travel there myself, as I have no brothers and could trust no one else to handle the situation for me." She'd have gladly let the Commodore go in her stead, and the retired officer had certainly offered, but with his advanced age and bad leg she'd feared he might not survive the trip, and she would not put the dear old man in danger like that, not when she herself was perfectly healthy.

"And that was when Carlyle—then Raven Mane—took you." There was no accusation in his tone, but still she felt her mouth firm and her chin rise.

"He captured our ship, and took myself and my maid hostage," she confirmed. "Therese fought back, and was cruelly slain for her efforts. I bided my time instead. Fortunately, I was worth more to him intact, and so he did not attempt any liberties. If he had, I would have fought, and most likely been killed as well."

Reid dipped his head in acknowledgement. "Instead you convinced his crew to turn on him, and took over his ship." Was that admiration in his tone?

"I did indeed. And then, knowing the state my father had left us in, even with the investments now being run properly, I turned pirate myself." She refused to turn away from his gaze. "I kept my crew under control, weeding out those who would not abide my rules, and did not allow any unnecessary violence, nor any indiscretions. If a ship surrendered, we merely took their cargo and left them unharmed and their vessel intact."

He nodded at that. "Yes, I'd heard such, and seen it so myself since. But you did still steal from them."

"I did. I had not intended to continue, however. I thought only to return home, some money in hand, and put all that behind me. Instead I found us in direr straits then expected, such that I was forced to return to piracy along our own shores. Though, if I am being wholly honest, I did not regret taking up the role once more. There is a freedom in it, and a sense of controlling my own destiny, that was otherwise lacking." She lifted her cup again, peering at him over its lip. "And now you know all my secrets. But I do not know yours, do I?"

Reid laughed. "You do not give up, do you?" he asked, but some of the light had returned to his eyes since the grim start of their conversation. He turned serious again, however, as he continued, "Very well. I had an older brother. Liam. Ten years my senior. He was . . ." He frowned and corrected himself. "A hothead. Impulsive, erratic, quick to anger, quick to act, with no thought to the consequences."

Bella did not point out the obvious similarities to herself. "You said 'had,'" she noted instead. "I'm sorry."

He nodded. "Thank you. Yes, he died a few years ago. His own fault, though not by his own hand. He was always getting caught up in this scheme or that one, Liam was. He threw himself into whatever caught his interest—and it almost always blew up in his face." Reid reached for his cup but did not drink, merely staring into the tea there as if it were a scrying pool revealing his past. "I had to save him from himself, many times. And then, finally, I could not. Matters unraveled too fast, tempers flared, and by the time I arrived on the scene Liam was dead. A barroom brawl, they said, but really it was a falling out between him and the men he'd invested in. There was nothing to be done for it, however."

Bella leaned forward and rested her hand on his. "That must have been awful for you. And you must have been so young, too." If they were a decade apart, and it had happened several years ago . . . she had a sudden image of a teenage Reid, all gawky limbs and long face, trying to pull his older brother away from folly.

"I was." He set the cup down again, untasted. "I joined the Navy soon after. I was determined to do something good with my life, but also . . ." He met her eyes. "I desperately needed that kind of structure, those rules. A knowledge of what was and was not allowed. A clear pattern of behavior."

Yes, she could see it now. "That is why you are so . . . circumspect," she said, as everything became clear to her. "You react to situations but do not instigate them because you need to know what is happening, and understand your place in it all. You cannot bear to leap in, for fear of disaster." He had seen the results of such behavior from an early age, and had fought against it, both outwardly and in himself. And that had conditioned him against being bold—brave, yes, but never bold.

Talbot's taunts that one day came to mind. "You and Davis were classmates at the academy," she noted. "She was bold, even aggressive, while you were supportive, strategic. Yours was the sounder course, but she took the credit when things went well because you were able to redirect her energies, just as you had done with your brother."

Reid nodded. "Yes. Winnie was fierce and fearless, but careless. I was cautious to the point of indecision. But once she'd committed us to an action, I had no choice, and thus I could set aside my fears and deal with the matters at hand. We were the perfect team. But, as you said, she received the bulk of the credit. I was dismissed as too timid for proper command."

"And yet, you have captured the dreaded pirate captain Ravenous, and his fearsome ship the *Hunger*," Bella pointed out. "That must stand to your credit."

His smile was both warm and faintly bitter. "I had a good deal of help, and it was not my plan."

But she refused to dim her own smile as she told him, "I will happily cede you all credit for it. You deserve it. There is a time and a place for boldness, but often it is the cooler head that prevails."

They were still sitting there, smiling at each other over their cooling tea, when Abigail finally entered. "Well," she stated, wrapping one of Bella's dressing gowns more securely around her shorter, rounder frame and taking a seat beside Bella on the couch. "I see that I have missed many things. Perhaps you will catch me up— once we have more hot water? And some sandwiches?"

Bella laughed and hugged her friend. It was so good to have her back again, and the rift between them mended! "Yes," she promised. "I will tell you everything."

But her smile was still directed at Commander Reid as she said that. And he was still smiling at her in return.

Chapter Thirty-two

ABIGAIL SAT BACK, ABSENTLY OPENING THE battered fan Bella had happily returned to her and waving it before her face. "Goodness!" was all she said for the moment. And, again, "Goodness!"

Bella tried not to laugh, and she noticed Commander Reid struggling to keep a smile off his face. "Indeed."

"That's . . . I mean . . ." Though not as quick with the verbal riposte as Bella herself, it was rare to see her friend at such a loss for words. "But really, Isabella, what a tremendous lot has been going on with you under the surface!" she finally burst out, gasping for breath afterward.

"Yes. I am sorry. I wanted to tell you, of course," Bella rushed to assure her. "But I couldn't. It would have put you in dreadful danger—as it evidently did anyway." Besides which, there had seemed little point in recounting it all when she'd thought to give it up, and afterward it just became harder and harder to share the longer she continued.

Abigail nodded. "No, I quite understand that now, thank you. Though I suspect you also worried I'd tattle it to Nellie, or to Stephen, or even to Mary Winstead or the Tremont twins." Her laugh was slightly rueful. "I suspect I am not known for my great discretion." Bella did not argue, earning her a gentle slap on her wrist from that same fan, though Abigail did not appear truly angry. Nor did she stop speaking, now she'd begun: "I am impressed, though. Truly. How awful that must have been, being taken captive! And poor Therese!"

"It was awful," Bella readily admitted. "The absolute worst days of my life, save perhaps when Mother died. But then I was a child and barely understood. This time I fully comprehended the fate in store for me."

"And you did not let it paralyze you," Reid pointed out quietly. "Many a man and woman would have. So frozen by fear they could not act at all, not even to save themselves. Not even if presented with far greater chances than you had." He dipped his head. "You did not give in. You persevered—and you triumphed. Few could have done the same, in your place."

She inclined her own head, acknowledging the compliment.

"But to have that same fiend turn up here," Abigail cut in, shattering the moment. "I can hardly believe it!"

"At least he will trouble me no more," Bella replied, before glancing across at the officer there. "He will not, correct? He has been fully detained?"

"Argus Carlyle and his crew are in custody, and will be taken back to London for trial and sentencing," Reid assured her. "He will never set foot outside and unshackled again, much less captain a boat." His tone was calm and serious, but his brow was furrowed.

Abigail noticed at once. "You don't look pleased about that, Commander," she commented. "I'd have thought it'd be both an enormous relief and a great point of pride, to have such a notorious villain in your custody."

Bella would have expected the same, and was equally puzzled until Reid replied, "Yes, you are quite right, Miss Montrose. And I am pleased. No, there's something else about the whole affair that's bothering me. Something doesn't sit right."

"I feel the same," Bella agreed. "I have been unable to put my finger upon it. It's something about Carlyle, though, I'm sure of it."

He nodded, and all three of them sat silent for a moment, her and Reid pensive and Abigail staring back and forth between them.

At last Bella's best friend could stand it no more. "What is there to think about?" she asked them both. "He was a pirate. You took his ship. He came after you. You destroyed his second ship and captured him. The end!"

The recitation brought Bella to her feet, as her scattered thoughts finally clicked into place. "That's it," she stated, stepping away from the seats to pace near the window. "His ship." Turning, she faced her friend and the man she desired. "When he was still known as Raven Mane, Carlyle captained the *Deadeye*, which I took from him and renamed the *Deadshot*. And it's a fine ship, the finest around."

"She is excellent, spoken as someone who's gone up against her," Reid agreed. "Light and fast and expertly crewed."

That earned him a curtsy—a little odd in trousers rather than skirts, but still she managed. "Yes," Bella said. "She is. But in an open fight she's no match for the *Diligent*, or any frigate. She was never meant to be." She paced a few steps more. "Still, I took her from him. I put Carlyle to sea in a rowboat, with nothing but his breeches and his boots." She grinned at the memory before moving on to her point. "How, then, did he find himself another ship? And not just any seaworthy vessel, but a Ship of the Line like the *Hunger*? He had no money, no crew, and if anyone had seen him wash ashore, no reputation. Yet he shows up here in the German Ocean with a monster like that?"

"Could he have stolen it?" Abigail asked, tapping her fan in her other hand. "Crept onboard, untied her ropes, sailed her away? Then found a new crew after?"

Both Bella and Reid shook their heads. "Even a schooner like the *Deadshot* takes a good half dozen men to operate it, minimum," Reid answered. "My own, you'd need a dozen at least. That ship? A score or more."

"So he didn't steal it, and he couldn't have bought it," Bella mused. "What was it he said? 'Thanks to a generous friend'? Someone got that boat for him. An investor—or a partner. Which means they might be the reason Carlyle came to England. The *Hunger* was making a name for itself in the Adriatic, so why leave all that behind?"

"You did," Abigail pointed out. "Or nearly so."

Bella smiled at her. "Yes, but I had reasons to come home—my father, this estate, and you. Does Carlyle have the same? Or did he come here because he was told to?"

"If you're right . . ." Reid shook his head, not so much in nega-tion it seemed as in doubt, or merely wonder. "Your own raids were civilized, even polite. The *Hunger* was a savage beast. Why would this mystery partner want that here off the English coast? Especially when it's so much more dangerous for them this close to home?"

Abigail reached for a tart. "Is it, though?" she asked, and Bella was impressed again. This more thoughtful side of her friend rarely emerged. When it did, Bella tended to listen. "Most pirates are in the Mediterranean, yes? Which means most of the Navy not cur-rently engaged in battle goes there as well. More fish means a better chance of netting one, after all." She raised the small pastry aloft, as if in toast. "That means coming here is actually the safer chance. Less interference, and probably less competition."

"She's right," Bella agreed. "Back in the Aegean, I had to watch for Navy ships constantly. Here, there's only yours to worry about. So this partner decides matters are too unstable there, and has Car-lyle bring the *Hunger* here."

"Here indeed," Reid said. "He could have picked any spot along the coast. So why here in particular? Especially with the *Diligent* already in residence. Is there some great treasure they were search-ing for?"

Bella laughed. "All of it. Our captures here have been far richer than those back in the Mediterranean. Fewer ships, perhaps, but more heavily laden, and with more valuable cargo."

"Cargo. Yes." Reid had his hands on his thighs, but his fingers had begun to tap. "Very few ships have slipped past you of late, and even fewer have managed to survive both of you together, or at least sail through unscathed each and every time. But there is one that's made several trips and never once been attacked—it's a frigate, though a civilian vessel rather than military." He frowned. "I believe it's named the *Safe Return*? Certainly it's lived up to its name!"

Now it was Bella's turn to frown. "That is Mister Fletcher's ship," she reminded Reid. "We did see them unloading, that day at the docks. And later he told us how, every time the ship went out, his heart went with it." She looked to Abigail. "There was something else about him," she admitted. "When I was in London, I chanced to meet his fiancé—only, she is not. She barely knows him. They met because of her father, Sir Desmond Grove."

Reid rose to his feet. "Sir Desmond Grove?" he repeated, staring at her. "He has a great deal of influence over maritime business. When we first arrived I put the docks under strict orders, no unnecessary deliveries or departures. I wanted to be free to chase you down without having to worry about other people, innocents, getting hurt on my account. But one ship was allowed to dock anyway. I had orders from my superiors about it."

"And that was Fletcher's ship," Abigail guessed. "He used Sir Desmond to gain access." She glanced at Bella. "He wanted to rid himself of any competition, so he used the *Hunger* to capture or destroy any ships you didn't clean out yourself. With his pet pirate gone, though, he'll have to worry about other ships coming in again, competing for sales—and about you going after him just like anybody else." She grimaced. "He may attempt to rid the seas of you first."

Bella laughed. "Others have tried, and some of them far better men." She directed a warm smile toward her commander. "Still, I'd rather not give him too many more chances, lest he have a lucky strike."

Reid nodded. "If Fletcher is involved, we will need to capture him for questioning," he agreed. "We need to know the details of his arrangement with Carlyle, and if there are any other schemes at work."

"And how do you intend to find that out?" Bella asked.

He grinned at her in response, shedding all his worry and doubt for a moment and appearing years younger for it. "I have a plan. But I'll need your help."

Now it was her turn to smile. "Then you shall have it. Always."

Chapter Thirty-three

WHEN REID RETURNED A FEW HOURS later, carrying a dark bundle under one arm, he found the manor's front door already rehung, the lock replaced, Abigail gone home to recover properly from her recent ordeal, and Bella in the drawing room poring over a map. "What's this?" he asked as he entered, setting his parcel down on a chair before joining her at the table. "Planning your escape?" His tone was light, however, and so she merely snorted in reply.

"Look here," she said, tapping a spot. "This is the mouth of the river. And here's Riverside, where your boat is docked." She traced her finger back down and to the right, following the land as it jutted out into the water, then up and along the coastline. "This is Hillington, and here is Crestmont." Her fingernail pressed down alongside a small notch, barely visible. "This is the cove where I have my ship." Even so recently as a day or two ago, she'd never have considered revealing that secret to him. Now, it felt right and natural to do so.

The commander was studying the map. "The detail on this is incredible," he said, running a finger over the fine lines here and there. "I've never seen anything so precise for this region."

"No, nor would you," she agreed. "It is my family's personal map, drawn many years ago by a cousin with a passion for cartography. But listen, the cove is cleverly hidden, you'd never find it from the water without knowing how. It's only big enough for a small ship like the *Deadshot*, though. The *Diligent* might be able to row in but certainly nothing larger, like the *Hunger*."

He took her meaning at once. She loved that about him, that their thoughts were so compatible. "Carlyle needed something like your spot, hidden away—he couldn't exactly moor his beast of a pirate ship out in the open. But you're telling me there aren't many spots like that in the area."

"Correct. In fact, far as I know there is only one, and as a child I explored the entire coastline from Scarborough to Mablethorpe." She slid her finger along the coast, north toward where a spur extended eastward. A short ways below that, however, she stopped. "Here, by Bridlington. There's a cove like ours, if not as well concealed, but much bigger. Big enough for a Ship of the Line, I'd say, and with room to spare."

"And you think, if his ship was holed up there, he must have come ashore from time to time, for food and drink and maybe company." Reid eyed the spot she'd marked. "In Bridlington." He frowned, straightening from his contemplation of the image. "But how can we know for sure? Or narrow it down to one establishment, if we do?"

She smiled and stepped back a pace as well. "Leave that part to me." Turning away, she paused to pat his cheek. "I won't be gone long."

Reid raised his own hand and cupped hers to his face. "I am trusting you to return," he said gently.

"Because you know I will." Her heart was pounding in her ears and her head felt light but not as much as her spirits as Bella left him there, cutting back across the lawn toward the gazebo as quickly as she dared.

It was growing dark, and the stairs were difficult to navigate with only her small lantern, but Bella managed it. Once at the bottom she hurried around and into the cove.

The *Deadshot* was there, as she'd hoped, and the men were all gathered around a fire on the small, rocky beach. "What news, Cap'n?" Gareth asked upon spotting her. "We done for?"

"I don't think we are, lads," she answered, stopping when she'd reached the little group. "Or, if we are, we may yet have some words spoken in our favor. But to do that, I need something from you all." Many of them stood straighter, and she smiled. "For now, just information. I know I had you all scatter whenever you left here, traveling only in small groups. Did any of you make it as far north as Bridlington?"

Bill and Gregor raised their hands. "We been there, Captain," Bill answered, and her pilot nodded.

"Good, good." Stepping up close to the two men, she directed her next question only at them. "When you were there, did you ever see a man, tall, bald, black beard, dark red cloak and hat?"

Her gunner frowned. "Aye, though can't rightly say how often," he offered after a moment. "Maybe half dozen times, in all?" He looked at Gregor, who nodded.

"I saw him too. That were Carlyle, aye? Didn't recognize him then, but he had a powerful presence."

Bella shuddered. "He did at that. Do you remember where you saw him, exactly?"

"The Dulcet Dove," Gregor answered slowly, then with more certainty. "Seen him drinking there a time or two."

"Alone?"

The pilot shook his head. "Naw, he always had company, whores and the like." He glanced about. "Except some of the time, it was men, and they were meeting at a table against the back wall, all business."

"Excellent." Bella smiled at them both. "That is a tremendous help." Without explaining further, she retraced her steps, taking great care to navigate the steps back up to Crestmont's lawn.

"They met at an inn called the Dulcet Dove," she declared as she returned to the drawing room. Reid was standing by the French doors, and she suspected he had been pacing the entire time she was gone.

Now, however, he smiled. "Nicely done! Then let me ready myself, and I'll be off." Going to the chair, he took up the bundle he'd placed there before. Unfolding that revealed a long, dark red coat and a matching tricorn. "Took these off Carlyle myself," he explained as he donned both pieces of apparel.

Bella studied him with a frown. "You've sufficient height, and though your shoulders are broader that won't be so evident in a dark tavern," she noted. "But you are sorely lacking in one area." She smiled. "Fortunately, I have the answer to that. Geoffrey, fetch Sophie for me, please. And have her bring her sewing kit."

The tall butler, who'd been stationed by the door to the hall this entire time and had shown startlingly little reaction to the news that his mistress was a wanted pirate, nodded and slipped out long enough to call up the stairs. A moment later, her lady's maid entered.

"You called for me, milady?" Sophie asked, curtsying. Then, rising, she glanced up for the first time and gasped. "Milady?" Evidently, although she had seen her mistress in these clothes before, it had not fully registered then as it did now.

"It's all right, Sophie," Bella hastened to reassure her. "It's merely a costume. You see?" And she pulled off the wig, fluffing out her short blond hair with one hand while the other offered the dark hairpiece. "I need you to remove a bit off the end and fashion it into a beard for the commander." She indicated Reid's chin. "Just here, and perhaps this far out."

Though the girl was no doubt confused by all this, she recovered quickly enough. "Oui, milady." Settling onto the couch, she used a small, sharp pair of scissors to snip a few inches off the braid's end. Then she spread that piece a bit, widening it to the size Bella had indicated. Next she took a small container of gum Arabic. "May I, sir?" she asked, waving Reid over. He nodded, approaching and lowering himself onto the nearby chair facing her, then stayed very still as she applied the adhesive to his chin before scrunching the bits of hair there. "Like so?"

Observing from behind the couch, Bella considered. "A little narrower and a little bushier," she decided at last, and the girl adjusted the makeshift beard. "Yes, that will do nicely. Thank you, Sophie."

Reid rose and, after nodding his thanks as well, moved over to the mantle, studying himself in the mirror there. "Not bad," he conceded, lowering his head so his features were in shadow. "Yes, not bad at all." He bowed to her. "I'd best be off, then. I'll send a boy to Fletcher, tell him to meet me at the usual spot at midnight. If I hurry, I can get there before him."

But Bella held up a hand to stop him. "Wait here a moment more," she instructed. She left the room herself, returning quickly with her father's old hunting cloak wrapped around her, the hood raised. "Right, let's go."

Her commander stared at her a moment, then laughed. "I won't be able to talk you out of this, will I?"

"Not in the least," she agreed, grinning.

He nodded, and bowed to her before offering his arm as if they were once more at a ball. "In that case, might I have this dance?"

"You may," she answered, resting her hand on his arm. They were both smiling as they exited the room, and the house, toward the cart still waiting beyond.

It was two hours to Bridlington, and would have taken far longer if Bella hadn't thought to send Walter to find a boy in Riverside to deliver that message. Fletcher had never been to Crestmont, and even if he had, their gardener kept mostly to himself, so she didn't worry about him being recognized and linked back to her. "We'd never make it all the way down there and back in time," she pointed out to Reid as he clucked the horses into motion and the cart rumbled forward, away from her home.

"No, you're right," he acknowledged. "Thank you."

They rode in companionable silence, and Bella took advantage of the night's chill to shift closer, until their arms were brushing together. "Do you think he'll show?" she asked as they finally

neared the town. It was quite late now, and only a few lights shone
here and there, but they could already see the inn at the far end
near the water, and it was still well lit within.

He nodded, though he didn't turn from navigating the cart
along the narrow street. "If we're right, and he really is working
with Carlyle, he'll come. He can't have heard about what happened to the *Hunger* yet, and I made sure the note looked urgent."
Rather than trust two people in sequence to remember the message correctly, he'd written it out on a scrap of old paper, using a
rough hand and quick, almost angry strokes of the pen. Bella had
been surprised at the clever forgery, but had to admit that it should
indeed do the trick.

Assuming they were right about Fletcher.

Halting the cart and hopping down to give the reins over to
a boy waiting outside, they entered the inn, both careful to keep
their faces hidden. It was not a large place, the taproom being a
single low-ceilinged room, and dimly lit from the fire and a few
lamps set out on tables. Reid pushed past those locals still out
and drinking at this late hour, making for the back, and Bella
followed. She veered off eventually to claim a table to one side,
while he continued on, finally planting himself at the backmost
chair of the farthest table, his back to the wall. Bella had readied
both their pistols along the way, working by feel in the near dark,
and she suspected he had his drawn under the table now. She'd
done the same, laying the half-cocked weapon in her lap where
she could raise it easily.

A serving maid approached, and Bella ordered a small beer,
so as to blend in. The drink arrived in a leather jack, and she paid
for it, sipping at the mild, fruity brew as she scanned the crowd.
Would Fletcher take the bait?

Reid had ordered as well, she saw, and they both sat there,
nursing their drinks, not looking at each other, for a good hour
or more. Then Bella heard the front door open. A moment later, a
man slipped through, heading straight for the back and the dark-
coated, black-bearded man seated there. He wore a heavy cloak

himself, the hood up to mask his face in shadow, but even in the dim light Bella could see his eyes were as blue as ever.

"Carlyle? What is the meaning of this?" Fletcher demanded even as he claimed the seat next to Reid's. "You sent that note? You know better than that!" He was keeping his voice down, but the merchant's words still reached Bella's ears.

"I had no choice," the man next to him replied, and Bella started, for Reid had put on a creditable impersonation of her old foe, his voice gone all rough and crude. "Navy's been hot on my tail. Need to lay low for a bit."

"What? No!" Fletcher grasped his companion's arm, leaning in closer to hiss at him. "That isn't the arrangement! I've got a shipment going out tomorrow! I need you to keep that damnable woman pirate away from it, and then to take out any competitors trying for London with their own wares!"

Reid yanked his arm away. "You don't tell me what to do!" He really did sound like Carlyle!

"Oh, no?" Fletcher was all but snarling now, the cruel expression strange on his usually amiable face. "Don't forget who got you that fancy ship of yours, my friend. You owe a great debt. And who has been supplying you with details on ships crossing the ocean? Without that, you'd be sailing about with no hope of finding anyone!" So that was how Carlyle had located his victims! Fletcher must have contacts in Denmark and other places sending him details on his rivals' ships.

She'd heard enough, but Reid was speaking again. "I'm the one taking all the risks here!" he snapped, starting to stand as if meaning to leave.

Fletcher quickly rose with him, grabbing his arm again. "You don't think the Navy would hang me right alongside you? We're all in this together, Carlyle. Right to the very end."

He started as the other man's free hand landed on his wrist, clamping down hard. "I completely agree," Reid told him in his own voice, tossing back his head to reveal his true features. "Thank you for stating it so clearly."

Fletcher stared, then tried to yank his hand away, but the commander had him in a tight grip. "No!"

As he struggled, motion elsewhere caught Bella's eye. Two men who'd been near the fireplace were shouldering their way toward the back. Both were big and burly, and hefted sturdy lengths of wood. So Fletcher had been cautious enough to bring some friends!

Fortunately, so had Reid—whether he'd wanted to or not. Slipping out of her own seat, Bella slid around behind the two men, drawing her second pistol as she did. "I'd stop there, if I were you," she warned, raising both guns and pressing a barrel against each man's scalp. "Otherwise, you're liable to regret it."

Feeling the cold metal there, the one on the left froze in place.

The man on the right, however, chuckled. "A woman? Put it done afore you hurt yourself, lass." He started to turn, raising the large fist not clutching the makeshift club.

And grunted, collapsing to the floor, when Bella whipped her pistol around and bashed him in the head with its heavy wooden handle.

"Don't," she warned his companion, who'd shifted as the gun had left his head. It was back in place now, however, and he obligingly ceased moving.

"Good. Drop the stick."

He did so.

"Excellent." She considered, but only for a second. Then, using the same reversed weapon, she knocked him out as well. He fell near his friend, and she grinned at Reid and the terrified-looking Fletcher over their bodies. "Shall we?"

"Indeed." Her commander had his own gun in plain view in his other hand, and prodded Fletcher forward with it, forcing the merchant to lead the way. "Crown business, tie them up and hold them someplace," Reid instructed the innkeeper as they passed the bar, drawing out a shilling and tossing it to the man. "I'll have someone collect them tomorrow." The man nodded, pocketing the coin. Everyone else made room as the three of them exited the inn.

Once outside, Reid tied Fletcher's hands behind his back before forcing him up and into the cart. That done, he and Bella reclaimed the vehicle's bench and set the horses into motion once more.

"I'll drop you off and take him down to Riverside," Reid told her as they rode out of town. "He can join Carlyle, all right, in the next cell over, until I can bring the whole lot of them down to London."

Behind them, Fletcher moaned at that. "This can't be happening," he muttered. "Everything was in place! We were nearly there!"

"It *is* happening," Bella told him over her shoulder. "And your plan is done."

He laughed bitterly at that, but said nothing more as they began the long journey back.

Chapter Thirty-four

BELLA WAS EXHAUSTED BY THE TIME Reid pulled the cart up to Crestmont. She had barely enough energy to stagger inside and up to her room, where Sophie helped her trade her pirate garb for a nightgown. She was asleep within seconds of resting her head on the pillow.

The next morning dawned bright and clear, the breeze from the open window crisp, and Bella took a moment, upon waking, to simply lay there, luxuriating in the feel of a warm bed and thick blankets on such a fine day. Then she remembered all that had taken place before and forced herself to rise.

"A bath, please, Sophie," she called out, and her lady's maid quickly poked her head in from the adjoining room to confirm the order.

Sometime later, feeling far cleaner and more awake, Bella dressed and went downstairs. She'd been impressed to find that, despite the late hour of her return, Sophie had managed to wash her Cannon Belle attire, and had half considered donning that but had instead opted for a simple day gown and an accompanying shawl.

Her father was already at breakfast, reading from an old travel journal of his, and beamed at her when she entered, making her even more glad she had not worn trousers and vest. "Good morning, my dear," he said as she crossed the room to kiss his cheek. "You slept well?"

"I did, yes, thank you, Papa. And you?" Returning to her own seat, Bella helped herself to eggs and sausage and toast, then accepted the cup of tea Geoffrey handed her. The tall butler seemed fully recovered from his own ordeal, for which she was grateful.

She had just taken a sip when someone knocked on the front door. Geoffrey excused himself to answer it, and returned a moment later. "Commander Reid for you, milady." His voice held neither condemnation nor praise, though she thought the old man looked ever so slightly approving.

"Thank you, Geoffrey. Have him join us, please."

"I am so sorry to disturb you both at such an hour," Reid declared once he'd entered, bowing to them both. "Lord Roderick. Miss Parsons."

Her father waved off the protestation. "Nonsense, my good man. You must join us. Pull up a chair. I remember all too well what Ayers said about Navy food."

That wrung a chuckle from the commander as he sat—and Bella did not miss that he placed himself close to her side. "Sir, you are not mistaken, so I will gratefully accept your invitation." For a few moments, they ate and drank in silence. But finally Bella could stand it no longer.

"You are most welcome any time, Commander," she began, and felt a happy heat at the quick, pleased smile that flashed across his face. "But I assume you did not call upon us just to break your fast?"

He laughed, then turned serious. "No, indeed. I have been thinking." He glanced at her father, at the table's other end, but he seemed engrossed in his old writings. "About our friend from last night."

Bella nodded, sipping her tea. "Was he difficult about his . . . new accommodations?"

"No more than expected," Reid replied. "Except when I brought him in and paused by Carlyle's cell. Fletcher went into an utter panic. He pleaded with me not to lodge him near the man, or any of the *Hunger*'s crew." He frowned down at his plate. "I offered, somewhat sardonically I will admit, to have his own men keep him company instead, once Hatcher retrieved them from the Dulcet Dove—and if anything he grew even more afraid. Would not calm until I'd placed him in an empty cell and promised that no one else would be made to join him there."

Now it was Bella's turn to frown. "I can understand not wanting to be in arm's reach of Carlyle—as you saw, the man has a temper and holds a grudge. If allowed to, I've no doubt he'd kill Fletcher out of spite, and to eliminate one more witness to his various crimes. But why be afraid of his own men?"

"That's exactly what I've been wondering," Reid agreed, efficiently buttering a slice of toast before taking a healthy bite. "And I'm forced to come to one conclusion," he continued after swallowing the mouthful. "Those men weren't his."

She thought back over the scene, remembering how they'd approached, and the merchant's reaction. "They weren't there to save him from you," she realized, feeling a chill. "They'd been placed to keep him from talking, even if that meant killing him then and there." She met Reid's eyes. "But Carlyle was already in custody. So unless he had those men there all the time, just in case . . ."

"Someone else sent them," the commander finished for her. He nodded. "And another thing. Remember what Fletcher said when he showed? 'Carlyle, what is the meaning of this? You sent that note. You know better than that.'"

"But that isn't how he said it," Bella recalled now. "He said, 'Carlyle? What is the meaning of this?' like he was surprised it was you—I mean, him—there. Instead of someone else. And 'You sent that note?' Much the same. He wasn't surprised about getting a note, just who it was from."

"Exactly." He finished his toast, washing it down with a swig of strong, hot tea. "Which means we have a third player in all this. And Fletcher may not have been the one behind it all."

Bella absently traced a finger around the rim of her cup. "No, he wouldn't have been, would he? Carlyle supplied the force, attacking ships at sea. Fletcher had the connections, both to get his ship through your blockade and to find out about competitors' ships. But someone else came up with the plan, and assigned the roles. Whoever that is, he recruited both of them." Another thought occurred to her. "This third party must have been responsible for getting the *Hunger*, too. Fletcher always said he had everything riding on each trip his own ship took, he wouldn't have had the funds to buy a Ship of the Line, or the means to steal one. We're looking for the one with the money, and the wits to put all of this together."

And, just like that, she knew who it had to be.

"It's Basil-White," she said, and had to shift her hands to her lap lest she snap the teacup in her rage. "He orchestrated all of this."

Reid was studying her, frowning still. "I'm not sure . . ." he began, but she cut him off.

"It has to be. Listen, he and Fletcher were friends, he introduced the man to us. And he showed up in Hillington first, around the same time the *Hunger* appeared off our shores. He has the money, and he was often gone for a time, which would have afforded him the chance to meet Carlyle. My crew said they'd seen him with men at the Dulcet Dove, rather than just one man—that must have been Basil-White and Fletcher." She scowled. "He has an accent, from living overseas. I heard similar when I was in the Mediterranean. If he was there, he could have met Carlyle that way, helped him get the *Hunger* after I stole the *Deadshot* off him. Damn it!"

Her father glanced up at the sudden outburst, and she waved and smiled to let him know she was fine, not continuing until he'd glanced away again, which gave her a few seconds to regain control over herself. She was still furious, however. "I liked him! And I never saw any of this!" Now, however, it all made perfect sense— except perhaps for his interest in her. Had that been genuine, or just another part of this scheme?

Reid's face had gone still. "I am sorry," he told her, his voice and posture far stiffer than it had been a moment before. "I am sure that is a great loss to you, to lose someone you had such interest in."

She couldn't help it—despite her anger, she laughed. "No, I was not . . . he was not the man for me," she promised, and was pleased to see a flush creep across her commander's face, and his stance relax, even as he showed her a sheepish grin. "I am just angry at myself for so misjudging someone, and for being so readily deceived."

"Ah." Reid attempted to cover his discomposure—and his relief—by taking up his teacup again. "Yes, well, I'll confess that I never liked the man much myself, but then I had my own reasons for such." She felt her heart flutter at the subtle hint, and smiled, winning an answering look of such clear and intense desire that she felt suffused with sunshine and joy despite the dark topic. "But you are correct, all the details line up." Finishing his cup, he set it down gently but firmly. "Which means we both know what we must do next."

"Yes." Finishing her own breakfast, Bella set her napkin down beside her place and pushed her chair back, allowing Reid to offer her a hand to rise. "Papa, the Commander and I have some matters to attend. Will you be all right?"

Her father started a bit, then smiled. "What's that? Oh, of course, my dear. You two young people go on, enjoy the lovely day. Commander, please do come again, any time."

Reid bowed to him. "Thank you, sir. You are most kind, and I am very grateful." That done, he gave Bella his arm and escorted her from the room.

She was inordinately pleased that this time he didn't even think of attempting to affect a capture without her.

Chapter Thirty-five

"I WILL NEED TO CHANGE," BELLA warned as they exited into the main hall. "I shan't be but a moment."

"Of course." Reid bowed, then began a perusal of the various busts and portraits hanging there.

Hurrying upstairs, Bella quickly shucked her current attire and donned her Cannon Belle clothes instead. Ah, it was always such a pleasure to feel the freedom of pants once more! Grabbing up her pistols and sword where she'd tossed them onto her vanity last night—creating quite the tableaux, those items of combat nestled among perfumes and cosmetics!—she bundled them with her hat and coat and rushed back down.

When she reached the bottom, the commander eyed her critically. "This time you are the one forgetting something," he pointed out, and she laughed, pulling her wig from the rest and fixing it atop her head. "Better," he agreed once she was done adjusting it in the hall mirror. "Though I must say, I prefer the blonde hair, myself."

Bella beamed at him. "Well spoken, sir. Now, shall we?" And she led the way outside. "Do we have any idea how and where to catch him?"

"Ah." Reid frowned. "Not really, no. I've only ever seen the man . . . well, around you, mostly."

"Oh, of course! Hold this!" And, thrusting her remaining gear into his arms, Bella raced back inside. "Geoffrey!" The family butler emerged from the dining room at once, utterly unfazed by her changed appearance. "Where is Mr. Basil-White's card, the one he left upon his last visit?"

The butler scowled. "I disposed of it, milady, as you seemed disinclined to accept his proposal."

"I still am," she assured him, but deflated somewhat. "The commander and I need to locate him, however. It is urgent."

A slow smile stole across the butler's lined face. "In that case, milady, I may relate that, according to said card, he is staying at the Hilltop."

Bella laughed and stepped in quickly to kiss the old man on the cheek. "You're a treasure, Geoffrey." She hurried back out. "He's at the Hilltop," she informed Reid, who was seated in a tidy little gig behind a handsome chestnut mare and leaned forward to help her step up to join him. Once she was seated properly, he flicked the reins and they set off at a good clip.

"I'm not familiar with the hotels hereabouts, though I believe I remember seeing that one," Reid commented as they exited Crestmont's grounds. "Good view of its surroundings, as I recall."

"Very." The Hilltop was one of the better hotels in Hillington, but not the largest or the fanciest—that was the Regal Arms. What the Hilltop had to especially recommend it was its location at the edge of town perched atop the area's largest rise, giving it a commanding view and a fresh breeze from the ocean. "We won't be able to surprise him there."

"No, but we can still apprehend him quickly, and one hopes quietly," Reid replied. "If he is indeed behind all this, he is a schemer, so perhaps he is less prepared for a direct and physical approach."

She nodded and patted her pistol. "I will shoot to wound, if I must shoot at all. But I will hope not to need it."

They rode on in silence, and soon reached town. It was not until Bella saw Mary Winstead emerging from the Grants' bakery that she realized she might have a problem. "Oh, bother!" Quickly she tugged her hat down low over her face, raising her coat collar for good measure. She could not be sure Mary had not seen her or recognized her, but prayed she had not.

Reid seemed to find this amusing. "A young lady riding alone with a man, I can see where you might worry for your reputation," he teased. Bella punched him in the arm by way of reply.

"This may seem funny to you," she whispered, "but I live among these people! How will I ever bear it—how will my father!—if they learn that I and Cannon Belle are one and the same?"

"Yes, I see," he told her. "I am sorry. Well, we are moving quickly and your hair and attire may be enough for people not to recognize you even if they do catch a glimpse of your face." He smirked. "Though if they do, it is your own fault for being so unforgettable."

She made to punch him in the arm again, and he pulled away, still laughing. The flirtation did help overcome her worry, but still she kept her face turned away every time they passed anyone.

Soon they were cresting the hill leading up to the old hotel. "Is Mister Basil-White in residence?" Reid asked the stable boy as he hopped down and handed the lad the gig's reins.

"Couldn't say, sir," the boy replied. "Sorry, sir."

Reid waved that off. He helped Bella down after him, and together they entered the hotel. The lobby was a grand affair, with its marble floor and vaulted ceiling, and their quick steps echoed as they made for the large, ornately carved desk at the room's back.

"May I help you, sir?" the man behind it asked Reid. He glanced askance at Bella in her strange attire, but finally unbent enough to nod. "Madam."

"Mister Basil-White," Reid stated. "What room is he in?"

"Room sixteen, sir," the hotel employee answered at once, straightening in response to the commander's martial tone. "Top floor, last door on the left." He pointed at the grand marble staircase occupying the center of the room, but Reid and Bella were already dashing toward it.

They raced upstairs as quickly as they could, then down the short corridor and around a maid to the last room, where Reid pounded on the door. "Basil-White!" he called out, his tone sharp. "Open this door at once!"

There was no reply.

A second knock produced the same lack of response. Reid tried the door handle, but it was locked. "We'll need to break it down," he stated, shifting his shoulders, but Bella laid a hand on his arm.

"Perhaps we have another option," she suggested. She turned back to where the maid was watching, wide-eyed. "We need this door open, please," Bella told the girl gently. "It's a matter of life or death." She produced a guinea from her vest pocket and held it up.

The maid paused a moment before stepping quickly over to join them. "Yes, ma'am." Accepting the coin, she produced a set of keys and used one to unlock the door. "There you are." She was already backing away as she said it.

"Thank you." Bella bowed Reid toward the door. "After you."

Laughing, he stepped through, pistol already in hand. But he need not have bothered. Though well appointed, the room was small enough to clearly see that it was unoccupied. A door at one end led to a cozy study, and one on the side to a private water closet, both equally empty.

"Damn, we've missed him!" Reid exclaimed. "But is he simply out and about, or is he fleeing arrest?"

Bella had been wondering the same thing, and suspected she knew the answer, though it was not the one they'd have preferred. "If those were his men last night," she said slowly, "the fact that they never returned to report in might have told him all he needed to know." A tea service sat upon the desk, a single teacup half-full, and she rested the back of her hand against the teapot there. "Still warm. He was here this morning, then, and not that long ago."

Reid nodded, biting back another curse. "Which means it's more likely his men escaped the inn this morning, whether by force or bribery, and came straight here to inform him we had Fletcher in custody. Damn. I should have taken them in last night as well. Well, nothing for it now." He sighed, holstering his gun and offering her a rueful smile. "I don't suppose you have some way of locating him a second time?"

She'd been glancing around the room, hoping for some sort of clue to the man's whereabouts, and now her eye fell upon an object beside the tea service. "I just might." She held up an old but hand-some and well-maintained brass compass. "What do you make of this?"

"A fine old piece," Reid replied, taking it from her for inspection before handing it back. "But what of it?"

"He said once that he abhorred the water and wouldn't set foot on a boat," Bella noted, still weighing the compass. "That's an odd thing to state so firmly. Unless it was a ruse. This is a mariner's tool, and not for show, either. Nor is it just a well-loved heirloom—it's been oiled recently. He was using this."

Reid nodded, once more catching her meaning. "You think he has a boat of his own, stashed away somewhere. If so, he'd surely make for it now. He can cut straight across the ocean, head for Amsterdam or the Netherlands, and we won't be able to do a thing to get him back here." He tapped his chin. "But you said there were many coves like yours, and we have no idea what kind of boat we're after, so we don't know which places might accommodate it."

Bella considered that. "Wouldn't it make more sense to use one you already knew, though? The cove by Bridlington could fit a sec-ond ship if it were smaller than the *Hunger*. And that way his men and Carlyle's could watch over each other's vessels."

"That does makes sense. But even so, he has a head start. We'll never catch him."

"Not before he can reach his boat, no." Bella turned toward the door. "But we each have ships of our own, and ours are nearer. We'll both head in that direction, angled upward to cross paths, and watch for any unfamiliar ships fleeing across the waters. With any luck, one or both of us will spot him before he can get away."

"An excellent plan." He tugged the door open and bowed. "This time, after you?"

Bella smiled and let him usher her through. She took the com-pass with her, just because.

Chapter Thirty-six

REID OFFERED TO DROP HER BACK home, but Bella had a better idea. "The commander requires a fast horse," she told the stableboy as he brought the gig around. She tipped him a shilling—she was out of guineas!—and he nodded, hurrying away to return with a handsome bay. "That will get you to Riverside faster," she explained, allowing him to help her up into the carriage. "I'll see you on the water. Good luck!" And, leaning back down, she kissed his cheek.

He flushed, but his smile was warm. "And to you." Then he was slinging himself into the saddle and, with a quick salute, urging his borrowed steed into a gallop. Bella set off right behind him but kept going through town when he turned off to cut around it. She drove as quickly as she dared, racing past startled townsfolk, and soon reached home, where she all but flung the reins to Daniel. "Mind this for the commander," she instructed as she jumped down and raced for the house, passing through it at speed on her way to the back lawn and then down the steps.

Her crew were milling about and startled as she burst in upon them. "To sea!" Bella shouted. "At once! We've a boat to catch!"

"What's the word, then, Cap'n?" Quince asked, even as the men leaped into action, racing for the *Deadshot* and readying her to depart. "This to do with the Navy and the *Hunger* and all that?"

"It does, aye," she answered as they hurried up the gangplank. She kept her voice loud enough for the rest of the crew to hear. After all, they were all in this together. "There's another ship behind the *Hunger*'s depredations, and it's making a run for the Netherlands to escape justice. I aim to stop it ever getting there."

"Begging your pardon, captain, but ain't that the Navy's job?" Tom called out, though to his credit he never paused in coiling the rope line.

"It is," she agreed, stationing herself in her usual spot near Gregor and the wheel. "We're assisting them on this." She grinned. "Can you believe it, lads? Us, working with the Navy? That'll look fine for us once this all shakes out, I'm thinking." She paused as if to consider. "Yes, 'privateer' has a lovely ring to it, wouldn't you say?"

Several of the men laughed, and a few even cheered. "That's our captain," Luke O'Dell declared. "Always with a plan up her sleeve, and always on the lookout for us!" That brought more cheers, and the *Deadshot* was in good spirits as it sailed from its cove, raising its mainsails and taking to the open sea.

"This only works if we help catch the villain," Bella warned. "So eyes sharp, all. It'll be starting from Bridlington and cutting straight across at full speed, I'm guessing it'll make for Amsterdam, but beyond that I couldn't say, so you see anything, sing out."

"Aye aye, Captain!" the men rang out, and she smiled, feeling both the thrill of the chase and the joy of a good ship with a loyal crew. This was the life!

She hoped she wouldn't have to give it all up.

They'd been out on the water an hour or more when Isaac called down, "Ship ahoy! To the starboard side, same direction as us, we'll cross paths soon!"

Bella aimed her spyglass in that direction and soon caught sight of the sails, and a hint of red and blue at the mast. "Aye, that should be the *Diligent*," she announced. "Good. Don't worry, lads—this time, they're on our side!"

Even so, she couldn't help feeling a moment of trepidation as the frigate neared them, particularly since she could now see that its gunports were all open and cannons readied. That anxiety eased somewhat when a familiar figure in Navy blue waved from the other ship's bow. "Ahoy, the *Deadshot*!" Reid called. "Any luck?"

"None yet," Bella shouted back. "But we should be crossing their route soon!" She'd set Gregor a bearing a little north of Denmark with that intention.

Reid nodded. "I've an idea," he yelled across. "Trust me?"

She smiled, though he might have been too far away to see. "Always!"

His answering smile was easily visible despite the distance. "Then keep going, and watch for me from the north." With that, he called something to his men, and the *Diligent* sailed on past. He saluted as they crossed, and Bella executed a curtsy in response. Then they were seeing the frigate's stern, the Navy ship swiftly increasing the distance between them until the *Deadshot* was alone once more.

"North?" Quince asked once the other ship had gone. "But our quarry's heading southeast, ain't it?"

Bella had understood, however. "Aye. And we're apt to find them first. Which means they'll have eyes on us. With any luck, they won't see the *Diligent* coming up on them from behind. Particularly as it's nearing noon, and the sun'll be overhead." It was a good plan, and a bold one, more in her line than her commander's. Perhaps she was finally rubbing off on him.

Her first mate nodded and got back to work, keeping the men on their toes, and Bella trained her own eyes on the waves once more. They had to catch Basil-White before he could get away. They had to!

"Ship ahoy!" came the call from above, and Bella immediately snapped to. She'd been lost in thought, the steady wind and waves and strong sunlight lulling her into a semi-daze, but now she was alert again. "Ahead and to port, on course to cross us!"

Moving to the port railing, she scanned the water. Yes, there! "I see it!" she replied. "A brigantine, by the look of it!" A good choice, she knew—that class was roughly of a size with a frigate, but with a shallower draft. Maneuverable, fast, and with more carrying capacity—and more guns—than a schooner like the *Deadshot*. Yes, Basil-White had planned carefully indeed.

She had no doubt it was his, either. Who else would be fleeing across the German Ocean at this very moment? And at this precise angle, from Bridlington to Amsterdam? No, it was him; she was sure of it. And a brigantine would have been able to squeeze into that same cove with the *Hunger*. Everything fit.

The approaching ship must have seen them as well, because it suddenly slowed, its sails slackening a little to ease its headlong rush. At the same time, a dark shape rose along the main mast. "They're raising their flag!" Isaac announced, the lad's young eyes as sharp as ever. "It's a Jolly Roger, but one I've never seen before!"

Bella studied it as well, and was equally unfamiliar with it— at the end of its crossed bones sprouted long, bell-shaped purple flowers, with dark berries clustered below them. Staring through his own spyglass beside her, however, Quince let out a low moan.

"No. Oh, blazes, no!" her first mate muttered. "It can't be!"

She shifted to study the sour-faced sailor, who looked even more stricken now. "What's the matter, Mister Quince? Whose flag is that?"

He gulped, and when he replied his voice was a hoarse whisper. "That's the *Nightshade*'s banner, Cap'n. I seen it once afore, long time ago." He shook his head. "But nobody's seen that flag for over a decade!"

"The *Nightshade*?" Bella stared at him. "That's impossible. That was the ship of—"

But her first mate nodded. "Aye, Cap'n. Of none other than Captain Hemlock, the deadliest pirate ever to sail the Mediterranean!"

Chapter Thirty-seven

BELLA HAD A QUICK DECISION TO make. Did they attack, try to evade, or mimic the approaching ship and slow enough to speak? There was no sign of the *Diligent*, and with ample time to prepare, she knew there was no way the *Deadshot* could go head-to-head against the oncoming brigantine. Accordingly, she tapped her first mate on the shoulder. "Loosen the sails, Mister Quince. It appears they want a word, and I'm curious to meet this legend—and find out what he's doing in my ocean." She projected her voice enough to carry back to her crew and infused it with all the confidence and nonchalance she could muster. That was the first rule of being a good captain, after all:

Never let your men know how badly you're quaking in your boots.

Like now, when Quince studied her a second before giving a firm nod. "Right you are, Cap'n." His voice, too, was strong and steady—and intended for their audience. "Slacken sails!"

The *Deadshot* slowed her pace, going from a headlong rush to a gentle drift. It was very civilized the way the two ships' bowsprits passed one another only yards apart. The image put Bella in mind of medieval jousts, particularly those where two knights showed mutual respect by deliberately not engaging.

She hoped that might be the case here. At least for now.

"Drop anchor!" came the cry from the other ship, and Quince echoed it, both ships settling there upon the waves, so close their railings were almost touching.

"Ahoy, the *Deadshot*!" a familiar, lightly accented voice called out. It came from the figure standing by the *Nightshade*'s helmsman, dressed smartly in a deep purple coat and matching tricorn, the color so dark it was nearly black. They were near enough now for Bella to make out the familiar auburn hair and hazel eyes of Charles Basil-White.

"Ahoy, the *Nightshade*!" she replied, stepping over to her own railing to see and converse better. "Why, Mister Basil-White! What a pleasant surprise!" She bowed, one captain to another.

He laughed and returned the gesture. "Indeed, Miss Parsons! Most pleasant indeed!" His laughter at her expression sounded more genuine. "Yes, I recognize you despite the wig and the clothes, though both are quite fetching, if you'll allow me to say so."

"You may." He had always been direct, but Bella was glad for the sun and the wind, both of which could explain away her blush. "So it seems you have overcome your lifelong aversion to sailing," she noted, hands going to her hips as she swept her gaze along the length of his ship. It was a handsome vessel, to be sure. And its gunports were all open and prepared for use, as was her own, though the *Deadshot* boasted far fewer of them.

Basil-White tipped his head in response. "It was less a personal preference than a paternal command," he confided, as easy as if they had been standing before the church or sitting in her drawing room. "My late father did not wish me to take to sea."

"To follow in his footsteps, you mean," Bella guessed, and was pleased to see a frown pucker his brow for a moment before he smoothed it away. "Your father was Captain Hemlock," she went on, the riddle unraveling as she spoke. "He disappeared from the Mediterranean years ago, I'm guessing to take his plunder and return to England, with you in tow. Was Basil-White his name before, or did he take that on as well, creating the guise of a proper gentleman?"

"Very good, Miss Parsons," her former suitor replied, applauding gently though with a hint of mockery. "Well reasoned indeed! Yes, you are correct in all points—even the name. He was born

Tom White, but became Thomas Basil-White for the voyage home and kept that name once we'd arrived. His most fervent wish was that I not take up his former career, and so while he lived I was forbidden from even sailing for anything but business." He grinned. "I took lessons in secret."

"And once he passed away, you felt free to claim his mantle for your own," Bella stated. "I am sorry for your loss."

He nodded. "Thank you. Yes, well done. But I did not wish to return to the Mediterranean, not when I was already so well established here. So I set my sights on conquering the German Ocean instead." His smile was suddenly less charming. "You were part of those plans, though admittedly an extremely pleasant one."

"Oh?" Bella wrinkled her nose at him. "How so? My father has squandered most of our money, and his title would pass to my son, but not my husband." A faint motion out beyond the *Nightshade* caught her eye. Was that a speck on the horizon? She tilted her head, lowering her voice so only the nearby Quince would hear over the waves. "Tell Isaac not to call out if that's the *Diligent*," she warned her first mate. "Then have men stand ready at the sails and the anchor." They might need to move in a hurry. "But do not hide what you are doing," she added as the thought came to her. "Let them see and wonder. Keep their eyes upon us."

Quince nodded and slipped away as she returned her attention to Basil-White, who was already replying. He did not seem to have noticed her quick aside.

"I am well aware of your finances, perhaps better than you know," he said, and his smile was definitely oily now. "Including that strange new debt you recently incurred. How unfortunate! And how fortuitous that you might have a wealthy suitor at just the right moment!"

Anger washed over Bella, sweeping away any embarrassment or anxiety. "You engineered that! You were gone at just the right moment and returned at the perfect time to take advantage of it!"

He dipped into a sweeping bow. "Exactly so. I must admit, I'd hoped you would be home when the message arrived so that I could comfort you then and there. Instead you were out of town, and I had to impatiently await your return. As it was, I barely had time to beat you to Crestmont once my men spotted you arriving in Riverside."

"But why?" she asked again. Her gaze darted past him for half a blink. Yes, that was definitely something approaching from the north! And on her own ship, there was a wave of noise as men scurried about, readying themselves. She could see the sailors of the *Nightshade* tensing in response but kept her own focus on Hemlock. "What did you stand to gain?"

"Besides a lovely young bride?" Basil-White smirked at her. "And even more respectability? There was one thing that truly motivated me. One thing you could offer that no one else in this region could."

She glared at him, and then the answer hit her like a thunderclap. "The cove! You wanted Crestmont and access to the cove beneath it!"

The newly made pirate captain nodded. "Correct. My own recent berth is too far away and too public. Yours is far better suited. With it, the *Nightshade* could strike at any time and then wholly disappear." He leaned on the railing. "It still could—and the *Deadshot* right alongside it. Imagine what a pair we could make! Captains Hemlock and Cannon Belle, raiding as one! We would own these waters!"

For an instant, despite herself, Bella was tempted. And Basil-White saw it.

"I would never make you give this up," he promised, and in that at least he seemed earnest. "Why should I, when it is one of the things I most admire about you? Your boldness, your fierceness, your strength—only a fool would try to wipe those away. You and I would be true partners, on land and at sea—fully respectable at home, utterly feared upon the waves. Think about it!"

It was an enticing vision. But Bella already knew the flaws to that plan—and the biggest one by far was the man offering it to her.

"You are too duplicitous by far," she told him now. "I could never trust you not to be plotting against me. Besides which," she tossed her head, "you are not the man I love." Oh, it felt good to say that aloud!

Basil-White's lips curled in a snarl. "And where is he, then, your precious Commander? Oh, yes, your interest in him was obvious. Else I would not have needed to fabricate that debt to sway you. But will he love you? All of you? Or will he try to tame you?"

The *Diligent* was now nearly upon them both, darting forward along the *Nightshade*'s other side, and Bella allowed herself to grin at the surprised suitor-turned-pirate. "Why don't you ask him yourself?" she said sweetly.

Then she spun on her heel. "Raise sails!" she shouted. "Raise anchor! Ready cannons!"

"What?" Basil-White straightened, confused. He turned, and was still close enough that Bella could see him blanch at the sight of the Navy frigate bearing down upon him. "To arms!" he shouted, racing from the railing. "Raise anchor!"

His sailors rushed to port, readying guns, but the *Diligent*'s men already had theirs out and raised, sighting across the narrowing gap, even as the frigate slowed and angled to allow itself a better shot. "This is the HMS *Diligent*!" Reid shouted from the bow. "Lay down your weapons and surrender, or be fired upon!"

Meanwhile, the *Deadshot*'s sails were billowing, catching the wind. With the anchor safely stowed, Bella's ship shot forward, its hull nearly scraping the *Nightshade*'s as it slipped past.

"Fire!" Basil-White screamed. "Fire at them both!"

"Fire!" Bella shouted in response.

"Fire!" Reid echoed.

Explosions burst from all three ships nearly simultaneously.

The *Nightshade*'s starboard cannon were aimed at the *Deadshot*, but Bella's smaller ship was already more than halfway past. The rear guns all missed completely. Several of the forward cannon struck her ship, however. Luke O'Dell cried out and went down. Gareth was felled as well, along with a few of the others.

The *Deadshot*'s own guns struck all along the *Nightshade*'s side.

Railings shattered. Cannons exploded. Holes appeared along the bigger ship's side.

On the other side, most of the *Nightshade*'s cannon missed the *Diligent*, which was still slightly behind it.

Whereas the *Diligent*'s aim was precise, its angle perfect, for its full volley to strike the entire length of the brigantine before it. Bella heard a massive rending noise as an entire section of the *Nightshade*'s hull burst into splinters.

"We're hit, but naught below the waterline!" Quince reported once the sound and fury had ceased, the air thick with gunsmoke. "*Nightshade*'s taking on water, though!"

"Surrender!" Reid insisted again. "We will bring all of you away safely!"

But Basil-White laughed. "Safe, to stand trial and hang?" he shouted back. "Never!" Bella could already see his men yanking back the cannons to ready them for firing again.

"Fire again!" she ordered, though she hated to do so. Not out of any further regard for Basil-White in particular but simply out of respect for human life. Still, if it was him or her—or him or Reid—she would not hesitate. She already knew Reid would be doing the same.

This time, the cannons were more staggered. But the *Deadshot* had passed the *Nightshade* and swiveled around along its front so that her broadside took the pirate ship across its bow. The *Diligent* remained angled near the brigantine's stern. And the *Nightshade* itself had very little shot against either of them, though it still made the attempt.

When the smoke cleared, the *Nightshade* was clearly listing, and beginning to go down. "Surrender!" Reid tried again. "Spare your men's lives, at least!"

"Never!" Basil-White reiterated. One of his sailors made as if to protest, and Bella watched as her former suitor drew his sword and ran the man through. "We go down with the ship!" he insisted, hefting his pistol in his other hand. "Or you can die right here and now!"

His men seemed less inclined to perish by drowning, however. They rushed him. He shot one, clubbed another, ran through a third. Then they had overwhelmed him, carrying Basil-White to the deck. "We surrender!" someone shouted. "Please!" There was a loud clatter as the pirates of the sinking *Nightshade* threw down their weapons.

Bella watched, satisfied, as the *Diligent* crept forward, coming alongside the brigantine. "Take us home, Mister Quince," she instructed. "Time to patch our wounds and see what today's efforts have wrought."

But she spared a quick smile and salute for her dashing Navy commander as he led his men onto the sinking ship. And felt warm as he returned both with enthusiasm.

Yes, today might have turned out very well indeed.

Chapter Thirty-eight

THREE DAYS PASSED, AND BELLA HEARD nothing.

"He has forgotten me," she moaned to Abbie, who swatted her on the shoulder with her ever-present fan. The two of them were, as always in the Crestmont drawing room—which, at least, was no longer in any danger, the mysterious "Elias Crawford from Leeds" having utterly vanished, along with his false claim. "He has moved on with his life and wants no part of me."

That received a snort from her friend. "First, I'd have thought at least a part of you might prefer it that way," she pointed out delicately, sipping at her tea. "After all, if he has truly forgotten you, then your secret is no longer in any danger." But Abbie waved all of that off. "Which is all beside the point, since he's no more forgotten you than you have forgot how to breathe."

"Then why has he not been to see me?" Bella demanded, attempting to glare at her friend—a fact made all the more difficult by the fact that Abigail currently had lemon curd at the corners of her mouth, courtesy of the lemon tart she had just consumed. "Whether to arrest me or to woo me, I'd have thought there would be something!"

"Perhaps he will do both," Abigail suggested archly. "After all, there are those who like to claim that marriage is much like imprisonment for a young lady of decent wits."

Bella growled and was contemplating throwing a cream puff— though that would be a horrible waste of Margaret's talents!— when Geoffrey appeared at the drawing room door. He bore a letter upon his silver tray. "This has just arrived for you, milady," he stated, crossing the room to present it to her with a deep bow. "From a Navy man."

"Oh!" Bella grabbed it up. "It's from him!" She held the folded and sealed missive up, trying to divine its contents and what effect they might have on her—only to have the letter rudely snatched away by a giggling Abigail.

"Shall I spare you the torture and read it for you?" her friend taunted. "Or put you out of your misery altogether by consigning it to the fires unread?" And she danced closer to the fireplace, where a merry blaze burned behind the grate.

"No!" Bella lurched to her feet but Abigail darted off, still laughing like a fiend. What followed was a merry chase around the room, which only ended when Abigail ran out of breath and flopped back on the divan, allowing Bella to finally reclaim her prize. To avoid any chance of losing it again, she broke the seal and tore it open.

"Well?" Abbie asked after a moment. "Is it to be Heaven or Hell?"

"I . . . don't know," Bella admitted, reading the short note again. "The pleasure of my company is requested for a trip to London tomorrow morning. I am to present myself at the *Diligent* at dawn. And I may bring a maid or chaperone if I wish, though one is not required."

"That's . . ." Abbie sat up, still gasping a bit, and fanned herself a moment. She frowned. "No, I don't know either. Does he mean to arrest you and escort you to London in chains, there to stand trial? But if that were so, what about the rest of your crew? Surely they would be punished as well, and far more harshly than a lady of noble blood." She waved Bella over. "How does he sign it?"

Bella reread that part, feeling a thrill as she did so. "Ever yours, Nicholas Reid, Commander, HMS *Diligent*."

Her friend smiled. "Well, that's all right, then. He'd not be leading you to your death and say he was ever yours."

"No, I don't suppose he would. Yet it is still curious." Bella tapped the letter against her cheek, thinking. "There is nothing for it but to accept his kind invitation, of course." She glanced over at Abbie. "Will you come with me? I don't think I can put Sophie through another boat ride, and I should value your support."

Abigail smiled. "Of course. I haven't been to London in ages, and only by coach. This shall make a refreshing change." She batted her eyelashes at Bella over her fan. "And all those handsome sailors, with no one to fawn over them because you only have eyes for their commander. Whatever shall one do?"

Bella laughed. "I have most certainly corrupted you," she stated with mock sorrow. "However shall I live that down?" But, inside, she was extremely grateful and took Abigail's hand in the hopes her friend would see that. Because, despite the warm salutation, she was not entirely convinced tomorrow would not end with her in chains—or worse.

The next day, Bella dressed in a comfortable sea-blue traveling gown and then took the gig to go get Abigail. The two of them drove down to Riverside, stopping just before the docks. Reid himself was waiting there for them and smiled upon seeing them arrive.

"Miss Montrose," he said, greeting Abigail first as he helped her from the gig. "How lovely to see you again. I hope you are fully recovered from your ordeal?"

"Quite so, thank you, Commander," she replied with a curtsy. "I hope you do not mind my accompanying Bella today."

"Not at all," he assured her. Then he turned to Bella. "Miss Parsons. I am very happy to see you." A smile tugged at his lips. "I feared you might have set sail without me, and then I'd have had to chase you down."

She grinned down at him before accepting his hand. "That does sound like fun. Perhaps later." She thought his fingers lingered in hers a moment, just as his eyes stayed upon her, and felt flushed despite the sharp breeze. "I hope your men survived the encounter well?"

He nodded. "A few minor injuries here and there, and at least one of my crew will have a handsome scar from it. Yours?"

She returned the nod. "Luke O'Dell will most likely walk with a limp, and Gareth may never recover full hearing in one ear. The rest took only scrapes, cuts, and bruises. So, to London, then?"

"Indeed." He smiled, but Bella thought there was a wobble to it, as if anxiety plucked at its edges. Still, there were no manacles in sight as he led them down the dock and up the gangplank, and when they reached the top Alex Hatcher greeted them with his usual cheer despite a bandage around his head.

"Miss Parsons, a pleasure as always," the lieutenant stated, bowing. "And may I have the honor of being introduced to your lovely friend?"

Reid stepped in. "Alex Hatcher, Abigail Montrose. There. Now ready the ship to cast off. We must be in London by nine." He bowed to them, his gaze again staying on Bella. "If you'll excuse me." Then he'd hurried off.

Hatcher just laughed. "Don't mind him, he's all a-flutter. But if you'll follow me, I'll show you to the best seat in the house." And he gallantly offered his arm to Abigail, who was as pink as an early sunset.

The spot he showed them was the same where Bella had sat before, on their journey back up here, and after they'd both thanked him the lieutenant hurried off to see to his duties. "He's quite handsome," Abigail said softly once he'd gone. "And very nice."

"He is both of those things, yes," Bella agreed. "He is also Reid's closest friend, so I daresay he is as fine a man as he appears." She smiled at her friend. "And quite taken with you."

"And why shouldn't he be?" Abbie fanned herself. "I may not be a pirate captain, but I'm still quite the catch!" She giggled, which set Bella off as well, and they were still laughing as the *Diligent* raised anchor, piled on sail, and glided from her berth, down the river and out to sea.

Though she'd rarely been on a boat, Abigail proved a natural at it, and the two of them happily chatted during the short journey, enjoying the fresh air and sunshine. Reid stopped by once they were underway, to make sure they were well situated and to offer them tea, but then resumed his usual post near the helm. Bella could hardly blame him. Nor, given his frequent glances her way, did she think he was deliberately avoiding her, as he had the last time she had been on this ship. Still, she wondered what lay in store for them at the voyage's end.

They reached London at half past eight, and Bella was startled to find her commander approaching her even as sailors tied the ship to the mooring posts. "I apologize for any unseemly haste," he began, "but you and I have an appointment at nine, and it would be best if we were not late. Would it be terribly improper of me to ask you to accompany me straightaway, with Miss Montrose to follow at a more leisurely pace?"

Bella rose to her feet, smoothing her skirts. "Not at all. Abbie, I'll see you soon." She brushed her cheek against her friend's, then followed Reid off the ship and to a waiting gig. They set off at once, at a swift canter, and Reid threaded the small carriage through bales and carts and workers with ease, though his hands were tight on the reins. "Is everything all right?" Bella asked him once they'd escaped the docks and were rushing through the city proper. "You seem agitated."

At first he did not answer, but finally he sighed. "I am sorry. This meeting, it will determine both our fates, and while I hope for the best . . . I do not truly know how it will all fall out."

Bella wanted to ask more, but a cart had just backed into the road and her commander was busy avoiding a collision. So she stayed quiet, letting him concentrate on getting them to their mysterious destination safely. At least, she told herself, whatever would happen next, she would face it with him at her side!

What seemed eons later and yet also mere moments past, Reid slowed the gig outside a large, grand old building of yellowed brick. "What is this place?" Bella asked as a Navy officer by the massive black door helped her down.

The man saluted. "This is Admiralty House, ma'am. I trust you have an appointment?"

"We do, yes," Reid replied, returning the salute. "With the Admiralty Board at nine."

The other officer nodded and rapped on the door with his fist. Two Marines opened it from the other side, and they were shown through, into a beautiful front hall with cheery yellow walls, handsome white columns, and a grand red-velvet-carpeted staircase. "You'll want the first drawing room, sir," one of the guards stated once Reid had given their names. "They're waiting for you."

"Thank you." Taking her arm, Reid led her down the hall, to a door just past the stairs. "I would tell you not to be frightened," he said as he slowed to a stop there. "But I know you are fearless. Still, I am with you." He squeezed her hand, then opened the door and stepped aside to let her enter first.

Bella did so, finding herself in a tasteful room with red brocade wallpaper and framed portraits between the white doors and column-flanked windows. A long table dominated the space, directly beneath a grand chandelier, and she might have taken it for a small dining room if not for the lack of food and the serious mien of the seven men seated along the far side, watching her. Four of them wore Navy uniforms, each with epaulets covered in more stars than Bella had seen below the night sky. A gentleman with a long face and dark eyes and hair approached her.

"Miss Parsons." He bowed. "I am John Wilson Croker, First Secretary to the Admiralty. If you'll allow me to show you to your seat?" She nodded, curtsying in response, and then followed him to the center chair on the unclaimed side. Reid made to sit as well, but Croker waved him off and he was forced to stand at attention off to the side instead.

"Miss Parsons." This was from the man at the far end, a sturdy, distinguished-looking officer with a high forehead and graying hair. His epaulets were the most heavily adorned of them all. "Robert Dundas, Viscount Melville and First Lord of the Admiralty. It is a pleasure to meet you at long last."

"Lord Melville, it is an honor and a pleasure," Bella replied, curtsying while seated. "My lords." She nodded to the other men.

One of them rapped his knuckles on the table. "Shall we dispense with pleasantries?" he asked, his words heavy with a Scottish brogue. "We've heard some serious things about ye, young lass. Ye're a bleeding pirate!"

Bella lifted her chin, antagonism giving her courage as always. "I have engaged in such practices, yes," she admitted. "I was forced into that trade as a way to survive and to preserve my honor."

"Yes, we have been apprised of such," one of the other officers commented. "Horrible that you were forced to endure such, and cheers for having won through it! Your bravery and perseverance does you and our great nation credit. But you did continue to prey upon innocent ships even after you'd secured your freedom." He said so in such an avuncular manner she almost expected him to wag his finger at her.

"I did, yes," she acknowledged. "It was necessary in order to cement the loyalty of my crew, that I might then direct us toward home."

"Yes, home," the Scotsman cut back in. "Where ye attacked ships yet again! Including good English vessels!"

But another gentleman waved that off. "Surely mistakes were made," he commented, his words also tinged with brogue but not as heavily. "Accidents happen. Who alive can say they have not had a similar misfortune? But perhaps we should focus on the positives instead?"

Lord Melville nodded. He had a kind face, which was difficult to reconcile with both his title and his position. This man was the head of the entire Royal Navy, and the Crown's top advisor on all naval affairs! Yet now he wore a slight smile as he said, "Yes, Commander Reid has informed us that you were instrumental in the capture of not only Captain Ravenous, a famed and feared pirate, but also the equally infamous Captain Hemlock, who had engineered an entire plan to dominate the German Ocean and our own western shore. Most impressive, Miss."

"She also rescued one of our merchant ship's crews," one of the remaining officers pointed out. "And helped uncover an officer who was most unfit for duty—and then helped stop her and her lieutenant when they escaped custody!" All of the officers were nodding, and Bella thought she saw respect on their faces, one ship captain to another.

The first Scotsman was still scowling, however. "The penalty for piracy is death!" he insisted. "Or are we just ignoring our own laws, now?"

"No, no, of course not," Melville replied. He looked at Bella—and winked. "And yes, pirates are put to death. But privateers? Ah, that is a different story."

Bella held her breath. Could it be?

The First Lord of the Admiralty continued. "You raided a French ship, the *Mère de Nacre*. And a Dutch ship, *Overvloedige Golven*. That was well done. We are at war with those countries, and several others. And, with Commander Reid, you defeated a rogue Ship of the Line. Very notable." He tapped the side of his nose. "The French and their allies, particularly Italy, Denmark, and Norway, must not be allowed to strengthen their navies. We must deal a blow to them upon the water whenever and wherever we may, and a large part of that comes from capturing their supplies. But our Navy cannot do this alone—we are too constrained by orders and politics. Thus, we must rely upon our brave privateers."

He glanced over his shoulder, and the First Secretary, Croker, approached him, carrying a leather folder embossed with the royal seal. Melville accepted that, glanced at its contents, and then slid it across the table toward Bella. "This is a Letter of Marque from the King himself," he explained. "It forgives any past trespasses you may have committed, and authorizes you to attack foreign ships upon the water, and to do with the spoils as you wish. You may not attack English ships in future, however. Is that understood?"

Bella nodded. "Perfectly, Lord Melville. Thank you." She reached for the folder, clutching it to her and trying not to tremble with relief.

"Very good." She was sure she saw both sympathy and approval in the First Lord's eyes. "You and Captain Reid will work together to keep the German Ocean free of our enemies, him by policing it officially and you by raiding any belligerents. I trust that will not be a problem?" Yes, he was definitely smiling at her now.

"Not at all, sir. I am happy to serve my country, and delighted to partner with Captain Reid." She had not missed the change in title, nor the way he started slightly at her statement, or the smirks from a few of the assembled admirals and lords. Well, let them. She did not care who knew of her affections!

No one commented, however, other than the Viscount, who dipped his head. "I am very pleased to have met you, Miss Parsons," he told her with what seemed genuine warmth. "The Admiralty—and the Crown—thanks you for your service. I wish you all success in life, and all happiness." That was a clear dismissal, and Bella rose to her feet, which at least allowed her to curtsy fully.

"I am honored in your faith in me, Lord Melville, Admirals, gentlemen," she replied. "I will not let you or the Crown down. I wish you all the best as well." They all nodded or saluted, though the one Scotsman gave a bit of a huff as he did. Then Reid had stepped forward and, with a salute to his superiors, had offered her his arm.

Bella let him lead her out. She was in a bit of a daze, and only recovered as they were settling again into the gig. Had that really happened? But she had the folder gripped to her bosom, assuring it had. Salvation indeed!

Chapter Thirty-nine

BEFORE BELLA EVEN KNEW IT, THEY were back at the docks. Abigail was waiting for them there before the *Diligent*, Hatcher at her side, and waved as she and Reid approached.

"There you are! Lieutenant Hatcher suggested there was little point in pursuing you, so we waited here instead." Her keen eyes swept over Bella. "I fail to see chains or stocks, so I will assume this mysterious meeting went well?"

Bella shook off her shock enough to nod. "It did. Very." She held up the folder. "I have been pardoned, and am officially in the service of the King as a privateer."

"Oh, well done, Bella!" Abbie hugged her tight. "After all that dreadfulness with Davis and Basil-White and, well, everything, I knew they could not help but forgive you!"

Bella had already turned to the man at her side. "You pleaded my case, did you not?" She studied him, all but daring him to deny it.

But of course Reid was made of stronger—and more honest— stuff than that. "I did," he admitted freely and without evident embarrassment. "I pointed out the difficulties you had faced, the choices you had been forced to make, and the ones you made freely. Like returning to save my crew and me from the *Hunger*. Risking your own life to save Captain Hodge and the crew of the *Sea's Midwife*. Working with me to stop Winnie and Talbot, and then to go after Fletcher and Basil-White. Hardly the acts of a bloodthirsty and ruthless pirate." He was grinning over that last bit, and Bella found herself smiling back.

"You are hardly one to talk, Captain," she replied, stressing his new rank. "You risked your career and your reputation by not only *not* capturing me for trial but by teaming with me against those same adversaries."

He started to reply, but was interrupted as Hatcher whooped and grabbed him in a hug, lifting Reid off the ground. "Captain?" the young lieutenant shouted. "Captain? About bloody time!"

"Yes, thank you, Lieutenant," Reid stated, trying to maintain some dignity while being twirled about like a kite. "The Admiralty chose to overlook any derelictions in favor of accomplishments, and have promoted me at last."

"You hear that, lads?" Hatcher shouted up at their ship, finally setting his friend and commanding officer down. "It's *Captain* Reid now!" That brought a resounding cheer, and applause from those other officers, sailors, and workers on nearby docks. Reid was trying for decorum, but he was grinning now as well, as were they all.

"It is good to see the regard your men hold for you," Bella told him fondly. "That is the mark of a good captain indeed." She curtsied, which she seemed to be doing a lot of today. "It will be an honor working alongside you, Captain Reid."

"And you, Captain Belle," he answered with a bow. "I look forward to our partnership."

"Is that what they're calling it now?" Abigail murmured, loud enough for only the four of them to hear. "How modern of them!" Bella swatted at her friend, who only giggled in response.

"Yes, the Admiralty has officially assigned us to work together," she stated, struggling to keep her own smile in check. "They feel that we are well suited."

Reid nodded. "I would agree." He shifted to face her fully, and Bella felt her heart race at the look in his eyes. Resolute—and something more, something that warmed her from the inside out.

"Miss Parsons," he stated, "I wish to apologize for anything I have said or done to offend or upset you. In truth, though I was startled to discover your hidden occupation, I have been impressed from the first by your courage, your vivacity, and your quick wit.

It should have been no surprise to learn that you were in fact the pirate Cannon Belle, who is renowned for those same qualities— and who, though reputed to be fierce, has only ever been proven to be fearless." He reached out and caught her hands in his own—his were chapped, calloused, the hands of a man who earned his way rather than relying upon others to do so for him, and she thrilled at their touch. "When we quarreled, it tore at me," he admitted more softly. "When we parted on ill turns, it made me nearly sick to my stomach. But when you were in danger, I realized I could not bear to lose you."

"What are you saying, sir?" Bella asked, though she could barely force the words out, her throat was so full, as were her eyes and her heart. She clung to his hands, and he to hers.

"I love you," he answered simply. "You are the only woman for me, and I wish us to be partners in life as well as work." Then, never releasing his gentle but firm clasp on her hands, he lowered himself to one knee, right there on the docks. "Would you do me the very great honor, Miss Isabella Parsons, of becoming my wife?"

Gazing down at him, Bella allowed her own feelings to show at last. "I love you as well, Captain Nicholas Reid," she replied. "And nothing could make me happier than to marry you."

Rising to his feet, Reid took her in his arms and kissed her, tenderly but with hints of the passion that would eventually follow. Beside them, Abigail and Hatcher cheered, and above them the crew of the *Diligent* shouted out congratulations as well.

They embraced a moment longer, and then Bella pulled away, though she was careful to keep his arm around her. "You will need to speak with my father," she told her newly minted fiancé. "He will approve wholeheartedly, of course, as will the Commodore. And you must write to your mother. We should visit her as soon as possible, so that I might present myself for her approval." A thought occurred to her. "Perhaps, once we are wed, she might be willing to relocate to Crestmont? She would have excellent care there, and I'm sure would be all the better for the fresh sea air, the company, and being able to see you more often."

The look Reid gave her then made Bella wonder how she could have ever doubted his feelings for her. "That is extremely thoughtful of you, and most generous. I am sure she would be delighted, as would I." He glanced up at his crew, many of whom were making gestures for them to kiss again and some of whom were offering less than polite suggestions as to what they might do next. "Ready the ship to make sail!" he called up, and all along the railing his men straightened. "We return to Riverside at once!" Then, offering Bella his arm, he smiled. "After all, we have a wedding to plan, and enemy ships to pursue."

Bella laughed. "Yes, my crew will be dismayed to learn that English ships are now off limits, but more than happy to make up for that by chasing down every French or Dutch ship to dare enter our waters." And to know that they had a continued livelihood, one they could perform openly. Those who wished to could even find homes, marry, have children, and still continue as part of her crew. It was better than she could have hoped, and Reid— "her" commander—had helped make it possible. She leaned into him happily as they followed Abigail and Hatcher up the gangplank—and was it her imagination or was her friend relying upon the engaging young lieutenant's support a bit more than was perhaps strictly necessary?

The sun was shining brightly now. The day was clear, the air crisp. The *Diligent* smelled of wood and tar and leather and salt, and Bella breathed all that in, choosing to stand with Reid by the helmsman rather than huddling on the seat at the bow. This was where she belonged, and soon she would be back on her own ship, steering its course. Even as she and Reid charted the course of their new life together. Bella knew it would not always be easy—they were both strong-willed, and both had their own ideas. But she was not worried.

After all, she was Cannon Belle, newly minted privateer to the English Crown, captain of the *Deadshot*, Terror of the Mediterranean and Scourge of the German Ocean. She could overcome any obstacle.

"Would you care to do the honors?" Reid asked her, and she laughed, then raised her voice.

"Raise anchor, up sails, and for home!" Bella cried.

And the ship leapt across the waves, her heart leaping right along with it.

The End

About the Author

AARON ROSENBERG IS THE BEST-SELLING, AWARD-WINNING author of over 50 novels, including the Twin Cities Cryptids urban fantasy series, the Areyat Islands fantasy pirate mystery series, the DuckBob SF comedy series, the Relicant Chronicles epic fantasy series, the *Dread Remora* space-opera series, and, with David Niall Wilson, the O.C.L.T. occult thriller series. His tie-in work contains novels for *Star Trek*, *Warhammer*, *World of WarCraft*, *Stargate: Atlantis*, *Shadowrun*, *Mutants & Masterminds*, and *Eureka* and short stories for *The X-Files*, *World of Darkness*, *Crusader Kings II*, *Deadlands*, *Master of Orion*, and *Europa Universalis IV*. He has written children's books (including the original series STEM Squad and Pete and Penny's Pizza Puzzles, the award-winning *Bandslam: The Junior Novel* and the #1 best-selling *42: The Jackie Robinson Story*), educational books on a variety of topics, and over 70 roleplaying games (including the original games *Asylum*, *Spookshow*, and *Chosen*, work for White Wolf, Wizards of the Coast, Fantasy Flight, Pinnacle, and many others, the Origins Award-winning *Gamemastering Secrets*, and the Gold ENnie-winning *Lure of the Lich Lord*). He is a founding member of Crazy 8 Press. Aaron lives in New York with his family. You can follow him online at gryphonrose.com, on Facebook at facebook.com/gryphonrose, and on X (formerly known as Twitter) @gryphonrose.

Piracy, mystery, and adventure awaits a pair of . . . brothers?

Sundra is a prince running for his life.
Ruhi is a young woman disguised to seek her freedom.
When they are captured by pirates, they claim to be brothers.
Now the pair has to navigate cruel masters, mysterious murders,
missing mages, vicious feuds, and violent storms.
But at least they have each other.

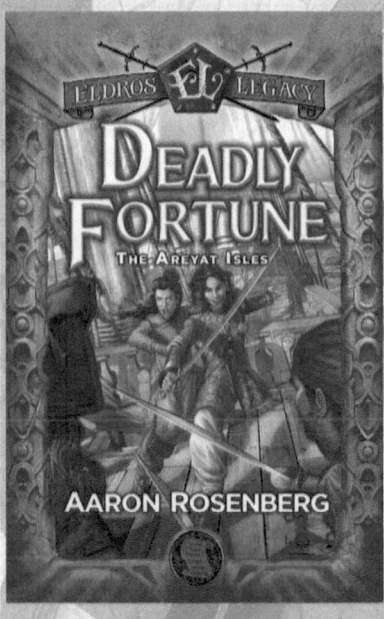

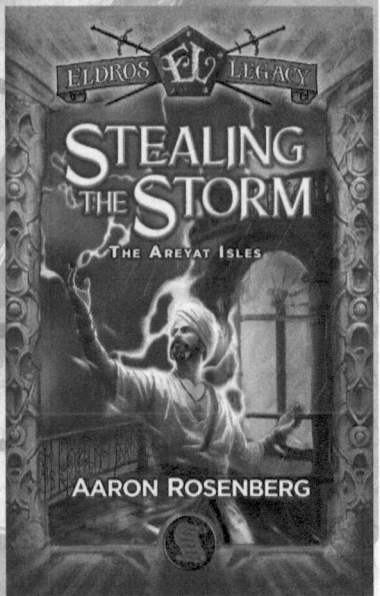

WHEN MAGIC DIES,
ONLY THE DEAD HOLD MAGIC.

Once, the empire of Ritakhou was full of magic. But since the Schism, the realm, renamed Rimbaku, is a pale whisper of its former majesty. Now the only magic is the Relicant Touch, a power allowing talents to be drawn from *aishone*, relic bones that are jealously guarded and widely coveted.

Kagiri and Noniki leave their tiny village with a few aishone and all the hope they can muster, but the world is a larger, more dangerous place than they ever dreamed. Forced into a dark bargain that may cost them not only their lives but their souls, their fates intertwine with an emperor, a warrior, a graverobber, and a killer in ways none of them ever imagined, ways that could reshape the Relicant Empire forever.

This is the first book in The Relicant Chronicles, the Anime-esque epic fantasy series from international bestselling author Aaron Rosenberg.

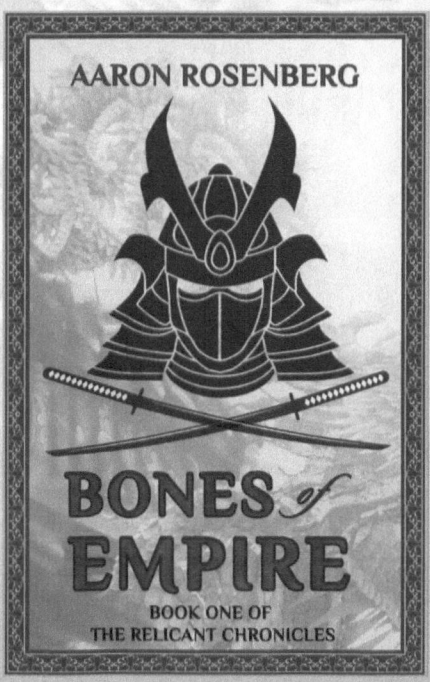

AARON ROSENBERG

BONES *of* EMPIRE

BOOK ONE OF
THE RELICANT CHRONICLES